HAND OF THE KING'S EVIL

The Fifth Book of Outremer

CHAZ BRENCHLEY

2003
50TH
ANNIVERSARY

ACE BOOKS, NEW YORK

HAND OF THE KING'S EVIL

An Ace Book / published by arrangement with
the author

PRINTING HISTORY
Orbit edition / December 2002
Ace mass-market edition / October 2003

For information address: Orbit,
a division of Little, Brown and Company (UK)
Brettenham House, Lancaster Place, London WC2E 7EN.

ISBN: 0-441-01110-1

ACE®
Ace Books are published by The Berkley Publishing Group,
a division of Penguin Group (USA) Inc.,
375 Hudson Street, New York, New York 10014.
ACE and the "A" design
are trademarks belonging to Penguin Group (USA) Inc.

PRINTED IN THE UNITED STATES OF AMERICA

10 9 8 7 6 5 4 3 2 1

Praise for the Outremer series:

"The praise that greeted Chaz Brenchley's *Tower of the King's Daughter* in hardback was considerable, with particular praise being lavished on the prose . . . here was a fantasy sequence to rival the most impressive in the genre . . . *Feast of the King's Shadow* is similarly impressive. Atmosphere is . . . conjured with tremendous skill in this book, never, however, allowing it to swamp the adroit plotting . . . This is fantasy exactly as it should be: ambitious, highly coloured, and supremely confident in its grip on the reader's kingdom . . . From its first confident chapter . . . Brenchley's grasp of his colourful narrative never falters, and his descriptive powers are exemplary."

—*Orbit*

"The intensity verges on horror at times . . . Compelling reading."

—*Locus*

"Chaz Brenchley's striking new epic fantasy series [is] a revelation. The atmosphere is so well described you can almost taste it."

—*Starburst*

"A refreshing (and necessary) change . . . The recipient of a British Fantasy Society award, Mr. Brenchley [has] a never less than skillful style and turn of phrase . . . Along the way there are all the adventures a discerning fantasy reader could wish for and Brenchley's concise, muscular prose makes the story flow, free of genre clichés . . . Recommended."

—*SFX Magazine*

"Drama and spectacle to spare. Brenchley's prose is clear and vivid . . . His ability to integrate the magical and uncanny into his more grittily realistic portrait of life on the outposts of Empire grounds his fantasy in a wealth of believable detail . . . thorough and striking . . . captures with brutal verisimilitude the harshness of life within a despotic religious/military community . . . Brenchley the horror novelist and Brenchley the fantasist come together in perfect alignment . . . the kind of dark, painful power rarely seen in the literature of heroic fantasy."

—*Cemetery Dance*

"As with all Brenchley's novels, the prose is beautifully crafted and a joy to read . . . I can't wait to see what happens next."

—*Northern Review*

Also by Chaz Brenchley

The Books of Outremer:
THE DEVIL IN THE DUST
TOWER OF THE KING'S DAUGHTER
A DARK WAY TO GLORY
FEAST OF THE KING'S SHADOW
HAND OF THE KING'S EVIL
THE END OF ALL ROADS

Visit the series website at
www.outremer.co.uk

βλεπομεν γαρ αρτι δι εσοπτρου εν αινιγματι
τοτε δε προσωπον προς προσωπον αρτι
γινωσκω εκ μερους τοτε δε
επιγνωσομαι καθως και επεγνωσθην

—THE FIRST EPISTLE OF PAUL THE APOSTLE TO THE
CORINTHIANS, 13, 12

THE CHAPEL HAD been altered since he was first here, last here, since he'd belonged. Fifteen years ago, that was: years of hard exile, for all that he'd been back in his own country and serving his own liege lord. They had stripped him naked and sent him away from this place, had turned their faces from him and closed the gate behind him as he stumbled out. The taste of that shame was fresh and bitter still in his mouth, fresher even than the memory of cold rain against his skin as he'd run weeping down through the dark. He'd cut his feet on sharp stones, bruised his shoulder against the wall of rock and felt neither cuts nor bruises, only the wind and the rain and the immeasurable shame. A young man then, he'd thought his life was over, he couldn't live with this. If he'd missed a turn, blinded by the night and the rain and his tears, if he'd fallen from the road no one would have cared, none in the castle and himself least of all.

Fifteen years. When he was driven out they'd still been building, raising new walls higher than the old; this chapel, like everything in the original fortress, had been left all but untouched for lack of time or men to work on it. He remembered the rough raw plaster where heretical mosaics, Catari blasphemies had been chiselled out by the pious men who first won the Roq and claimed it. The word then was that it did honour to the God, when the very walls of His chapel showed how they had been wrenched free of black religion and consecrated to His service.

The word must be different now. It was called the Knights' Chapel these days; he supposed the knights had paid, or their families or sponsors. They must have paid handsomely. He knew little of such matters—in Elessi they kept their chapels simple, white walls and dark wood, only the candles' flames to stand in the eye and remind a man of his God—but the lamps and vessels here, even the high candle-stands were silver where they were not gold. The walls had been plastered and the plaster painted; everywhere he looked he saw images of the saints and their deaths, or else images of the God's victory here and throughout the Sanctuary Land. The glory of Ascariel glimmered jewel-bright behind the altar.

It was all alien to him and he liked none of it, but he came here none the less. The great hall was too public and too familiar, it held too many memories. Every day since his arrival at the castle he had come; he had spent hours on his knees in the darkest corner he could find, relying on cap and shadows to obscure his face from all but the God. There were few to see, in any case. They might call it the Knights' Chapel, but the knights used it seldom. Brothers came in sometimes, alone or in pairs, for private prayer and meditation or else for confession; their murmuring voices offered little distraction and no one gave him more than a sidelong glance, no one challenged his right to be here.

Only once had he been singled out and spoken to directly. That had been a challenge, perhaps: to his faith, perhaps, and to his betraying soul. His reply had been a confession, but nothing that could soothe or cleanse.

STILL, THE ENCOUNTER had gifted him with hope. So he still came to the chapel daily, he still locked himself in private prayer like a man who walked a wilderness alone. In many ways he was alone, more so than he had been these fifteen years: his lady charge was gone, and his troop after her. She'd slipped his guard and run with strange companions, heretics and worse. Her lord husband had led the search for her, with Marshal Fulke of the Ransomers hot at his side; different spurs drive different men with equal fire.

No trace had been found, no tracks, no rumours of their passing. At last the baron had gone back to Elessi, and taken all his men with him; only Blaise he'd left at the Roq, "in case she should return, sergeant, in case she should be found. A familiar face to greet her, and sharp eyes to watch her welfare . . ."

Sharp eyes to watch her straying feet he'd meant, and Blaise had understood him perfectly. Twice now she'd slipped her guards and fled, shaming her husband in the eyes of all; she shouldn't be allowed a third adventure, but gossip said that the preceptor of the castle had an eye for her beauty and would make an unreliable custodian. It was wisdom to leave a man of Elessi, to be sure she could be kept until she was collected.

It was cruelty to name Blaise as that man, to leave him so alone beneath the burning-glass of his own disgrace. The young baron couldn't know that, though; if his uncle the elder baron knew, he kept his counsel.

Blaise had been offered a private chance of redemption, right here in the chapel; that was all he had to cling to. The conversation was burned into his brain. His faltering confession, the history of his time within the Order, and then:

"I was stripped naked and sent into exile, Magister. Forbidden the habit, and the service of the God. And I, I have lived with that all this time, but I do not think I can bear it any longer."

"You must. When you endanger a brother, you betray the Order. There can be no remission."

"No, Magister. I know. But . . ."

"But that is not to say that you cannot serve the God, or the Order. Many men do, who do not wear the habit."

"I am no knight, Magister."

"No, but we have other servants yet. The time is coming, when we will need more fighting men than are sworn to us. I dislike to accept mercenaries, but when I must, I will. Will you fight with us, brother, when that time comes?"

"Not for money, Magister!"

"Well, you may do what you will with the pay. I cannot put you in a habit, but I can put a sword in your hand and give you a place in the line, if you will take it."

"Yes, Magister. I will take it. And thank you."

"I am not finished yet. That time will come, but it is not here yet. Will you serve me and the God in the meantime? Without a habit and without pay, without honour or recognition, in secrecy and obedience even when you hate what it is that I ask you to do?"

"What will that be, Magister?"

"It may be this, it may be that. I cannot say. I do not explain myself; but I want private servants sworn to me in silence. Will you be one among them?"

"Magister, I will."

"Good. Listen for my voice, then, and obey when you hear it. The time will come. Serve the Lady Julianne and serve her well, until I call you; then serve me better . . ."

*   *   *

AND SO HE had waited out his time, enduring day by day, hour by hour, moment by terrible moment. He had exercised his body and his horse in order to be ready whenever that call should come, regardless of the pain it cost him to ride or sweat among the brothers, where he was no brother now. Otherwise he had held himself apart, as a guest ought. He attended the noon service whenever he could bear to, praying in the gallery with other strangers; he fetched his meals from the kitchen and ate in solitude, in his own rough quarters; and every day he came back to this small chapel, to spend hours on his knees before the God and to hope, almost to pray for another visit, another conversation with the one man who could save him.

ALMOST, HE HAD given up hoping. Almost he thought he had been forgotten or dismissed, that the chance once offered had been withdrawn again. But he did devoutly believe in second chances, his faith required it; the God's sign glowed before his eyes, a path that turned and turned and came back always to the centre.

And so he did come back always to the chapel, even on his darkest days, at his most despairing; and so at last he was rewarded.

ON HIS KNEES in the shadows and the silence, his belly clamped around its perennial hunger—he lived like a guest but ate like a brother penitent, bread and porridge and no meat, no midday meal, no satisfaction—and his mind clamped around its perennial sense of loss, he heard the whisper of a robe that brushed the floor. He tried piously, hopelessly to pretend that this was not what he had been listening for, that his thoughts had been entirely on the God; and failed, as an honest man must when he lies in his heart.

The soft sounds came closer, till he could hear the footsteps beneath the robe, till he could hear even the man's quiet breathing. He held his own breath, still not quite daring to hope; the man knelt beside him, and murmured a brief prayer in the old tongue.

Then, at last, Blaise lifted his eyes to look. And saw in the lamps' glow what he had dreaded not to see, even now: the robes of a master, the balding head above defiantly uncovered before the altar of the God, the thin pale face turned towards him.

"Magister . . ."

"Sergeant. Are you still willing to do as you said, to serve me?"

"Yes, Magister. Of course."

"Good. I have a mission for you."

"Magister, I have been ordered to remain in the castle here, against the Lady Julianne's recovery . . ."

"She will not be recovered now, or not to this place. She is long gone from here. You are right, though, you must defy your lord's command to obey me. Will you do that?"

It required barely a moment's thought. "I will."

"Listen, then. There is disease abroad in the Kingdom, a plague that no medicine will cure; I believe that it is a curse from Surayon, the Folded Land. There is also a man who follows this plague from town to town. He heals, he says by the touch of a saint's hand; he says he is no saint himself. He also preaches, and he is gathering an army of the poor and dispossessed about him."

"To what end, Magister?"

"I do not know; but he preaches against Surayon, as all true believers must. I want my man among his people, Blaise. I want to hear everything he says, to see everything he does. His army is nothing, a peasant rabble, a joke; but he may be a weapon I can use . . ."

ONE

A Shadow Behind the Eyes

THE FLOOD HAD not reached so high as this. Neither had the men of the house come up here since, to tramp wet mud from dirty feet across the gritty floor. The only signs to be read had been left, must have been left by those she hunted: her enemy, her friend.

"Look," she said to Sherett, who held a lamp above her. "A bare footmark here, the touch of a robe against the opposite wall there; neither one has had the time to dry. He brought her this way, and not so long ago."

"We are all of us barefoot," the older woman said mildly enough, "our feet and robes are wet. A restless man, a thinking man—a hungry man perhaps, looking to see what food might have been stored here and forgotten?"

"There is none—and after that feast, who could be hungry? Besides, this is not mud." She had it on her finger now, a little of the dark damp stain she'd found and followed from mark to scattered mark. She sniffed it, nodded, held her hand high. "Taste."

Sherett did that, touching tongue to finger's tip. "Blood," she said. "Julianne's?"

Elisande managed a smile, slightly. "Even I don't know the girl that well. She can't be dead," *she can't be,* "or why would he carry her body away? He left the guards he killed. This is their blood, I think." *And you can taste their bodies if you want to, to compare. Not I . . .*

"He might have left her somewhere else."

"He carries her, across one shoulder. Why else would the one side of his robe brush the floor, the other not? Her weight drags at him." She was a big girl, Julianne: little shorter, little lighter than Morakh who had taken her. He was all desert, that one, all bone and leather and no water in him. Bone and leather and black spite to match his black robe. Elisande would like to find a black thread to prove it, but it must have been him. The men who'd watched at Julianne's door had second mouths for throats. Morakh had killed others that way, swift and silent. Besides, who but a Dancer could face two alert companions and surprise them both, get behind each in turn . . .?

She'd been with Sherett when the news reached the women's quarters, a message sent from Hasan, *come quickly,* no more than that. No more had been needed. They'd left goblets of *jereth* heretically unfinished, had gathered up their skirts and run through the crusting mud on the valley floor to the house of the Beni Rus. There they'd found a mill of men in the hallway, furious and aimless, weapons drawn and voices raised. In the Sands, they'd have been more cautious; they would not have wasted their anger so. She knew what to blame, all that water, and a hopeless fight survived: relief and wet feet had made them slippery of discipline.

There had been more order on the upper floor, but still no direction. Even Hasan had been pacing, to and fro across his carpets. Julianne's bride-gifts had lain scattered from their tray; of Julianne herself, there was nothing.

Sherett had been quick, sensible, controlled. Only her eyes had given her away, and those briefly.

"Hasan. What has happened here—a thief?"

"She has not run away. Not this time. Two men are dead, the Dancer's work . . ."

"I saw." The bodies were wrapped, but the stains on the stone spoke. "If you don't calm those headhot fools below, they'll forget the Dancer and blame the Saren or the Kauram, anyone they can see. There will be war here in Rhabat, and that will consume us all. You go down, go now. Organise the men, search the valley. Pointless, I think, but do it, put them to work. Send messages abroad, if any mount of ours survived the flood: your wife is stolen from you, no Dancer should be trusted. Anything, but keep the tribes from fighting."

He'd looked as though he wanted to fight the tribes himself, all at once and by himself; but even this outrage, even the loss of Julianne couldn't take his eye for long from his greater goal. A tribal war would destroy any hope of the war he sought, perhaps for another generation or longer, his chance lost. He'd nodded, turned, stridden away.

Sherett had fingered the scattered jewellery, stooped to retrieve a piece or two, said, "These must be counted and checked, to see if Morakh has stolen aught else but our sister. Not now, though. Let the men search below; they will make a lot of noise and find nothing. You and I, Elisande, we will search above."

*   *   *

ELISANDE HAD BEEN thinking that there was nothing but solid rock overhead, that Hasan's chamber stood at the height of the house. She'd been mistaken, forgetful. There were corridors that climbed higher yet, leading to store-rooms that were little used, ultimately to a great cistern where rainwater from the occasional storms could be collected. A web of channels had been cut through the rock, to draw it down from the plateau above; she knew that, she should have remembered. Only yesterday she'd fetched water herself from the cistern in the women's quarters. Why was she, why was everybody being so *slow . . . ?*

All of those drains were wide and high enough to accommodate a man, if barely. They must be, necessarily; how else were they cut? Elisande had squirmed through a few in her time, following giggling friends. And Morakh's trail did lead to the cistern. The air was cool and damp; Sherett's lamplight showed a low roof above a dark, still pool. The water looked deep, and chilly. Elisande suppressed a shiver as she gazed about. The cistern was encompassed by a narrow walkway; to left and right, it was overhung by spouts carved from the rock of the walls. Above each spout was black emptiness. An agile man could haul himself up, a strong man no doubt could boost a girl so high; a thin man could insinuate himself into either of those channels. Could he drag a girl behind him? Well, perhaps . . .

Where a thin man and a tall girl could go, so could a skinny short girl. She thought about that, shivered again, and found her eye caught by the water.

And laughed, a little shrilly perhaps, and said, "Esren."

A shimmer in the lamplight, an intricate coil of air as fine as her friend's hair plaited; the djinni was there at her word. "Lisan."

"I think you will know where Julianne has been

taken." It was a quick-learned habit, almost second nature now not to ask questions.

"You are right."

"Go after her, fetch her back. If you had to slay the Sand Dancer to achieve it, I would not much mind that."

"Neither would I; but I may not do it."

That was a surprise, but *don't ask why not!* "Well, so long as you restore my friend to me, that one can die later." At her dagger's point, for preference.

"I meant that I may not do what you require. The daughter of the King's Shadow must seek help from otherwhere."

Elisande gaped. Her mouth moved soundlessly for a moment; then, "Spirit, you swore to obey me . . ."

"I swore to come when you called me and to act at your command. That is not necessarily to say that I would obey your commands."

Was it not? Well, perhaps not; but the difference was as fine as a single one of Julianne's hairs, and should have been as easy to snap except that Elisande had a question now, *why will you not obey me in this, as you have whatever I asked before?* and it burned so brightly in her head, so hotly on her tongue that she could think of no way not to ask it.

And then had no need to ask, because the djinni offered her an answer regardless. "Lisan, close your eyes."

Startled, she did so; and heard its thin voice again, "Tell me what you see."

"Nothing. A darkness . . ."

"Show it to me."

"I cannot!" Her eyes snapped open again, glaring.

"No. It is neither day nor night, it has no existence outside your own mind; and yet you see it, it is there. Similarly, I cannot walk in the place where the Sand Dancer has taken the Shadow's daughter. He took her from here to the plateau above; but now they are not quite in this world, nor yet in the land of the djinn."

"I don't understand."

"You have seen how the Sand Dancers can move when they choose, unseen from one place to another."

"Yes." They flicked in and out of view, they were here and then they were there without seeming to cross the ground between; but, "Only short distances, though, only moments of time," only long enough to pass from one man to another and be behind each of them in turn, convenient to cut their throats.

"Yes. The effort costs them, and they grow uncertain of finding their way back to the world if they linger. This one is half-mad, though, and knows he will be hunted. He has risked much to seize the Shadow's daughter; he is risking more to keep her."

It was the risk to Julianne that concerned Elisande. She said, "I still don't understand where they are, that you cannot reach them."

"You know of four directions in your world, north and south, west and east. Conceive of a fifth that has no name, that stands an equal distance from each . . ."

That made sense to her, suddenly. "I know of this; it is how we have Folded my land, out of the reach of our neighbours. But the djinn can visit us in Surayon, when they choose to."

"Indeed. Surayon exists where it always has, within its borders, and we can find it there. The border, though, where the shift is active—neither human nor spirit can find that. The Dancer Folds the land as he goes, and he walks within the crease. As long as he does so, he is beyond me."

Elisande still found it hard to credit, she'd grown so used to djinni omniscience. Djinni honesty, though, was an article of faith; Esren would not, could not lie. So she gave one more glance to the darkness of the narrow rain-channels, and felt a shudder of relief that she need not claw her way through those in pursuit of her friend. Then she thought suddenly of Julianne's being trapped within a worse darkness, sucked helpless into the space behind her eyes. Dizzy and confused perhaps, terrified certainly . . .

"Esren, wherever they are now, they must be headed somewhere, Morakh must have an ambition in this world. However mad he is, he must come back to what is solid," *he must bring Julianne back,* "and you can surely see where he will touch ground again."

"Perhaps; though I have been long detached from the spirit-weft, and my vision is uncertain."

"If we get closer, you may see more clearly. They went to the plateau, you said. Take me there, Esren. Quickly, before the men get so far."

She felt herself swept up and almost closed her eyes again, against the expected swirl of dark as Esren opened some strange pathway to the stars. Except that she was afraid of that particular darkness now behind her lids, and so she held them wide; and so she saw the rush of Sherett's lamp and the racing shadows of the passage beyond as she was carried back, all the way back to Hasan's chamber. She saw a blur of startled, bearded faces, his men, the man himself.

No time to speak to him, to any. She was carried out of the open window, into the night and up, high above the narrow valley. Briefly she did have time to think how Julianne would have hated this hellride, and yet to yearn hopelessly to have that girl beside her. Then the broad stretch of the plateau lay below her, blacklit by a blaze of stars.

She'd been slow, it seemed, despite her urgency. One man was ahead of her, alone, a shadow on the bare rock; her mind caught hold of the word, *a Shadow indeed,* and she whispered, "Esren, set me down. With him."

*   *   *

IT WAS STRANGE, how she seemed constantly to forget about Julianne's father. Or else not so strange, because he was such a self-effacing man in many ways; and then again perhaps not strange at all, because a girl could get into the habit of discounting fathers altogether. It was a hard thing to remember that some mattered, and to their daughters too.

She set bare foot to chilling rock and stood beside the King's Shadow with her djinni at her shoulder, a golden glitter in the dark. At least she knew how he had come here ahead of her, long ahead of all the rumpus; with his title came his power, or some of it. Like the Dancers, he could cover distances in a single step; unlike the Dancers—or so it seemed, or why else would Morakh have wriggled his way through narrow channels to reach this height?—he could step through air or rock or whatever stood in his way. Sometimes, she thought, he stepped through his daughter; in him, she could not quite contrive to resent it.

Sometimes, as now, he seemed to step out of his title and power and all to be a man again, simply a man and a father.

"Coren? Can you tell which way they are going? Esren can't."

"Can it not?" A question, but aimed at her even in his distraction; he was not a man to be careless, at such a time or anywhen. Even so there was a note of surprise, almost disbelief in his voice, and his eyes did seek the djinni for a moment.

"It says not. It says they walk in the crease where the world Folds, which is like the dark behind your eyes, nowhere at all, it says it cannot find them . . ."

"Well. I wasn't aware that the djinn had such poetic tongues."

"The djinn do not have tongues at all," Esren said, "unless they choose to do so. Like human poets, though, they sometimes seek to describe what is, in words that their listeners can understand."

Elisande felt that she hadn't understood one word in three, but that wasn't important now, though Coren seemed to feel that it was. She called him back to what truly mattered, repeating her question impatiently. "Do you know where they have gone?"

"West," he said certainly, turning to face towards the Dead Waters. "That much I can feel, though Djinni Tachur is right, they have touched this land only fleetingly."

"Can you follow them? And take me with you, if Esren cannot?"

"I can follow, but not I think as fast as they are moving. Definitely not, if I have to carry you. It's been a long night, Elisande, and I will not risk your life." *As Morakh is risking Julianne's* were the words he did not add, because he did not need to.

"Well, you go, then," enough of this standing around, "and Esren and I will follow you, as best we can. Or," another thought, suddenly, "Julianne said that the King could place you anywhere," *like a chess-piece,* she had said. "Can you not ask him . . .?"

"The King could lift me up and put me exactly where they will next touch to earth," Coren confirmed wearily. "But this is not his Kingdom; and no, I cannot ask him. He acts as he pleases. My daughter's health and welfare are perhaps not his priority. Let us see what there is to be seen, from the rim of the plateau . . ."

THE KING'S SHADOW stepped into a hazy golden light, and was gone. Elisande half-moved to go after him, but checked herself as the light dwindled; instead she called to Esren, and rode the wind to the high escarpment where she and Julianne had stood the previous day to watch how the djinni sucked up the waters of the sea.

Quickly though they'd come, Julianne's father was once more there before them, standing on the extreme edge of the cliff. He spoke without turning his head, without shifting his gaze from the dark glimmer of the water far below.

"Djinni Tachur, I cannot be certain, but it is my impression that they came to this place, that they stood exactly here."

"It is so. The man and the girl were here, and they climbed down."

"No," Elisande blurted instantly, "she could not, she is terrified of heights . . ."

Even as she said it, though, she remembered Julianne's glazed wonder at herself just hours earlier, her stunned murmur, *Elisande, I climbed a mountain.* The proof of that had been written in her hands: cracked and broken nails, skinned palms . . .

"What she could do once, she can do again," her father said, as though he could read Elisande's thoughts without even looking at her face. Perhaps he could. "If the djinni says she climbed, I think we must believe it. They are in any case not here, and he could not have carried her. Shall we go down?"

HE WENT, WITHOUT waiting for a reply. Again the night shone with the light of his leaving, again Elisande followed by her djinni's grace, gliding down almost within arm's-reach of the cliff: She found some measure of consolation in the thought that Julianne would have had to climb only some of the way; from perhaps halfway there were steps that had been carved into the rock centuries before, to give access to the caves that pitted its face.

But still, the image of her tall friend stumbling down at Morakh's heels, bent one way or another to his will— no, there was small consolation in that.

The Dead Waters had some life tonight, a slow surge and swell that lapped over the quay's edge, last vestige of the day's fury. How long would it take, she wondered, to calm a sea after it had been ripped from its bed and let run back? Less time, she thought, than it would take to calm Coren de Rance, who had had his daughter ripped from him and did not yet have her back.

This time he did at least turn his head to acknowledge her arrival. "There is no trail from here that I can sense, only that call to westward; but I do not believe that even a Sand Dancer can dance across water, any more than he could dance down a cliff."

You had no trouble coming down that cliff without climbing. Could you not have passed something on to your daughter, more than stubbornness and guile . . . ?

"They must have gone the other way, up the tunnel."

Julianne's father was the soul of patience, or so Elisande had thought him. Tonight, it seemed he lacked the patience to pace even the shortish distance to the further end of the quay. He walked in light; she ran after him, and if she seemed lighter on her feet than she expected, if each leaping step seemed to lift her higher and carry her further—well, no doubt anxiety and strangeness and urgency could explain that. No need to give credit to the djinni.

Rank and salt-soaked air had her gasping regardless, before she reached his side. She thought he'd already opened the hidden door to the climbing tunnel, but he denied it: "No, I found it so. Proof positive, I think, that they came this way. Sand Dancers trace their steps in strange country, but they still need an earthly path to follow."

Which you do not, so why can you not hunt them

quicker than they can flee? No point in posing the question; he was as elusive as the djinn, and as dangerous to hold a debt. She gazed blindly into the absolute black of the tunnel's opening and spoke hesitantly. "There was an 'ifrit, Marron said, guarding the further end . . ."

"I do not think it will have kept its watch."

"And if you are wrong? Esren cannot kill it, face to face." Spirit could not touch spirit and survive.

"If I am wrong, then I will meet it. Face to face. I have slain an 'ifrit before this. But if I am wrong, if it lingered past the flood, then I think it stayed to meet Morakh and my daughter. Like the djinn, the 'ifrit have some sense of what will come."

His misty light, his brisk step into it, his sudden absence, gone before the light was gone. No such easy walk for her, to rise from sea to peak. Rather a blind and sickening rush, turning and turning until her stomach rebelled. It had been a long slow ride down this tunnel that brought them into Rhabat, their way lit by guttering, failing torches. Now Esren dragged her in the opposite direction at terrible speed. Her desperate eyes sought something, anything to fix on in the utter dark, and found only the thin golden rod that was the djinni at her shoulder. But that too was spinning, spinning against the twist of the tunnel in a way that jerked her eyes out of rhythm with her belly. She closed her eyes, swallowed against a thin sour saliva, swallowed again . . .

JUST IN TIME, something solid kicked at her bare feet, kicked again. Her startled eyes sprang open and she saw rock, solid rock plunging beneath her. No, it was she who was plunging, staggering, falling towards it—except that she felt the djinni's strength grip her body until she could catch a tentative balance. ·

At least she didn't feel sick any longer, only giddy and

furious. She drew herself up cautiously, tried to outglare the djinni and said hissingly, "Esren, when I asked you to take me up, I meant straight up through the air, as you had brought me down . . ."

"Indeed. I wanted to try the tunnel."

Was this what it had meant, that it would act at her command but not necessarily in obedience? She foresaw a lifetime of such journeys, its will set against hers; and gritted her teeth, and said, "We will discuss later the terms of your oath to me. In the meantime, enough of folly. Tell me where Coren is."

"The King's Shadow is yonder, at the cliff's edge beyond the temple. You should go carefully, you are not yet steady on your feet."

That was humiliatingly true. She stepped forward with exaggerated care, past the simple temple that guarded the tunnel's mouth, past a crumpled heap of clothing that she thought might hide the body of the imam who had served as watchman before the 'ifrit came—and no, there was no 'ifrit now, unless Coren had killed it or driven it off—and so came to where Julianne's father was an unshifting statue, a silhouette against the glory of the stars.

Keeping a sensible, almost a Julianne-distance back from the drop, she asked softly, "What do you see?"

"Pestilence, and war," he said gravely. "I do not see my daughter."

"No." Even those brilliant stars couldn't hope to give light enough for mortal eyes to find her, even from so high a vantage-point. "We need Marron," she went on, giving voice to a hopeless yearning, "his sight might find some mark of her . . .?"

"Not even his, I fear. And Marron is in the land of the djinn, with Jemel. Leave them there, Elisande."

Oh, she would, she would. Desperate for something, anything to wash the bitterness of defeat from her mouth, she said, "Esren, you may be able to see more clearly from this height, to find some echo in the spirit-weft . . ."

"The weft does not echo, Elisande," any more than its voice could echo, so cold and unbreathed as it was, "and I am still untuned to its touch. There is perhaps something, though. There is perhaps a castle, and an army. To the west."

Oh, not the Roq, she thought in desolation, *let us not have to return to the Roq again.* But Roq de Rançon lay a long way further north than west. "There are no castles in the Sands, and no armies." None bar Hasan's army of the tribes, at least, that he meant to lead against her own land, unless Julianne could stop him. "She cannot be in a castle."

"No. But she may be, in time to come. I can see no more clearly than that."

"To the west lies Outremer, beyond the Sands," Coren said heavily. "There are many castles there, and more armies than a man could count. Come, this is pointless. We will not find her by staring into the dark, nor by chasing vainly through the desert. We should go back. I need my bed, and you yours, Elisande. For what little is left of the night, at least."

He didn't move, though, not yet; which gave her time enough to say, "Take me with you, Coren," as though she thought he should not go alone. She doubted if she had fooled either one of them, the man or the djinni, but he nodded graciously and took her arm and led her into his golden gleam of light.

TWO

A World, A Man Unransomed

ANTON D'ESCRIVEY STOOD on the height of the wall at Roq de Rançon, and knew himself possessed; and could not truly have said which of two spirits it was that possessed him, nor which was good, which evil. He knew what his Church would say, he believed that he knew what his God would say, and in this at least they would speak with one voice. Put him to confession, though, or put him to the question, dig for the deepest truth in himself and he could not be certain what his own voice would answer.

He stood in the last of the daylight, when it was dark already on the plain below. He saw the glimmer of torches on the road, a late patrol riding in. He could hear their news later; for now his eye reached further out, looking perhaps for some other light, some hint of life among the distant hills.

He saw nothing, only purpling shadows on their peaks

and unbroken black beneath. Every day for weeks he had stood here, and seen the same. It was wasted work to climb so high, wasted time to look for what would not be there. The preceptor had opened the King's Eye more than once at his urging, and no, there was no sign of the escaped heretic, nor of the baron's runaway wife, nor of his own treacherous squire. They had vanished in the chaos of that dreadful night: vanished by magical means for sure. The sorcerers of Surayon must have cast a blanket of darkness over that party of small souls, so dark that even the King's pure light could not find it out . . .

So they said, at least, in the halls and the guardhouses; and so Anton believed, because he must. And yet still he came up here high, each evening; and still he watched for some touch of light that might perhaps be a fire, might just possibly be a sign of one soul's returning.

Hopeless watch, but the knight kept it none the less; and did not turn until the great bell called the garrison to prayer, just as the sun fell from sight and that sea of shadow below swept up to engulf him.

HE MIGHT HAVE said his prayers there on the castle wall, with Marron's whisper in his head for company. To silence that distracting voice, he might have moved a little along the wall to join the guards who must watch and pray together. He might have gone back to his own chamber and prayed alone, as he used to do.

But times change, and men must change with them; old habits must be cast off, when men dress for war.

Anton took the stairs rapidly and then strode through the wards and passages of the Roq until he met the tail of his confrères, a slow procession winding into the great hall, torchbearers before and behind. He joined that procession, pacing in steady step with his brethren and leaving his head uncovered, as some half of them did now in sign of extra oaths that they had sworn.

Briefly, he remembered the occasion of those oaths. After he himself had caught and confronted the runaways in the stable yard, after they had laid him low with some numbing, bewildering spell on his mind—*after Marron had refused to leave them and come to him, but never mind that now; this was sanctified ground, or that was*— and after he had recovered himself and run to the broken gate and seen them riding out, even after so much, he had gone back to the stables and discovered worse.

He had discovered the stalls where a squad of men had been waiting as guards and grooms, where they waited now in an eternal stillness and a bath of blood. Some evil curse had torn them, flesh and bone; and the few bound and terror-stricken survivors had accused Marron himself of doing this thing.

Marshal Fulke had declared that the source of the work was Surayonnaise, whatever the instrument. There in the stables, among a breathless crowd of men, he had called not vengeance but justice on that wicked state; he had declared a holy war, and asked who would ride with him.

Used to orders, unused to invitations, the Brothers Ransomers had hesitated. It had taken the knights, the nobles' sons to push forward first, to make a path that the brothers could follow.

First among the knights—necessarily first, for his own squire's sake, who had been first cause of all this horror—had been Sieur Anton d'Escrivey.

Soon now, any day now, the long ride would begin. Until then, Anton lived as he had not before, side by side and sharing with his confrères. First among equals, his superiors said, though he was not aware of that; he thought himself only a hypocrite and weak, drawing needful strength from others.

They would ride, and they would find Surayon; and they would destroy it utterly, and that was good.

He did not expect to find Marron within its borders, and that was good.

He did expect to find Marron, somehow, somewhere, sometime; and that too, the God forgive him for he himself could not but that too was good, and hungered for.

IN THE GREAT hall, on the dais that stood below the sign of the God, Marshal Fulke stepped forward to preach to all the Ransomers, brothers and knights together on their knees.

"My brothers," he said, his voice soft but carrying, like the whisper of a whip in the air before it cracked, "all these weeks I have been telling you of the evil nestled like a worm in the heart of Outremer, that nestles also in the heart of each one of you, eating at your virtue. All these weeks you have waited to hear me cry you forth, like hounds upon a hunt. A month back you saw that I was right, when those you had welcomed here turned to sorcerous wickedness, and many brothers died. Since then, you have ached to wreak the God's vengeance on the vile, to ride against the heresy that is Surayon.

"You need wait no longer. The time is now, and you are the hand that shall strike, hard and clean into the heart of sin, a light to drive out darkness.

"How can I know this so certainly, you want to ask? I will tell you. I have been granted a vision; I have seen our enemy, as clearly as I see your thoughts, your hopes, your doubts.

"This last night I rose from my pallet and walked abroad while you slept, or else I dreamed that I rose and walked; I cannot tell whether my body in truth left my cell, or whether it was only my spirit that was called forth by the God. No man saw me or spoke to me, no hand touched mine unless it was the God's own hand that gripped me.

"However that may be, I felt myself drawn to climb high, to a place on the walls where I might overlook that ancient tower which has no doors or windows, to which the King himself gave a name when he was here, the Tower of the King's Daughter.

"As I stood and gazed upon it, it seemed to me that I saw a light shine out through the very stones of the tower. They turned to mist and faded, to leave a doorway where there is no door.

"Out from that doorway, I saw a flood of creatures come: demons I would call them, from the pits of hell. They were black and many-legged like spiders, and they glistened in an unearthly light.

"I saw them swarm up the wall behind the tower, where there is no walkway and so we set no guards. They were so many and so fast, they seemed to flow like water, like a foul and shining river over the wall and so out of my sight.

"When they were gone, the tower's stones were restored, and the glow died back to darkness.

"I have thought all day on what I saw, I have prayed and fasted, and this is my reading of it. There can be no doubt.

"Whyever it was built and whoever built it, that tower now stands in our eyes for the Folded Land, for Surayon. Think, my brothers! Only think, and you will see that it must be so. No doors, no windows—it exists and yet it is sealed to us, we can gain no access to it. Only sorcery could lead us through its walls. Is this not also true of Surayon?

"And yet, we know, the evildoers of that forsaken country pass its borders to mingle all unrecognised with us. We had one of their kind in our own captivity, under our guard some few weeks since, until he was released by powers beyond our reckoning. You all know what price we paid in that escape.

"What I saw, though, what the God showed me in His kindness was more than a few wicked men stealing out to work mischief among us. It was what we have long feared, what the Surayonnaise have long been preparing for behind their hidden borders. It was an invasion, an army issuing forth to wreak havoc in the Kingdom, to challenge the rule of the King himself.

"By the God's grace, we have been warned; by your strength and faith, we can forestall it. More, and better: we can use this knowledge, this chance to strike at last against that canker that lurks at the heart of our land.

"One man may slip silently, unseen through a curtain; an army cannot. The sorcerers of Surayon must open their borders to send forth their strength. If we are there and ready when they do, we can pass inside; and then the God's vengeance will be ours to enforce.

"I have spoken with the preceptor, and this is our plan. Already birds are flying, messages have been sent; the lords of Outremer will rally at this news, we will build an army of our own to meet the men of Surayon. Even magic-workers are mortal and may be slain. But we, the Order of Ransom, knights and brothers both will hold ourselves apart from that battle; we will ride into Surayon as soon as the way is clear, and there we will work the God's will against that heretic people, and so bring the King's most wayward daughter back into the heart of her family, from where she has been too long lost. Prepare yourselves, my brothers, cleanse bodies and minds, confess if that is needful; you must come pure to your trial, and we march in the morning."

THERE WAS MORE, but Anton's attention drifted. He remembered how he had seen Marron and the others, the night they fled—how they had been grouped in the court below his window, at the foot of that same Tower of the King's Daughter, all lit by a glowing ball of fire. They had looked like travellers balked, or warriors defeated. That had been his thought then, and was still his thought now. He had wondered ever since, why there? It was the furthest part of the castle from the gate, not guarded perhaps but overlooked by all the knights' windows, a nonsensical place to meet. Unless they'd had some other objective, another way to leave perhaps, some mystical door that the prisoner from Surayon could open, except that they had found it closed against them . . .

He thought that what Marshal Fulke had seen was no sleeping vision; he wondered if perhaps it was not either a visitation from the God, but rather simple truth. This was a land of miracles and magic, and not all beneficent. There had been ample proof of that, when Marron had slaughtered his troop in the stables. With a blood-demon by all reports, a monster of terrible strength—something that he had perhaps come by within the tower? For sure the boy had owned no supernatural powers earlier, Anton himself could testify to that; only the native charms of shyness and beauty, a pair of eyes that could snare a man's heart . . .

It might be blasphemy, he thought, to question a divine vision. It was certainly disobedience to his vows, to question the affirmation of his superior. Well, let it be so. One further sin on his conscience, what did that matter, one among so many? And no, he would not be confessing it before they marched.

HAVING NO SQUIRE now, he made what use he could of his confrères', what little time he could beg their servants from them; but was still kept busy on his own account, packing and preparing for what could be months in the field.

It wasn't until the following morning, when the castle and all the chaos of a dawn march lay hours at his back, when he had at last the peace of a steady horse below him and the silence of his brethren all around him, that he found the time and the space to think a little. Even that silence had been slow in coming, for all the rigour of the Order's rules. Young men who ride to battle will be talkative, and his fellow knights spoke to Anton now as though he were one of their own: only a little older than most and a finer swordsman than any, a favourite of Marshal Fulke's too and so very much worth their time. He was still not used to that. A sudden popularity was hard to deal with, harder to set aside.

Eventually, though, the weight of cloak and armour under a fierce sun beat down the most insistent tongue. With his hood drawn up and its rim hanging low to shade his eyes from the glare, Anton could feel himself alone amid a crowd, as he had been for so long before this. *Before Marron . . .* For some few years he'd all but hidden at the Roq, given implicit licence to hide by virtue of his name and fame. Or infame, rather, the truth and rumours that attached to any whisper of that name. He'd rarely left the castle walls, except to patrol the borderlands where there were none to whisper, only wild tribes who fled at sight, the occasional Sharai raiding party to be tracked or attacked. His recent venture east as part of Julianne's honour-guard had been curtailed, but had still reaped a taste of trouble among the Elessi.

Now, though—now he was headed directly into the heart of Outremer, and could not hope to escape the public eye. All down this long road there would be petty grandees offering food and wine and hospitality, offering their sons to the adventure, perhaps throwing their marriageable daughters into this lordly company.

Above all there would be constant arrivals, recruits come to join this building army. The Order might make the hammerhead, but every hammer needs a solid shaft. There were swords, bows, axes in their hundreds aboard the wagons at the column's tail. Any man who offered would be armed and welcomed to the march; every lordling who answered the preceptor's summons would be given his place of honour, and would mingle as of right among the knights. Anton could no more lie about his history than he could hope to hide his face. Anton d'Escrivey rode out into the world again, after so long a silence; let the world make what it would of the fact, of him. He would be interested to see the results.

And might see them sooner even than he'd budgeted for; a group of men was waiting at a crossroads up ahead, two of them mounted and the rest afoot. Some minor noble and his eldest son, this ought to be, with a dozen retainers, all that their estate could spare. First to join, and they would carry that like a banner, Anton thought: *before the horde, before our liege lord even, there were the Ransomers and there was us, they treated us like brothers . . .*

So much so that Fulke himself rode on ahead to greet them, to offer honour where it was so manifestly due, so manifestly expected. He could be a diplomat, then, as well as an inspired preacher; whether he was or could learn to be a soldier, that was yet to be seen.

THERE WAS—OF course!—a shrine at the crossroads; there was also, *mirabile dictu,* a spring that still gave water in this height of summer. Or not such a miracle, perhaps: he'd grown so used to the drouth of the Roq and its lands of dust, he'd forgotten how fertile the Kingdom was in its long lie between the mountains and the sea. Even one morning's ride south into Tallis, a rising purple shadow to the east gave better protection from the desert wind and the drifting sand. There was more roll than jut to the hills, more soil than rock, more green than grey. The spring was a slow bubbling pool rather than an over-running freshet, and they daren't let the animals near for fear of their hooves churning it into an undrinkable mire, but if the column rested for an hour—and if the brothers and squires worked all that hour, fetching and filling with their knees in the mud—every horse and ox could be re-freshed. *Never lose a chance to water your mount* was an order ingrained into every man of the Order, after a few months' service at the Roq. Of course, they would pause.

And of course the knights would not scurry about with their boys and their black-robed comrades, after they had all knelt before the shrine to say the midday service with Marshal Fulke. Of course they would gather in a separate and superior group, to eat and talk quietly among them-selves. And of course Anton would linger with them, sooner than make a target of himself, one man apart from all. And of course the noble's son would drift away from his father, towards the young men whose dress and ar-mour bespoke their rank, whose bearing and demeanour must seem so attractive.

He was an open-faced, cheery lad, no older than the squires who were busy tending their masters' horses, six-teen or seventeen at most, and he was possessed of a tongue that wouldn't stop wagging. Anton was more ac-customed to shyness and quiet obedience among the young; this boy was almost a revelation, certainly a re-minder that he was riding into a different world.

". . .This isn't my place, not really, it ought to be my brother's, to ride with Father; but he's been sick for weeks, he's had the fever, and our mother wouldn't let him come. He swears he's well enough now, but he's thin yet and he can't stop coughing. So Father said I could come in his stead. Mother was against that too, she thinks

I'm too young, but he said he wouldn't ride alone while he had two sons and one strong enough to bear arms for the King and the God. It's what I've always wanted anyway, always. Not Roben, that's my brother, he has a farmer's soul, Father says, he loves our land and never wants to leave it; it's a blessing, *I* think, that he's been so ill. Now that he's getting better, I mean. He can stay, as he really wants to, and I can go to the war.

"Roben would never make a soldier anyway, but I think I will. I mean, I hope so. I've never been afraid to fight. Not that Roben's afraid, I don't mean to say that; nor a weakling either, it's just that his heart's in the land, do you see what I mean . . .?"

"Emphatically," Raffel murmured. "Halben, a soldier's first duty is service—which is generally taken to include standing quiet among his betters, as a good servant does. Do you think you could manage that?"

"Oh. Forgive me, sieur. My mother always says I was born with a brook running out of my mouth, but . . ."

"I'm sure she does. It's all right, lad, I was teasing. It is true, though, that a young warrior should look first to serve; have you ever thought of offering your service to the God? As we do, I mean, as knights of the Order?"

"All my life," the boy said simply. "Father wouldn't countenance it, though, he says it's too expensive. If I had been the elder, then perhaps; I think he would have liked to see my brother take the white for a year, and earn his badge. But Roben doesn't want it, and Father won't pay for me to stand in my brother's place."

"He may change his mind, if he sees you do well with us." Even from where he stood on the edge of the circle, Anton could see the look on the boy's face, and guessed that that idea had already occurred. He hid his smile better than some of his confrères, but then lost it completely as Raffel went on, "If you cannot make your vows to the Order, you can at least offer us your service before we come to battle. One among us has need of a squire, if you would be willing . . .?"

Of course Halben was willing, his speaking face said so even before his thrilled voice could confirm it. Anton felt his own face darken in response, with that clouding scowl he'd seen so often mirrored in others' wide and frightened eyes. For once he took the necessary moment to dispel it, before he pushed his way through the mill to where he had least intended to find himself, the centre of the circle and the focus of each man's gaze. Raffel wouldn't frighten, after all, and the boy was an innocent in this, he didn't deserve even the margin of Anton's anger.

He didn't deserve even as much as Anton must give him, here and now.

"A soldier's duty is to serve, perhaps; a soldier's wisdom is never to volunteer, at least until he knows to what he has promised himself. To whom. I am the one my brother speaks of so casually. When you have heard my name, you may not be so eager to stand as my servant."

"Sieur, I will gladly attend any Knight Ransomer who thinks me worthy . . ."

Perhaps there was some trace left after all of Anton's scowl; the boy stuttered into an unaccustomed silence, as their eyes met.

"It is not your worthiness that is in question, Halben." Anton tried a smile, but even he could feel the bitterness of it as he went on, "I am called Anton D'Escrivey. If you have not heard that name, you should ask your father's advice before you commit yourself to it."

No need for that, transparently. The boy had heard the name, and some at least of the stories attached to it. He went first pale, and then scarlet beneath his farmer's tan; his feet carried him backwards seemingly against his intent, while his arms flailed to shape excuses in the air, while his tongue ran loose and desperate. He should not give himself against his father's express desire, his father would in any case require a squire's service of him, his mother had always cursed him for a clumsy oaf who couldn't serve a cup of wine without spilling it, and usually on whichever poor man it was whom he was serving . . .

By the time the lad had squirmed his way through the press of men at his back and scurried off to join his parent, still apparently crying alibis to the wind, Anton had a better hold of his temper.

"Raffel," he said, "that was not fair."

"Was it not? Then I apologise. But you could not have hoped to keep the secret longer than a day or two, Anton. There will be many more who join us, and there must be some to know you, you have not changed so much . . ."

"I have no intention of keeping secrets. I meant that it was unfair to the boy, to offer me as the fulfilment of his dreams. He was all on fire with delight, with this chance and this company; likely now some part of him wants to creep home to his mother. *He* will know that he can never be quite comfortable with us again, even if you do not."

And never a word about his own discomfort, or his own distress. To have been offered a lively younger son as squire and companion, a boy who couldn't stop talking about his brother—no, that had been neither fair nor kind. Anton must needs confront ghosts with every mile of the ride, and it was the ghost of his own brother who overshadowed all. Almost, he could find himself longing to be back at the Roq again, and only yearning for Marron's impossible return. Almost . . .

ALL AFTERNOON, SMALL groups of men joined the column, petty nobles and landowners with their retinues. There were enough youngsters among them that Halben found his courage, left his father's side and spread his whispers widely: *you see that man, that one there, the dark head and the haughty glare? That's Anton d'Escrivey. Yes that's right, the fratricide who fled his brother's body and his father's wrath to hide in the arms of the Order. They say he's a boy-lover too, that his brother caught him at it and so died; and he asked me to be his squire, me . . .*

That much Anton could live with, as he must do. There would be weeks more of it to come. He urged his mount and a few chosen companions forward, to ride in the column's vanguard and so escape the sidelong glances, put some little distance between himself and the muttering boys; but that only provided the chance that broke him for this day. They met a priest on the road and gathered about him for his blessing, threw back their hoods to show the strength of their vows—and Anton saw an accusing finger rise to point him out, heard his own infamy declaimed.

"You! I know your face and style, however you mask yourself in holy robes. I had heard that you ran to the Ransomers for sanctuary, that you sought to flee the King's justice by buying a place among their ranks; I had not thought to see you ride out so brazenly, in defiance of all honour. You are a marked man, Anton d'Escrivey. Your dress and vows may shield you from your deserts, though it is shame to the Order that it granted you so much favour; they will not shield you from your disgrace."

"My disgrace is my own," as was his sudden fury, though that at least he did try to mask behind the chill of a long-practised voice, "for me to carry as I may. My soul and honour are given, not sold, to the God. As are yours, if your own dress speak you true. My sins have been confessed," or some of them, those that the world twisted in whispers, "and I have served penance for them all. Do you not believe in redemption, that the Church says may be granted to all who repent?"

"I believe in the King's law, that says murderers shall answer for their crime, and suffer death when it is proved against them."

"So do I, but the God's law takes precedence even over the King. Besides, I am sorry to disappoint you, but I have never yet been a murderer. Now stand aside, or I may have a better case to answer." He could keep the anger out of his voice, but his body rebelled against control; his hand touched the hilt of his sword Josette.

"Would you threaten a priest, sworn to the God's service?"

"No, but I see no priest here. Only a man whose words deny his robes, who sets public gossip before the teachings of the Church, whose blessing would taint our venture. Stand aside, or I will ride you down."

He urged Alembert forward; the man scurried to the side of the road in a swirl of skirts and dust, as Anton's companions closed around him. At their backs, they heard a shrill curse sent against them. Some made the sign of the God superstitiously against brow or breast; Anton kept both hands on the reins and his eyes firmly on the horizon.

"Anton, was that well done?"

"No, probably not. But it has been done, and may need to be done again and yet again before we come to Surayon. You need not ride beside me, if you fear the curses of the stupid."

It was a sign of how things had so recently changed for him, that his confrères laughed at that and promised to stay close. It was a sign of how he was not so immune as he had thought himself, that he led them deliberately slowly until others could catch up, Marshal Fulke among them.

"Magister," he said then, "the sun will be setting in an

hour; it might be good if some few of us rode a little ahead, to find a place where the army may camp for the night. Unless you know this land . . .?"

"Not I. All Outremer is new to me. But I had thought to press on until we reached Allansford. We will be late, but we can say the service as we ride, the Order has dispensation to do that on campaign; and the preceptor's messengers told men to gather there . . ."

"All the more reason to avoid it until the morning. If we arrive tonight, in the dark, it will be chaos and we'll get no rest. Come the light they'll be looking for us, and we can arrange the column as we wish."

Fulke nodded slowly. "Ride on, then, see what comfort you can find. The knights will want ground to pitch their tents, and the animals will want water. You know what is needful, Sieur Anton. Go and seek it, with my blessing."

Was there perhaps an extra meaning to that, as though the marshal had met a raving, cursing priest beside the road? Anton wasn't certain, but he said his thanks gracefully before he spurred forward.

ANTON KNEW THIS country little better than Fulke did. He had travelled all the length of Outremer, which few of his generation could claim, but only the once and only to reach Roq de Rançon, to be as far as the land could take him from any word of home.

Now he gazed about him as he rode, and saw fields of corn and millet on either side. Alembert's hooves splashed through streams in the valley bottoms; where the land rose too high and dry to support crops, ancient fig and olive trees spread their twisted branches above twisting roots. He began to wonder whether they would find any stretch of ground clear enough to make an encampment for even this small force, these few hundreds of men; whether they might not after all have to ride on in the dark till they came to the township at Allansford.

After another valley with an infant river in its cleft, though, there came another ridge; and the road climbed higher than ever yet, through olive-groves to a rocky summit too bare to nourish any tree. There was no water, but the beasts could be picketed along the river-bank below while the men made camp on the height. If the baggage-wagons must come up with his confrères' tents and kettles, no doubt the brothers could haul them.

"This will do," he said, turning his eyes southerly and seeing nothing better in the long, late shadows that cloaked the road. "Torres, will you ride back and tell the marshal what we have found? Quickly, before the sun sets? Say your prayers with him; and tell him that we will make a beacon here, to catch the eyes of the Order and promise rest after a long day's ride."

He had no right of command, but the knights listened to him now, where they had only laughed before. Torres nodded, turned his mount and went swiftly back down the ridge.

"Come, then! Hewers of wood and drawers of water we must be, while the sun lingers. Raffel, will you take the horses down to drink?"

"Gladly, if Tomas will assist. Give me your reins here. A knight may care for his mount and his companions' at need, but gleaning wood is brothers' labour. Brothers or peasants, and I am neither."

"There's no disgrace in labour. Brother." A hard word for Anton to say, and he meant it hardly. "And would you deny our confrères a light to fix their eyes on, a sign of journey's end? They'll welcome it, I swear to you . . ."

He spoke lightly, teasingly against Raffel's pride, but Anton meant it deeply. It was what he had looked for every night from the castle walls and been denied, what he had truly never hoped to see, a glimmer of hope in the darkness. He could offer to others what no one offered to him, and that was another change in him, he thought.

SHERARD CARRIED AN axe at his saddle-bow, but would not use it. "No sense in angering the master of these lands. They are not our trees to fell. And if they were, still I would not touch them. Older than us, older than the Kingdom: some of these olives are older than your family, d'Escrivey, or mine. Some might have been rooted here before the God walked this country. Would you cut that thread of history, would you kill a tree that the God Himself might have seen and touched and eaten from, for the sake of a fire on a hot night?"

"Not I," Anton murmured, smiling. "Olives as old as these will drop their branches under the sun's weight as a boy with cracked knuckles drops his sword. Let's gather what they've let fall, and be thankful."

COLLECTING WOOD MEANT unaccustomed labour, scrambling over steep slopes with uncertain footing, dragging awkward branches. Anton was not the first to strip off his heavy cloak and mail, nor the last to envy Raffel and Tomas their easier task with the horses.

Eventually, though, Anton could strike a light from flint and tinder, to coax a fire into life. As the boughs began to catch, he straightened and turned his back to the rising flames, in time to see the last red touch of the sun flare across the distant line of the sea.

Back at the Roq, Frater Susurrus would be tolling the hour, calling brothers and guests to service. On the road, Marshal Fulke would lead his army's voice in prayer as he led its body towards war. Here there was only Anton to do that work, and only his few companions to hear. That would not matter to them, nor to the God; he wished that it did not matter to him. He remembered praying in his own quarters, with Marron's soft voice joined to his; he remembered one morning when they had prayed together as they lay together in his bed. The Church would call that heresy. At the time he'd thought, he'd even said that the God would not. Now he wasn't so sure, he wasn't so proud in himself; all that he was sure of, he would hear Marron's whisper answer him every time he led anyone in prayer again.

It had to be done, though, none of these would steal the lead from him. And so it was done, and he hoped that their spirits could draw some comfort from it; his own could not. He could have thrust his arm into these leaping flames beside him and watched it blacken and wither, felt its slow death; he tried to thrust his haunting affection for Marron into the furnace that tempered souls, and felt nothing beyond a queasy wrongness. *As though Marron has no place in the God's eye, for sin or for salvation—* but that again must be heresy.

"Go down," he said after the last words of the appointed ritual had died into the night, after they had stood respectfully silent in the firelight for a minute longer, after he had sought and failed to find any sense of solace or release within himself. "Go down and meet the men in the valley, when they come. I will tend our beacon."

They went, with smiles and warm words but also a prompt obedience, all three of which Anton still found hard to fathom. Had he really changed so much, to force such a change towards him? He didn't believe so. Perhaps it was that the world had changed around them all, demanding new dispensations . . .

NEW, BUT NOT so new. He still found himself alone on a height. The fire blazed, the wood crackled and spat, he felt his skin tighten in a rush of heat; in a rush of memory he heard young boys screaming as they died and almost saw Marron's face this night as he had seen it then, across a distance and through the flames, frozen ice-hard and close to shattering.

Then he heard the tread of booted feet climbing the road, one man alone. That could only be one man. The road drew him up into the light; Anton bowed—just slightly, a touch more than a nod, as though he were on horseback still and saluting from the saddle—and said, "Magister. I hope that you find this satisfactory. It's a hard bed, but every man has a blanket, and we can spread as far as we need along the ridge. I thought it best to leave the horses below; if we watch from up here, we can see any danger that threatens long before it reaches them."

"What danger do you imagine, Sieur Anton, in the heart of Tallis? We are far from Surayon."

"That is not our only enemy, Magister. We are just one day's ride from the border, and we left a much-reduced garrison behind us."

"Do you think the Sharai will know that, and raid at our tail?"

The question forced a reluctant smile. "No, Magister. But I am a soldier, and I have watched from a high place for years now; perhaps it is become a habit."

"No bad habit, for a soldier. I do not criticise your choice, Sieur Anton. Tell me, have you ever fought in a war?"

"No. Skirmishes only, and that one night at the castle . . ." There was an obvious question leading on, but only impertinence could ask it.

"Nor I," Fulke said, gifting him the answer regardless. "We are soldiers by training only, I know the frustration of that; but the God will use us in His time, and I believe that time is now. Come, I have something to show you. Do not be afraid."

He produced a candle from his sleeve, a candle of

white and black tapers intricately plaited into one; stooping, he snatched a brand from the fire and lit its several wicks.

"Forgive me, Magister, but I have seen the King's Eye opened before, and found nothing in it to be afraid of."

"I think you will not have seen how I intend to use it." And then, a seemingly irrelevant question, "Why do you call me Magister, as the brothers do? The Rule does not require it of knights."

"They are not life-sworn to the Order, as I am."

"No. A curious creature you've made of yourself, Sieur Anton—neither true brother nor truly knight, despite your dress. Well, let it stand. The God will dispose all, when He brings us to the test. In the meantime, watch and learn."

Fulke murmured a few words and passed his hand across the candle. Its feeble yellow light grew incandescent in a moment, as its flickering flames stilled and rose like white-hot rods of steel.

This was nothing new to Anton, familiarity had almost—almost!—worn the wonder out of it. He couldn't understand the marshal's words, nor see how those words could cause these things to happen, but he was no superstitious peasant, to fear what he could not understand. The Sharai practised forbidden magic, the Surayonnaise were sorcerers, and a sensible man would fear both even as he fought them; Fulke was the God's man, a priest as much as a warrior, and what he wove here was miraculous and blessed.

What he wove was light, bending those columns of rigid flame with word and touch and gesture until they spread out and down like fingers, until they broke apart into a thousand threads that glowed like golden wire. The threads made a tapestry, an intricate image in the air; Anton saw the whole of the Sanctuary Land, all of Outremer spread out before him like a map.

"See," Fulke said, and the map moved and swelled, fraying into invisibility at its edges as the centre spread wider and more detailed, "here is Surayon where we are bound, where we hope to come. Nothing can be Folded in the King's Eye."

There it was indeed, couched between its mountain walls: smallest of the five states that made the Kingdom, little more than a single broad valley. Despite himself, Anton bent low to peer at it. Any more detail, and he might be looking to see the arch-sorcerer, the Princip in his palace, working at his spells . . .

"That is not what I mean to show you, though," Fulke said. Surayon swirled away; for a moment Anton felt like a hawk, swept from his soaring by a wind too strong to beat against. A wind driven by another man's will, and that will strong enough to break him, feather and bone, if he tried to resist its forcing . . .

Almost he managed a smile then; he didn't often think himself bird-delicate or vulnerable to storms. But he didn't often have a companion like Fulke, so focused, so determined, so certain of his course. It occurred to him that they could both perhaps benefit from a little self-doubt, a passing touch of humanity.

And then there was no more time for thought, as he stooped—yes, very like a hawk—and was dragged down once more towards this strange and glowing landscape, this map of wonder. A moment's disorientation, where he had to remember that he still had a body and that it was under his command, that he could draw back from the King's Eye; he did so, and a frowning effort helped him to identify the land laid out before him. That had been Less Arvon that had just rushed past him, swifter than any hawk could fly; this was Tallis now, and not so far from where he actually stood on solid rock and earth. A day's journey to the east, perhaps, a day closer to the rising mountain-range.

It rose, or he fell; or neither of those, but it appeared so. He saw hills and valleys etched in light, and it was more and more like falling as his field of view narrowed to one particular valley that seemed to open and engulf him; detail massed before his eyes, and the surrounding hills loomed high on either hand. He lost sight of the horizon and couldn't properly see even the ridge he stood on, for this dazzling tapestry thrown over.

What he could see was a river that ran like living, livid gold, not yet at its natural size but soon, surely, if it and he drew any closer. He could see no sign of man's work in the valley, no trees or planted fields, though the true land was fertile and farmed; when he squinted, he thought he could make out a roughness on the hillsides, as though the King's Eye were sharp enough to delineate individual rocks. Nothing moved among them, there was no sign of anything that lived.

He had thought himself familiar with the King's Eye, he'd boasted so, but he'd never encountered it like this: only as a map, a chart scrolled with lines of light for ink upon an unseen parchment, or else as a model showing all the shapes of hills and cities. This was something entirely other, where a man might find his map burn like a fiery landscape all about him. *You will not have seen how I intend to use it,* Fulke had said, and Anton would not argue with him now.

"What is this," he murmured to the man at his side, "what have you brought me to?"

"The heart of a miracle," Fulke replied. "Here, take my hand, and follow close."

Anton couldn't turn his eyes from the glittering marvel that had swallowed him. Like a hawk come to ground, he stood now on the river's bank or so it seemed, although he could not hear the water's movement. If it were water. He had heard stories in his childhood of a land where rivers ran with molten gold; he'd never thought to see it, never truly believed it till this moment.

He felt Fulke's fingers close around his, and grip tightly. He could almost find comfort in that, though not enough. When the marshal tugged at him he resisted, or his body did, lacking his consent to move. It was only Fulke's soft laugh that impelled him to take one step forward, and then another.

IT WAS AS though he had crossed a border he could neither see nor sense. He was wreathed in steam suddenly that seemed to be rising from the river, which was hissing now beside and below him, though it had appeared quite silent before. Even the hot, swirling steam had a golden gleam to it, dazzling and stinging his eyes. He blinked, rubbed at them and found his skin damp to the touch. Cautiously, he touched his tongue to his finger; the acrid, burning taste of it made him spit.

Again, Fulke laughed. "Do not try to drink the water, Sieur Anton. It would be fatal to you."

"Where are we?"

"In Tallis, as you saw—and yet not in Tallis, as you might find it by riding. By the God's grace and the power of the King, we are granted a passage into the Eye at need, into any place that the Eye can show us."

"Even into Surayon?"

"Aye, even there," bitterly. "But there is like this, a golden desert country in the God's eye, not the land given to us for our habitation; and we have found no way to step from this to that. Even the God does not grant us wings, Sieur Anton," for all the world as though he knew how that hawk's image lingered. "If I blew out this candle, you would find yourself back on the ridge, beside your blazing beacon. I shall do so shortly, and you will. One may walk beneath the lid of the King's Eye, and so come safely to the place one seeks; one may use it as the preceptor does, to overview any part of the Kingdom and what moves there; or one may use it as I have tonight, to come to this half-land that resembles our own, and is not."

Anton nodded, striving hard to appear calm in the grip of wonder. "What point, then, in the journey? Why have you brought us here?"

"For a meeting. We should find a man here, to whom I have taught a little of this skill. He is no priest, but if his faith is as strong as he proclaims it, if he serves the King-dom and the God, he should have managed to cross from our world into this. It is a useful attribute, to have a place to meet that is hidden from enemies and doubtful friends alike; why else would the God and the King between them have given us this blessing?"

That didn't answer the greater half of Anton's ques-tion, *why have you brought me with you, why seek me out for this?* He held his peace, though, and simply followed Fulke a short distance away from the river, till they were free of the clouds of steam.

Then, "Blaise!" Fulke's voice echoed strangely in the flat, lifeless air. "Blaise, if you are here, show yourself!"

A shadow moved from behind a rock upslope of them—but no, it was not a shadow. A man, rather, in dark, drab clothing. With a start, Anton recognised the name, and then the man. Blaise had been the Lady Ju-lianne's sergeant at the Roq; did he now serve Marshal Fulke? Seemingly so. The strangeness of that, though, was overborne by something stranger, as Anton's first thought caught up with him. The man cast no shadow as he stumbled down towards them, both hands wrapped protectively around a candle. A glance up at the sky con-firmed what should have been impossible, that there was no sun to make shadows.

Anton had only ever seen Blaise dressed according to

his rank and allegiance, as an Elessan soldier; it was plain
from his greeting to Fulke, an awkward "Magister", that
he had once worn other garb. Easy to guess that Blaise
had been a brother once, had lost the right to wear the
habit and now clung to what little was left him. Less easy
by far to divine what service he did Fulke and the Order
now, dressed as he was in rough homespun such as any
landsworn peasant might wear, gabbling as he was in
what seemed to be terror barely and badly disguised.

"Magister, I have done as you bade me, but I don't
know if it is an angel or a devil I follow, I cannot tell; and
this place your power has brought me to, it is as hot and
dead as hell itself, I cannot be easy in it . . ."

"None the less, you must learn to use it as I have
shown you, as you have tonight. Not my power, Blaise,
but the God's; or the King's, rather, given by the God's
grace. Trust, and do not be afraid."

As well tell a rock not to stand, Anton thought, or a
river not to flow. Even here, those laws applied.

"We will be swift, though; we ought not to linger
where we can come only on sufferance. Tell me briefly,
then, whatever you have seen and done these last days."

"Magister, I found the wandering preacher, and his
band. I have not joined them, quite; they are saints all, I
think, or else they are possessed. They do not speak to
strangers, I have never seen them speak among themselves. But I am not the only one who follows at a distance."

Fulke frowned at that. "I want you close. Have you
heard him preaching?"

"Oh yes, Magister. The plague runs ahead of him, and
he follows it from village to village. At every halt he
heals the sick—I have seen that, and it is terrible: one
touch from the relic that he carries and even the dying,
even the damned are whole again, our own people or
Catari, no difference—and then he speaks. He speaks of

war as you do, war against Surayon the cursed, the Folded Land. Then he moves on. Those he has healed, those he has touched join with his disciples; others follow. We are not an army to make war with," at last a glimpse of the soldier through his fear, "there are old men and children, women too among his disciples, and they carry no weapons; but the number grows every day. Even a rabble may be dangerous . . ."

"Even a rabble can win a war, if it is armed with faith," Fulke responded. "Have you learned his name yet, or whence he came?"

"No, Magister. He never says."

"Get closer, then. Speak to him directly, ask him outright. Find a way. He has claimed a share of my war; it may be that he is a weapon of the God, to swing the fight to us."

"Or an instrument of devils, Magister, to turn it against us. There is something cold in him, and in his people."

"That too, it may be so. Find out, Blaise. However you need to."

"Magister, I will try . . ."

"To try is to fail before you begin. Do it, Blaise. That is my command."

And then Fulke leaned forward and blew out the sergeant's candle, whose flame he had shielded so nervously within his palms. Nothing changed, except that the man was no longer there. There was no noise in his leaving, no swirl of light or shade; only his absence, so sudden that Anton wondered for a moment if he had ever actually been there at all.

"We are all phantasms, walking in a dream of light," Fulke said, with a thin smile that he threw at Anton like a challenge, the moment before he extinguished his own candle.

THREE

A Smudge of Light

MARRON FELT THAT he need be scared of nothing now.

With the Daughter in his blood and in his eyes, with Dard in his hand he could outfight any man, any number of men; with the Daughter in the air, in his sight, he could outrun man or spirit, slide between worlds as fast as sliding between one thought and another.

With Jemel at his side, he thought that he need neither run nor fight. He thought that the two of them together could simply walk away. They could go to the east, perhaps, where there was no Sieur Anton and no holy war; if they went far enough, beyond the wide stretch of the Sands, there would be no djinn and no 'ifrit either, and even the gods would be strangers to them both. They could become traders, perhaps, dealers in silks and horseflesh among the yellow men of myth. Jemel knew horses, and Marron supposed that he could learn. They could both learn about silks. They might even trade with the

Sharai, with Outremer, sending their baggage-trains west, sending messages to their abandoned friends but never coming back, no, making a new home and a new life for themselves in distant lands.

Or else they could be explorers, writing their names in legend as they traversed the land of the djinn. Even now, though, as they stood high above that wide and golden world with a hot marvel beneath their feet, even now Jemel was agitating for what Marron wouldn't and couldn't allow.

"Jemel, Jazra is dead. Why are you so keen to follow him, so quickly?"

"Jazra is dead," Jemel said, "and I do not mean to follow him at all. I'll wait till you are dead, and follow both. But Anton d'Escrivey I will send after Jazra, as soon as may be. It is my promise."

His voice was husky now, scarred by the deep scar on his throat. Likely he would always sound so young, then, younger than he should. At the moment he was acting also younger than he should, dancing his impatience on hot rock.

"Morakh all but killed you, and Sieur Anton is a better swordsman than Morakh. I have fought them both, I know."

"Morakh took me with a trick."

"And what, do you suppose that Sieur Anton is any more honourable? In a duel with his own kind, then yes, perhaps. But he will fight and kill an infidel any way that comes to hand. He has done so, you have seen. No, Jemel. He would overpower you, and you would die; and this time there would be no Elisande to save you. I think she would be angry to see all her work wasted."

"I should be sorry to make her angry at me—but I have sworn an oath, to seek my vengeance. If the God slay me instead, that is His will and must be endured. I said I would see you to Rhabat, and I have done that much and more . . ."

"What, do you want me to quit you of my service?"

"I want you to come with me, Ghost Walker. As you know. I came with you, this far."

"You did, and I am glad of it. More than glad. But I am the Ghost Walker, and I can't wander where I choose through Outremer in pursuit of my friend's folly." *Though I will run with you, far and far from Outremer, if you will let me.*

"You wander where you choose here, in pursuit of some folly of your own." Jemel's voice was sour, caustic enough to cut even the strings that had been twitching at him, so that at last he stood still and silent on the edge there. They had retraced some part of Marron's earlier journey in this land, that he had shared with Elisande; the great needle of stone was still far ahead, and there was only a long fall before them now. Under their feet, at their backs was the mountain cut and polished by the djinn: a mirror made to reflect the sky back to itself, dark rock that wasted its heart-heat in a sheen that showed nothing to nothing, to speak of the vast emptiness of this uninhabited world . . .

Except that the world was not uninhabited, and he should not think it so. Even as the thought did flit across his mind, Marron heard a susurration at his ear, the grate of wind on still air.

"Djinni," he said, a warning to Jemel as much as a greeting to the spirit.

"Half-human."

That turned him. It was a shimmer, a twist, an intangible string in the air but not of the air. In his own land it would perhaps have glittered as it spun, perhaps have gathered up some dust to make itself a visible body; here it did neither, and Jemel was probably not seeing it at all. Marron's enhanced eyes could find it, but barely.

"I have carried a few titles," *brother, squire, heretic, abomination,* "but half-human is new to me."

"You have that within you that is not human. I do not know the proportions, whether you master what you carry or whether it masters you; either is possible. I could dismember you, but that would teach me only that it survives what you cannot, and that I know already."

"Djinni Tachur." Easy to name it now. "If Elisande sent you to me, then I am sure there will have been a reason."

"There was. She required me to tell you that the daughter of the King's Shadow has been taken from Rhabat, by the Sand Dancer Morakh. I cannot find them. Neither could you, but she would like to see you fail."

No echo of Elisande's voice surviving in the djinni's, but something of the girl's desperation came through none the less. *Tell him that Julianne's gone, and how; tell him you can't help; tell him that I need him, urgently . . .*

"It will take us two days to come back to her, on foot." Longer, perhaps. Time was hard to judge here, and they had not hurried. They could hurry now, but not defeat the miles. He was a doorkeeper, no more than that; he could not overleap time or distance, in his passage between worlds.

"I will take you, if you will permit it. She ordered me to fetch you whether you would or no; some orders I am prepared to disobey, though, and that is one."

Too proud to be a slave, it would make a captious servant. That was for Elisande to confront; he'd watch when he could, and enjoy. In the meantime she had asked for him, sent for him, whichever. Marron said, "I will permit it, djinni," smiling a little at his own condescension even as he reached for Jemel's hand.

A whipping wind lifted his feet from the plateau, and he felt the sudden drag of Jemel's weight against his fingers. He tightened his grasp and hauled with easy, inhuman strength, yanking the other boy up to stand beside him on seemingly solid air, binding Jemel's body against his own with an arm wrapped around the narrow waist. Wide, startled eyes stared into his from an inch's distance; Marron smiled again for reassurance, *did you think I would let it abandon you?*

Jemel turned his head away. Marron gazed at tangled black hair and the tawny neck beneath, heard a broken whisper, half chuckle and half sob. "Look down, Marron, we are flying . . ."

Obediently, Marron looked. They were skimming like gulls over the flattened peak; for a moment he could see not a shadow but a dim reflection of his own body and Jemel's in the glittering gloss of its surface. Then they passed the southern edge, and he saw the landscape fall away. Suddenly they were at eagle-height or higher, so high now that he lost that rushing sense of speed. They might have been soaring like an eagle indeed until the wide golden land beneath them began to fade, to lose itself behind a swirling darkness. Briefly he thought that he had Julianne's disease, an unexpected terror of great heights.

The darkness grew to encompass them all, to block out the shimmering light. The djinni shone within it, though, visible now like a shaving of that same light, like a twisting hair of gold. Not Marron's head that was spinning, then, and not his sight that had clouded. At last he understood, this was how the djinni would make the shift from this world to their own. Unlike the Daughter, which simply ripped an open way between, the spirit was taking them out of the one entirely before it brought them to the other.

Out of the one, and into what? Into a nothingness that had no light, no heat. He was barely aware of Jemel's body pressed close against his, barely aware of his own; he wanted to feel himself pinched or punched or bitten, only to reassure himself that he could still feel something.

It was a dark and a chill and an inhospitable place, and Marron wanted no more of it. Would have preferred less, indeed, and a great deal less by the time he felt a bitter wind scour his skin, solid as a wall to lean against. He turned his head upward and saw familiar stars like a glory, like a blaze across the sky to welcome him.

BRACED AGAINST THE wind, he locked his arms around Jemel and kept his eyes fixed on the ground so far below. There were undulations in the sand that must be great dunes to those who had to cross them, that looked like mere ripples to him. He could see occasional breaks in the smooth still flow of them, that must mark outcrops of rock; he thought he could see a glimmering mirror to the east, the Dead Waters trapping the stars' light as they had trapped this djinni that carried him now.

It took a long time even for his eyes to find the slightest gleam, the faintest smudge of light among the dunes. He was barely sure of it; the djinni, though, must have been certain because they were descending suddenly, fast and straight. As he blinked into the wind, the glow resolved itself into a dying fire, with a single figure sitting huddled beside. Another lay on the ground at a little distance.

The djinni brought them down to the fire and set them lightly on the sand. The figure lifted its head and was Elisande, a blanket around her shoulders and an exhausted tension in her face, in her voice too as she said, "Thank you, Esren."

"Indeed." It said no more than that but stayed, a single golden thread in a gloomy tapestry. Its service done, it was only an observer now: curious, perhaps, if the djinn felt curiosity. This one might.

Elisande stood, and came slowly to him. He still had one arm around Jemel, but she rested her cheek briefly against his other shoulder and said, "You, too. Thank you for coming. Both of you."

"What else should we have done?" *We should have stayed and left you to your own concerns, we should have broken free*—but friendship was a snare, a cord that tightened against a struggle and would not break easily. Oaths he could break and had, but not this simpler binding.

She drew breath beside him, intending perhaps to answer what he hadn't really meant to be a question. Seeming not to find the words she needed, she just sighed and shook her head, touched his arm with chilly fingers and turned back to the fire.

"Tell us what happened, Elisande." That was Jemel, making some little play to claim his own place here, both as Marron's companion and one among her certain friends.

Again she took a breath, again she tried to speak. This time there were words, but weariness and worry held her spirit in defeat; she could tell them little more than the djinni had already. Julianne had been taken, on the night of her wedding, three nights since. The djinni had been unable to track Morakh and his captive; she and the King's Shadow had tried, were trying yet, but were having little joy of the hunt.

"We've scoured the Sands, by Esren's grace," she said, "and all we've found is the remains of a fire here, some signs that were hard to read, and this." She slipped something from her wrist and held it out to show him: a golden bangle studded with little gems. "It might have been one of Julianne's wedding-gifts. Coren thinks so, at least. We believe that they are with an 'ifrit. If it took a winged shape, it could have carried them anywhere by now. We didn't find this place until this evening, and the fire was cold by days. They must have stopped to rest and eat, an 'ifrit can't fly at Esren's speed, but . . ."

But they were long gone from here, so much was obvious. The chase was futile; and yet Marron could understand the need for it, the urge to be doing something. "Would they have crossed into Outremer?"

"Coren says not, he says that the King could find them if they went within his borders. He may be right," though her tone suggested doubt, either of the Shadow or possibly of the King himself. "But there is endless country they could hide in, this side of the border; and Coren's so tired, we both are. Speak softly, don't wake him. He didn't want me to send for you but I had to, I couldn't carry this alone . . ."

The King's Shadow might be tired, might be worn out indeed from his own anxiety as Elisande was from hers, but Marron was suspicious of his sleeping. He could hear the man's soft, steady breathing, and thought he could sense a wakeful, listening mind behind it.

"Why did Hasan leave the two of you," a girl and an ageing man, albeit a djinni's companion and a man of rare abilities and rarer friends, "to do his hunting for him?"

Elisande smiled slightly, where in a lighter mood she would have laughed aloud. Marron missed the laughter, had been consciously trying for it; he knew the answer before he asked the question. "Oh, he didn't. We left him, he couldn't keep up. The camels died, all of them, in the flood. Horses, too, though he couldn't have brought horses over this," and she sifted sand between her fingers while her other arm waved at dunes that ran to every horizon. "He went back to Rhabat, to try to keep the tribes together. He says that the theft of his bride from their own citadel is an insult to all the Sharai, not simply a matter for the Beni Rus. He says that if there are 'ifrit involved, it may need many warriors to retrieve her; he says that he will gather what camels he can from the local tribes, if he has to spend all the wealth in Rhabat to do it. Then he will follow, as quickly as may be. Esren carries messages between us, so he will know where to come. But we have to find Julianne first. If we fail, then Hasan will have his army at the gates of Outremer"—*at the gates of Surayon* she meant, or so Marron heard her— "and he will not waste that opportunity, with his men hot for fighting. Even if we do find Julianne and rescue her, he will still be there, with his army at his back; I don't think her pleading could hold his hand. There will be war, Marron, unless we can find her and rescue her ourselves before he comes. That's why I wanted you, in case . . . But I think there will be war."

So did Marron. So perhaps did the silent djinni, which would explain her hopelessness if it had been less silent earlier. A spirit with some sense of the future could spell doom to any prophet.

"Julianne's father is here," Jemel said suddenly, pointedly. "Where is yours?" His voice carried generations of tradition, of certainly in what was right and proper.

"He is with Hasan. For all I know he may be arguing still against bringing war to Outremer; if so, he wastes his breath."

"He should be here, then. Why is he not here?"

"I have a knife. He has a throat."

And that certainly was right, and wise in both of them. Elisande was as drawn as an overtight cable, and her father could make her snap at any time; at such a time as this, she might truly let fly with a blade where honed words would have contented her before. If not, his presence would still divide this little party into two, his and hers. Marron and Jemel would stand with Elisande, the King's Shadow with Rudel; youth would divorce experience, fire would fight with ice and they would travel more slowly and learn less.

Let him use his skills elsewhere, then, let him work yet on Hasan, *thus far and no further, pursue your wife but not your dreams, learn to live with Outremer* . . . It would do no good, Marron thought, one man's voice couldn't turn a tide; but let him try, at least.

Jemel grunted his understanding and turned the conversation abruptly to a more compelling issue. "Do you have any food?"

Elisande flashed him a sympathetic smile, her mood shifting in a moment to match his. She'd been in the land of the djinn; she knew how appetite was a stranger there but how it returned full force in this world. Even Marron felt hungry now, at the mere mention.

"Yes, of course. I'm sorry, I should have thought. There's plenty, Jemel—we've got bread, cold meat, cheese, fruit. Good bread too, not desert bake. Esren fetches it for us, with our fuel and water."

"You use a djinni to fetch water?" This time his tone was sheer incredulity.

"We have to; we've no camels, and we can't carry as much as we need." She was busy as she spoke, passing over a waterskin and crouching above a pack; Marron had only her voice and the set of her shoulders to read, but they were enough. Esren had let her down, through weakness or malice or for whatever reason; she was seeking any way she could to use it in humiliation, ageless and potent spirit reduced to a handservant . . .

THEY SAID LITTLE more after that. For a while their mouths were too busy, Jemel's and his own, they couldn't chew nor swallow fast enough to meet the demands of their raging stomachs. Elisande sliced meat and cheese for them, tore bread, found cups for water.

Then the simple weight of food inside them made them sleepy, just as her own long day, her several weary days and sleep-short nights all too visibly caught up with her. The night was cold, and she offered them her blanket, but they wouldn't take it. Jemel had slept out colder nights than this, he said, and sat out colder still with only rags to huddle in, no robe such as he wore now. Besides, the warmth of the other world was with him still, crept deep into the marrow of his bones. With Marron at his one side and the fireglow at his other, he'd be content as any sheikh within his tent . . .

Marron, of course, was never cold at all. He had his own otherworldly warmth that went deeper than his marrow, went to his soul except that what it found there, it could never warm.

So they arranged themselves, he and Jemel this side of the fire and Elisande that, lying close to the King's Shadow who still hadn't moved and who still, Marron thought, was not asleep. Better that way, perhaps: a man of his age and cunning ought to be wakeful, thinking, conceiving and plotting. Ought not to be chasing hard across an empty desert in pursuit of a long-vanished phantom and a captured girl. Let his mind run free in the hunt, and perhaps his body would fail at last to follow; perhaps he'd be so weary come the morning, they could legitimately turn on him all together, prove he was unnecessary, send him back to Rhabat to rest . . .

COME THE MORNING, Marron woke to find that old and exhausted man on his feet and active while their other companions still slept.

He had been active, rather; fresh young flames were licking at new-laid cakes of camel-dung among the ashes of last night's fire. Now he was standing atop a dune-crest at some little distance, standing like a monolith with its face set towards Outremer, when he should surely have been sitting close and taking in what heat he could to set against the ache in his bones and the morning's early chill.

Marron peeled himself carefully away from the huddled warmth of Jemel's back, with a silent apology for leaving it so exposed. He stood up and walked softly over the sand, feeling how the dawn wind whipped it against his ankles as he climbed the dune. Joining Julianne's father, he saw their two shadows strike a clear path due west, as though they laid a path that men should follow. Greyish dust swirled high on the gusting wind, while tawny sand skittered beneath in the slow, endless progress of the desert. *Give it a few thousand years more,* Marron thought, *and Hasan won't need his army, no need of all that fighting and dying that Jemel's so hungry for. The Sands will swallow Outremer and none but the Sharai will have the heart or the wisdom to live there then . . .*

He watched the shadows' long run in the low light, and might almost have been talking to one of them, certainly didn't turn his head to face the man beside him as he said, "Shadow? Tell me about the King."

"My name is Coren."

"I know, but—"

"But you have trouble calling men by their given names, when they carry titles. Respect is no bad sign in a young man; none the less, Marron, call me Coren if you can turn your tongue around the word. You are at least as important as any of us, and I would prefer it so. Jemel will follow your lead; Elisande is there already."

"Elisande gives no respect to anyone. Not even to the djinni . . ."

"That is not entirely true, though she'd like to know you think it. Come, this is not so much to ask, where there are so few of us caught in such a turmoil."

"Well, I will try. Must I call the King also by his name, to make you answer my question?"

That barb drew a quiet chuckle in response. "No, I'll not ask that much of you. I don't ask it of myself, though I used to once. Long ago, when we were two adventurers together I used to call him Marc, and quarrel with him for the sheer love of losing in a fight. These days, not— though one would still lose. Assuredly, one would lose."

"Tell me about him."

"What would you have me say?"

"Is he a man?"

"Oh, yes." The question didn't draw a laugh, though, as it surely must have done if it were as stupid as it sounded. "Trust me in this, Marron, he is most certainly a man. I've seen him bleed; I've *made* him bleed, more than once. I've seen him eat and sleep, defecate and for- nicate, which are the four prime motivations of mankind. If that's been worrying you, rest easy. He may be King of Outremer, with all that that implies, but he's human yet."

"I don't understand, then. All the stories I've heard, from you and others—how can he do what you say he does, if he's just a man like any other?"

"I didn't say that. He was never very much like other men. He's ten years older than I, so I never knew him as a boy; even as a youth, though, he had talents that singled him out. His father was a powerful man, but he was the youngest son of five, so had no hope of inheriting land or title. He spent his early manhood in a monastery, but was, ah, persuaded out of it; then he discovered an interest in travel and soldiery, making war against pirates and ban- dit lords. He took me with him, me and others; we hung at his tail like daglocks from a sheep, we little boys, we worshipped him. But so did older men, all those who fol- lowed him.

"When the cry went up for an army to reclaim the Sanctuary Land for the God, he was the obvious man to lead it. He was created Duc de Charelles for that purpose, because the lords and churchmen who declared themselves for the venture would yield to no lesser rank. It's a courtesy title, Charelles is a lump of rock in the ocean which offers no better harvest than gull-droppings, but a duke is a duke regardless.

"So he went to war again, this time with thousands in his train, but I was closest. It was a hard journey, and a harder fight: many battles, many deaths, a great deal of evil on both sides. But he held the army together, lords and church, until we had won Outremer. The Ekhed had governed the land for centuries but they couldn't stand against us, they retreated to their kingdom in the south; the Sharai fought us tribe by tribe, and tribe by tribe we drove them back into the desert.

"Then there would have been trouble, as all those ambitious men fell to quarrelling over the spoils; but my lord and friend summoned the Conclave. He called the nobles and prelates into one building, the Dir'al Shahan that had been the greatest temple in Ascariel; he made them leave their weapons in the porch, he locked the doors with his own hands and pocketed the key, and he made his own divisions of the land. He told them who would govern where, he showed them on maps, he drew the boundaries himself. In the course of one day he created the five states that you know and gave them to the most powerful of the lords. To the Church he gave nothing. He knew what trouble that would bring, and so he allowed the Ransomers their castles, and he made his own son Duke of Ascariel; that boy was always the Church's man, more than his father's.

"Himself he declared King of Outremer and demanded oaths of allegiance and fealty from all, would let no one leave till they had sworn. Then he sent them out and locked the doors again behind them. All that year, while the Kingdom settled into its new name, he was seen seldom outside the Dir'al Shahan; since then, never. For forty years he has ruled from isolation. I am his

Shadow, I speak for him, but even I see him rarely and only when he summons me. I used to be his friend, but now? I am not sure."

How does he eat and dress, Marron wanted to ask, *who serves him?* The question seemed trivial, though, against the sense of loss he heard in the other's voice; so he asked another, an easier question instead. "You have named him a man, a warrior and a diplomat; how was he made a magician, then, where does he take his power from?"

"That I do not know. I've never had the temerity to ask," *and neither should you, if I do not.* "He has great power, but the source of it is as secret as his life. He summons me, or more commonly he sends me; I do as I am bid, no more than that."

"And if he summons you today, this morning, now? Would you go, would you abandon your daughter to serve your king?" It was a question that turned and turned in Marron's mind, duty against love. He had answered it himself, he thought, both one way and the other; both had felt wrong, treacherous, bringing a deformity to the world. Both had broken what should have been most strong, had spilled what was most precious.

"Marron, when he summons me, he doesn't offer choices. I have abandoned my daughter before, remember? On the road to the Roq, and at other times too often to count. Not to such peril, I confess—but yes, I would go. I would have to."

All the more reason to find Julianne quickly, then, and rescue her if they could. Marron had another thought, though, another question. "Can you speak to him? From here, I mean, right now?"

"Not outside the Kingdom, no. He speaks to me, where and when he chooses. He has sent me from Marasson to Rhabat and further; I am only his Shadow, with a shadow's strength."

"Well, if he speaks to you before we have her safe, could you not ask him to summon Julianne, the way he summons you?"

Coren smiled faintly. "Oh, I could ask. I will ask, if the occasion arises. But will he answer me? I do not know. Years ago, yes—he would have risked his own life, perhaps his whole army for a child in danger. He has changed, though, since he came into his new title. Great strength and great responsibility will change any man; you know that, Marron, you have been changed yourself. Believe me, when I say that his alteration outweighs yours by all the distance of age and authority that lies between you."

Forty years, and a Kingdom: Marron could believe that without difficulty. He thought it ought to change a man beyond recognition; he thought that perhaps it had, by the touch of regret in Coren's voice. A friend lost, and perhaps a daughter too—they ought to command more than a touch, but the King's Shadow kept his humanity as hidden as his master, or tried to.

He was speaking again now, as his eyes remained fixed on the far horizon. "It occurs to me, Marron, that I may perhaps be able to guess where Julianne has been taken. If they are wise, they will not cross the border; I do not know how the King would react to that, so certainly neither does Morakh, nor any 'ifrit. There is a place, though, that lies on this line, and a little outside the Kingdom. I don't understand why they would head there, but every bare sign we find suggests it. There is nowhere else, at least, and I don't believe that they are running aimlessly, although I cannot see their purpose. Wake Elisande; this day may bring us answers, of a sort."

FOUR

Spirit Snares

JULIANNE KNEW WHERE she was now, at last; she knew what she had to fear.

SHE'D BEEN FRIGHTENED before—or had she?—when her body had not been her own, neither her thoughts: when she had felt her bones and muscles pull and shift all out of her control while her mind kept barely a thread's connection to what was real in the world, while it swam and sank in sickening oils, a haze of colours and shapes that meant nothing and touched her nowhere and yet were sickening regardless. She'd had no use of eyes or feet or fingers, her own skin had been alien to her and there was nothing in her head that she could claim. She had known somehow that she was moving; had she known also that she was afraid?

* * *

SHE COULDN'T SAY. What had come later—after she had been allowed her body again, after she had been let slip back inside her skin, when she had fallen back on rough rock and shivered frantically for more than the cold bite of the night and sobbed at the taste of harsh dusty air against her tongue and throat—what came then had been terrifying too, or so she thought now, looking back. There had been a creature, hard to see it clearly because of the way its black body sheened in the starglow but certainly it had been an 'ifrit, an 'ifrit with wings, longer and broader she thought than those that had attacked at Rhabat. Morakh had spoken to it, though she hadn't heard it speak nor ever heard that such spirits could; and then it had spread those wings and leaped from the clifftop—which was when she'd realised that there was a clifftop, and they were too close to the edge of it. Staring around in starlight she recognised the place, high above Rhabat and the Dead Waters, close to the temple and the tunnel's mouth. Marron had mentioned an 'ifrit, she thought, and a dead imam—but that was days before, and the 'ifrit had been defeated. Hadn't they . . .?

This one not, as it seemed. It had soared high, and swooped low; Morakh had hauled her to her feet, and she'd felt long claws bind themselves about her like a whip's coils as her body jerked like a whipped girl's, her neck snapped back, she was snatched abruptly into the air.

No comfort that Morakh was beside her, that they had this terror to share. She had dangled helplessly, eyes tightly shut, an unknown distance above a ground she could not bear to look upon; she had filled her mind with a constant repetition, a desperate litany: *I have climbed a mountain. Besides, they want me living, therefore it will not let me fall. Besides, this beast is burdened, weight will drag it down. If I opened my eyes, if it were daylight, likely I would see that there is not so far to fall, no further and no worse than falling from Merissa. I miss*

*Merissa. She gave me a smoother ride than this, and
faster too; I was never scared to fall from her. Besides, I
climbed a mountain . . .*

But had she been truly afraid or simply falling back
into old habits, hiding from what was new, being scared
of heights because that was so much easier than being
scared of an 'ifrit's claws around her belly, a dark and uncertain future? She couldn't say. All she knew was that
the steady chant of her own voice inside her skull had
lasted from those first moments of flying until she was
dropped on the sand, had kept her silent, had possibly
kept her sane. If anything in this madness could have
driven her mad, it was that first flight, and she'd survived
it. Therefore—perhaps—she could survive whatever else
might come until her friends or her father or either of her
husbands came to save her, as they must. The only real
certainty was that she couldn't save herself.

She had been dropped onto sand, and had opened her
eyes at the shock of it to see the sun just rising over a
rolling sea of dun and dusty dunes. Morakh was getting
to his feet beside her; the 'ifrit was crouching a little distance off, fierce red eyes glowing in a body from a child's
nightmare, glistening black and shaped for evil, too many
legs and wings that wouldn't fold as they ought to in any
creature of nature.

Morakh had slipped straps from his shoulders, dropping a faggot of fuel, a water-skin, a bag of flour. He'd lit
a small fire and baked desert bread on a stone; he'd
tossed a portion to her and she'd choked it down like an
obedient prisoner, despite its rank taste. Food was important, strength mattered. Water too, and so she'd swallowed grimly, though the skin had smelled rotten and the
water's sliminess had almost closed her throat against it.

He'd lain down to sleep, and so had she. No question
of his binding her arms or legs to keep her there, no need
for it; the 'ifrit had been watching, and spirit never slept.

She had eaten, she had drunk; she'd tried to sleep as well, but her body wouldn't be forced despite its aching weariness, nor would her mind be still. She had heard of captives so numbed with shock that they slept and slept and could hardly be roused, and seemed to sleepwalk when they were. She had envied them, yearned to imitate, but could not; might as well have been an 'ifrit herself for all the rest she had.

Not that she would have been let sleep very long, not long enough. Morakh had allowed himself only two or three hours before he stirred, grunted, rose. Julianne had kept her head down, watching in disbelief as he'd assembled his baggage and slung the straps about him, not moving herself until he'd kicked her to it. Already the horizon had been blurring till she could barely see where sand faded into sky; already the air was drying and burning her throat as the light dried and burned her eyes. No one moved in the Sands, while their shadows were this short.

No one moved, and so they would, and so leave pursuit behind them. The air would be cooler up high, if the 'ifrit could reach it; perhaps she would not die that day.

She'd still had a bangle on her wrist, part of the bridal treasure that she'd been playing with when Morakh had seized her. She let that slip to the sand as a sign to whoever came in pursuit, and otherwise stood quiescent beside her captor and simply waited as he did for the 'ifrit's claws to seize them.

AND SO IT had gone, on and on: flights in sunlight and in the dark, with her body dangling and her eyes tight shut, her mind focused on simple breathing, on staying alive. They'd come to ground more often than she'd expected, though it could never be often enough for her. At every halt she had been given water; at sunset and sunrise the Dancer had made a fire and baked bread. Her stomach had revolted, her throat had clamped, but she could be strong in this at least, she could force the vile stuff down. She'd tried to leave some token each time, though she had no more jewellery and the simple robe she wore had offered nothing that was clearly hers. A few threads picked from its hem and twisted together with hairs plucked from her scalp, the resultant string knotted into a crude double loop, the sign of the God in whom she had no faith at all: that had been the best that she could manage. Any woman of the tribes who travelled in the Sands would wear such a robe, of that deepest blue that filled the spaces between the stars; her people—Julianne's people now that she was married, married again, so newly married and how careless her husband was of her, to lose her so very quickly—the Sharai claimed it for their own colour, a gift from their own God. Any woman of the Sharai might have hair of such a length, and only a few shades darker than Julianne's; not for the first time in her life she could have wished to be a golden blonde, to leave a clearer message. But surely no woman else would leave the God's sign in this land, for any friendly eye that could find and read it . . .

SO SHE HAD done what little she could and suffered all else that had come to her, bad food and bad water and the constant, dreadful stare of the 'ifrit, which had seemed to see no more of her leavings than Morakh did, though she'd held her breath in terror every time she dropped another tiny tangle of thread and hair. Every time its claws closed about her, she had held her breath again, not to scream aloud as she was wrenched from the grip of solid ground.

By the time Morakh had used the last of his fuel, there had been scant water left in his skin and less she thought in hers; she'd felt parched and withered, wrinkled like a raisin. Either they must seek a well and a source of fire-wood, or else they were close to journey's end.

THERE'D BEEN SCANT relief in their arrival. Even with her eyes tight shut she could sense that the 'ifrit was descending, but what of that? It had done the same a dozen times already. She'd waited for the impact of crusted sand beneath her bare feet, the jolt that would knock her to her knees or send her sprawling. This time, though, they had plunged into a sudden, utterly unexpected shadow a moment or two before they struck ground; and what they struck had not been sand. Sandy, to be sure, but level stone beneath the grit. The shock of it had made her yelp aloud; it had also jerked her eyes open, as she'd fallen and rolled. She'd glimpsed walls, sky, more walls before she came to rest on her belly, aching and shaking all over.

Some kind of courtyard, long disused: they were stone flags that she had landed on, but they were cracked and broken under their coat of sand. Desert cold had been at them, since they were laid. Sitting up slowly, Julianne had seen rough-worked stones strewn around, where they had fallen from the height of the walls. Likely an earthquake had done that damage: it would take generations of frosts to do so much, cracking the mortar and shifting the stones fraction by fraction with every year that passed. She didn't think these walls had stood long enough. Even in the deep shadows of the courtyard there were toolmarks to be seen, the scars of axe and chisel. They looked quite fresh, cruder work than the Ransomers had made of the Roq but surely no older.

Then she'd felt Morakh's deformed hand grip the back of her neck. She had shuddered, once for the simple chill of his touch and again for what must follow, what she had experienced already, too much for any girl to bear.

His four fingers had seemed to sink through her skin and flesh, altogether into the bone of her. She'd thought she could feel his mind whisper against the beat of her blood, an alien rhythm that overrode her own. She'd felt uprooted, disinherited, soul thrust from its native throne; she'd lost all possession of her body, as she had in the water-channels and on the cliffs of Rhabat.

The sickness had closed in on her in swirling pools of colour, colours that ought not to exist, that she could not have given a name to if she tried. Perhaps she ought to try, perhaps she should list all the colours that she knew, give a focus to her thoughts: *no, that is not violet, nor umber.* She couldn't do it, though, could only slip and fall through oily nothingness, fall endlessly where there was nothing solid to be clung to.

IT HAD BEEN a long time, the longest time imaginable before she realised that she had ceased to fall. The stillness that engulfed her after was so absolute and so welcome, it took her a while longer to understand it. Only a sudden, desperate need dragged her mind back from its drifting; she felt herself shaking, gasping, rearing up against a terrible weight, and only as she dropped back, only the lancing pain as her head cracked against stone told her that her body was her own again. That was the heaviness she felt, the weight of bone and muscle. She'd forgotten almost how to breathe; that had been the need that had seized her.

She lay quite still again, but consciously so now, deliberately taking all the time necessary to fit body and mind together, to make them one again, her own, herself. For a while she did nothing but breathe. The air tasted dull, dusty, stale, but no matter.

Then she reached out into the extremities of her skin, fingers and toes, stirring them lightly, checking that each

twitched and danced to her own command and no one's
else.

Satisfied, she opened her eyes at last; and thought herself blind, perhaps, thought Morakh had stolen her sight
from her and kept it for himself. She needed yet more
time to understand that it was dark in here, wherever here
was; and that she was lying on her side and facing what
might be a wall or a corner. She couldn't see it, but she
reached out a cautious hand to check and was thrilled beyond measure when her fingers' tips touched stone just a
hand's span from her face.

It took an effort, a tremendous effort to move more
than that. She was scared of shaking herself loose from
her body again, she felt so ill-attached. But she edged
over onto her back and stared upward, and saw light.

Only a little light, a high horizontal bar of blurry grey;
that was enough for now, that was dazzling glory. She
thought that any more would have burned her.

She turned her head the other way and saw two glowing red coals looming high above her, set in uttermost
black; and that was the opposite of glory, that was despair, to recognise that she shared her cell with the 'ifrit.

IT DIDN'T MOVE, and neither did she. It didn't blink, although she had to. Trying to outstare a monster was no
game for a grown woman. She'd never been alone with
the creature before, but her sudden shortness of breath
was just a brief slip of control, no more than that. She'd
tried too much, too soon; she was still uncertain in her
body, forgetful of what used to happen naturally. She
could breathe like a normal girl, if she concentrated: in
and out, in and out, there, like that. She wasn't afraid of
the thing, why should she be? If it hadn't killed her in the
days they'd spent en route, it wouldn't do so now. They
were alone together, but nothing else had changed . . .

Were they alone? There was no sign or sound of Morakh in the dim light and the dead air of this chamber, but he could be still when he chose, he could be sitting directly behind her . . .

She was proud of herself for not jerking round to see, for sitting up slowly and turning her head as though there were no hurry in the world. There was certainly no Morakh. Now that her eyes were adjusting, she could make out the low shape of a door, but nothing else. She had been right, then, this was a cell and she was a prisoner; and her guard shared the cell with her, its glossy, ill-formed body cramped and awkward in this enclosed space. It had crouched as best it could into a corner but still took up half the floor, more. It made no sound, no creak of shifting chitin, no scrape of claw on stone, no stir of breath; its hot gaze never moved from Julianne.

She wasn't afraid of it, no. She was just slow, that was all, still disorientated, uncertain of her strength and its uses; no other reason why it seemed so hard to move herself, to stand and walk those few short paces to the door. Of course she didn't think the 'ifrit would pounce as soon as she twitched a muscle, of course she knew it wasn't going to eat her . . .

She'd seen a man, a known thief downed by a trained hound once in Marasson. She'd seen, felt, smelled his terror at the steady rumble of its growling, the bared fangs an inch from his throat. Many times she'd seen the palace cats and the mice they played with, how often there'd been no pleasure in the game because the little things wouldn't scamper but only stood immobile, fixed with fear. But she was not a mouse, far from it; and this spirit-creature might desire her death—if spirit could know desire—but it would not kill her now. Orders or instinct or plotting restrained it. She was captive, bait perhaps, a ransom-prize but no worse than that. Not a victim, not a corpse.

Not yet a corpse, and moving would not make her so. And so at last she stood, deliberately with her back to the 'ifrit to show how very much she scorned it, how little she was afraid. Those messages might be too subtle for the thing to read, but not for her; right now she mattered more.

She stood—a little dizzy, a little off-balance, her body still seeming not to fit too well—and shuffled her way to the door. It was locked or barred, of course, she was a prisoner. The 'ifrit too, then: but the 'ifrit apparently had no reason to leave, so long as she was there.

Questing fingers and eyes that squinted in the gloom could find no handle and no hinge, only the heavy wooden planking and the iron studs that held it all together. Patiently she picked at each with her nails, hoping to find one loose enough to draw out, a spike to make a weapon that might dim those fierce eyes that watched her as she picked. They were an 'ifrit's only weakness unless you had a blade blessed by a priest, which she did not. Or unless you were a djinni with a sea at your command, which she was not. She wasn't sure that a door-nail would be enough to kill the creature, and was fairly sure that it would kill her first in any case; still, she thought she might like the chance to try. If things turned out that way, if there came no sign of friends, husbands, rescue . . .

No surprise, though, that none of the nails would come to the picking of her own. It was a well-made door: solid timber neither green nor ancient, no hint of worm or rot that her fingers could discover and no sign of any give when she leaned all her weight against it.

She didn't pound her fists or kick it, nothing so petulant. She'd found what she expected and felt almost satisfied by that, almost pleased that her enemies hadn't let her down. She liked a puzzle, a challenge, something worthy of her father's daughter.

With the door so solidly closed against her and the

light so high out of reach, she wondered why she was being so closely watched. The 'ifrit were single-minded and far from subtle creatures, but she had no way out of here, so why did it waste its time?

She sat against the wall, as far as she could come from those eyes, and thought about it. Not long, no need to strain, she hadn't turned stupid yet. Among her rescuers—if she waited for them, if they came—she could count three at least who could walk into a locked cell and lead her out without chipping wood or stone or iron, without leaving a mark to show that they'd been. Her own father might step out of a golden nimbus at any moment, and she was a little surprised that he hadn't yet, she'd not thought him so slow. Marron could cross back and forth between one world and another; she'd like to visit the land of the djinn, she thought, even with that boy for company. And then there was Elisande, whose temper might not break down doors of its own accord, but certainly could when it was allied to her djinni's. They could come like Marron from that other world, and spirit her away there; she thought it more likely that they would come through the wall, and leave more than a mark behind.

Except, of course, that the 'ifrit was here, and the djinni at least should know that if the others didn't. Djinni Tachur liked to present itself as a poor stunted creature, cut off from the intangible current of spirit knowledge; Julianne wasn't at all convinced. She thought if that were true, then the djinni would have appeared long ago, riding the storm of her friend's fury to snatch her back to safety. That it hadn't come must surely mean that it knew an 'ifrit was keeping her company. A djinni and an 'ifrit couldn't meet in anger, without both being destroyed.

As long as the 'ifrit was guarding her, the djinni would not come. Nor her father, nor Marron: the 'ifrit would be ready for either. It had changed its shape, she saw. The cumbersome wings had gone, been resorbed into the body of the beast; it was armed now with giant claws like a lobster's, poised to grip and crush any man that ventured here in the moment of his appearance. She hoped that she was right about the djinni, that it would know and warn her friends; she'd rather be abandoned to her fate than see them come and try to save her, try and die . . .

She wouldn't abandon herself, though. If she couldn't be rescued, she'd simply have to escape. Despite the 'ifrit, despite Morakh's lurking presence somewhere beyond the door, despite whatever else might come.

The 'ifrit were said to share the djinn's foreknowledge; perhaps it knew in advance what she might try, and would forestall her. Perhaps it knew that its simple watchful presence would be enough. A never-sleeping monster should be adequate to guard an unarmed girl.

But no prescience was absolute, even the djinn could be mistaken or misunderstand. She would think and watch and plan, however fancifully. The 'ifrit might leave her alone eventually, Morakh might leave the door unlocked and unguarded, she might find a hidden tunnel beneath the flags she sat on, where a slender girl could wriggle out and her dreadful guardian not. There might be another earthquake, to bring the walls down and crush her captors and let her walk away . . .

Anything might happen; she would be ready if it did. In the meantime she rested, she closed her eyes once more against the glare of the 'ifrit, she forced her mind to think.

It would be useful, obviously, to know where she was. She could work that out even in the dark. She'd gleaned clues enough from the glimpses she'd had in the courtyard above, what she could see here below; she thought now that she could touch a finger to a map and say with confidence, "This is where I am."

All that she'd seen—the high walls with their battlements, the blunt square design of the doorway here, the way the door itself was made—all of that was her own people's work, no question. The Catari did not build in such a fashion; the Sharai did not build at all. This was a Patric castle, then; and yet it was in the desert, by all the blown sand in the court, not in Outremer proper. And it had been deserted, abandoned, some time since. She could think of only one place that answered such description.

WHEN THE SANCTUARY Land was won again for the God, the Ekhed who had been rulers there were driven out entirely. The settled Catari by and large accepted their new Patric overlords, finding them little harsher and in some cases kinder than what had gone before, or so Julianne's father had told her; their wild nomadic cousins the Sharai could be held back in the deep desert, on the far side of the mountain ridge that made a natural eastern border for the Kingdom. Raiding-parties were commonplace, but a fragile and unofficial truce developed quickly, supported by both trade links and diplomacy.

Except that there was one ancient settlement only a short distance to the east of the mountains, from where there was swift and easy access to the valley principality of Surayon, and from there to all of Outremer. The lords of the Kingdom were reluctant to leave it in the hands of the Sharai; they sent a force to seize it. The Sharai tribe that claimed that land tried to retake it time and again, was beaten back time and again. The Patrics built a castle; the sheikhs, united at last—the place had religious importance to them, as well as trading wealth—sent an army to lay seige. The Patrics were starved out and sur-

rendered, returning to Outremer under safe conduct; the
Sharai occupied the castle until the Duke of Ascariel led
his own men back to retake it.

And so it had gone on, turn and turn about, until
Surayon vanished within the mystery of its Folding. Now
the castle was more isolated than before and men of the
Kingdom more unhappy within its walls, seeing enemies
on all sides and malign magic at their backs. Given the
rumours of collusion between Surayon and the Sharai,
the nobles were doubly reluctant to lose their outpost, but
they found it ever harder to garrison. The King would say
nothing about it; at length they sent their own emissaries
to Rhabat and made a formal truce with the sheikhs. The
settlement should live as it had since time immemorial, a
place of prayer and trade; the Sharai would not occupy it,
and neither would the Patrics. The castle would stand
empty, as a sign of good faith from both parties.

AND SO IT had, so far as Julianne knew—until now, at
least. This must be that castle; there was no other.

It was called Revanchard, a name that raised doubt
and suspicion throughout the Kingdom: who knew, who
could say what evil the sorcerers of Surayon might not be
working there, or their cohorts the devilish Ṣharai?

Julianne knew, Julianne could say. Nothing, and nothing. There was only dust and rubble and emptiness, and
now a girl, a fanatic and an 'ifrit.

✠   ✠   ✠

IT SEEMED TO Imber as though he were losing time,
growing younger, falling back through years almost as
fast as the weeks passed around him. He felt himself fifteen again, passionate and helpless: mired in humiliation,
caught constantly between tears and rage and able to in-

dulge himself in neither. He craved to be sick, to have a killing fever that might legitimately keep him private in his grief and would make his family sorry to have lost him later. Instead he was robust, thriving, pale only in anger or sorrow; which meant that he was pale all the time except when he was blushing, which meant that he alternated all the time between white and scarlet.

His father, his uncle, his cousins: all had shown him a mixture of sympathy and fury, and all had brought the blood rushing to his face every time their eyes met his, because he knew what they were thinking, what they were saying between themselves. *Imber the love-lorn, marries the girl and can't keep her, she ran away before the wedding and ran again after, straight after their wedding night and he pines over her posy because he cannot find her when he should be raging at the insult to himself, to all his family, to us . . .*

He blushed because it was cruel, and also because it was true. Sometimes he could be angry with Julianne for fleeing him, for making such a public mock of him; and yet he loved her, he wished her nothing but well, he wished that he could find her to offer whatever aid was in his power, to bring her out of what trouble she was in. Then he was angry with his family for their blindness, for their being concerned only with honour when his girl must be in need of help. And yet he had loved them all his life, collectively they were still his wisdom as they always had been, and when he was rational he saw that they were right in this, that it was wilfulness and nothing more that took her from him, and insult that she left behind . . .

He hadn't been so muddled in his thinking since the year of his manhood, the year of first blood on his sword and first girl in his bed; but that wasn't the only reason why he felt so displaced in time suddenly, why he could fling back the flap of his tent in the mornings and almost feel an urge to rub a hand through his beard, to check his height against the pole and be sure of the ring on his smallest finger, to reassure himself that the last four years of growth, maturity, marriage had not been merely a dream.

He was young yet, but he had been younger; and not since then had he woken to days like this, days of tension and confusion and embarrassment all blended together to keep him in a ferment, when he was glad of simple things to do to keep his mind from chasing phantoms far away.

Simple things like fetching his own breakfast from the fire and eating on his feet with his confrères; like harnessing his own horse for the day's ride and grooming it at sunset, even cleaning his own tack under the stars. Troopers saw to the pitching of his tent, but he would gladly have done that too if he hadn't been so aware of his cousin Karel's eye on him in his shame.

Even the land they rode through was a reminder of his youth. At that age he'd been sent to ride the southern border of Elessi for a year with the regular patrol, wild lands and a rough apprenticeship for the future Count. Now he was back, watchful and anxious as he had been then, feeling the weight of another's critical gaze just as he had before. Then it had been the sergeant's, who commanded that patrol; now it was his cousin's, who commanded this.

Imber had spent days searching uselessly for Julianne, after her flight. Finding no certain sign of her, no trail that he could follow, he had at last returned to his father's house in Elessi to face the court's politeness, his uncle's rudeness, his own desperate puzzlement at how he had made Julianne so unhappy.

It had been pure relief when rumours reached the city about strange movements among the Sharai, all the sheikhs gathered at Rhabat and their tribesmen following. It must mean war, rumour and logic both agreed; and what more likely than a strike against Elessi, the hammerhead, the most vulnerable of all the states of Outremer? Let the Sharai but win Elessi, and they could ride into Tallis and so down all the length of the Kingdom, killing as they went . . .

Ambitious sheikhs had tried the same before, and had been rebuffed with many losses; Elessans were the finest soldiers the King had, everyone knew that. But they'd never had to face all the tribes united. It had been divisions among the Sharai, blood-feuds between tribe and tribe that had kept Outremer secure until now.

Every man who could be spared from other duty was ordered to the borders, north and east and south, especially south, where the desert rubbed its hot muzzle against unprotected farmland. No mountains here, to make a wall to guard.

Imber had leaped at the chance to ride with Karel and his troop: to leave squire and servants behind with the gossiping, fractious court, to leave fretful father and sour uncle to their maps and arguments, to spend the days staring into a searing dust-laden wind and half the nights sitting up with his cousin, twitching at every natural sound and trying never, never to think of Julianne. He almost hoped that the Sharai would come and find him; better to lose his life, he thought, than to lose the girl he loved. At least he could understand that, a bitter fight and bitter steel's touch at the end of it and so a sudden peace and no more blushing, if all his blood were let run out . . .

And that again was fifteen-year-old thinking, and he knew it; and thought it anyway, thought it deliberately, trapped in some strange mood between misery and defiance.

THIS DAY—RIDING miserably, defiantly a little distance ahead and to the south of Karel and the troop, courting danger and making a childish point of it, which his cousin was pointedly indulging—he scanned the smudged horizon as he had done times without number and saw nothing of what he hoped for, neither a moving shadow which might be a Sharai outrider nor a moving shadow which might be his Julianne unaccountably returning, as she had unaccountably left.

Closer to him, though, something was moving, and did snag his eye. Anything that moved in this drear, dead landscape was unusual, and potentially a threat.

This was only a dust-devil, though, a slender twisting pillar; he'd seen a dozen such since he came south. One had struck their campsite in the night, and ripped Karel's tent from its moorings. He watched this one for lack of anything else to fix his eyes on, and registered slowly that it was heading directly towards him. He nudged his mount to the side, out of its path—and saw it veer, and realised that it was moving against the wind, which surely ought not to be possible. Unless it was some trick of the Sharai, some touch of sorcery, a wicked conjuration sent against him . . .?

He turned his horse with a yell, saw how far he'd wandered from his companions and thought himself lost, even as he dug in his spurs. He had a moment to regret his bravado—this was not what he'd wanted even if he'd truly wanted that, there was neither honour nor satisfaction in being slain by a magical sending, without the chance to face an adversary blade to blade—and then the swirling cloud swept past him, steadied, and spoke.

It spoke his name, but he had no time yet to wonder at it; he was busy with his horse, which was rearing, screaming, terrified. It was all he could do to stay mounted; the beast backed away, entirely out of his control.

The dust-devil, apparition, whatever it might be hung motionless, except that its body was constantly in motion, a spiralling rope of dust and air. It stood between him and the troop. His horse was fighting the bit, straining to turn, to flee—but flight would take it and him south, where any evil might be waiting. Imber used spurs, reins, his mailed fist, everything he had to hold it still. When at last it subsided, quiescent and trembling, he lifted his head to face the devil, and heard it say his name again.

"Imber von und zu Karlheim, your wife has need of you."

Imber blinked, stared; its voice was high and carrying, quite inhuman.

"I—I do not know what you are." His own voice came out only as a whisper, it could surely not have covered the distance between them, except that the creature replied instantly.

"I am the djinni Esren Filash Tachur, and this is my message to you, that I am sent to carry: that your wife Julianne, who is daughter to the King's Shadow, is in need. If you would come to her aid, ride south to Selussin, to the castle called Revanchard. Ride swiftly; her peril is great, I am told to say. It may be true. The future is dark to me, but I at least cannot save her."

"Wait . . .!" he cried, too late; there was a sudden soft fall of dust, and he could see nothing before him except Karel thundering forward on his giant destrier.

Imber pulled off his mailed gauntlet, ran his hand over the prickling cold sweat on his face and wondered what in the world he should say to his cousin.

FIVE

A Healing Possession

BLAISE HAD THOUGHT that nothing could frighten him
more than the company he kept these days, until he made
his first journey into the King's Eye. When he was there,
he thought that nothing would ever frighten him more than
simply being in that place. Now he thought that he'd been
twice wrong. Soon he would have to go back, to report his
failure. He dreaded facing Magister Fulke; he thought that
the marshal's anger would be a more frightening thing than
any that he'd yet seen.

He had called them a rabble, the people that he followed, but that wasn't strictly true. A rabble is disorgan-
ised, and loud. This was neither. The preacher led and his
disciples marched behind—like an army, almost, except
that it was an army of the poor, dressed in rags and lacking weapons. More like penitents in a procession, then,
silent and involved, their thoughts turned to holy matters.
Except that the preacher only ever spoke about Surayon,

the need to crush heresy, to bring the God's light to un-believers. Which made it an army indeed, intent on victory.

Blaise walked behind like a camp-follower, just one among many. These really were a rabble. Some were relatives of those the preacher had healed. They had seen their husbands or wives or children called back from certain death, had seen them rise up and abandon family and village to follow the preacher, had felt drawn to follow in their turn. Blaise had spoken to a few of them and learned their confusion, their distress. Their loved ones shunned their company and would not speak. Those whom the preacher healed might as well have died, he thought, for all the good their resurrection did.

Others had heard the preacher speak, and answered more simply to the call. Men and boys had seized what weapons they owned or could improvise and set off to do what the long generation of their fathers had failed to do. They would pit knives against nothing, mattocks against magic, and Surayon would open before them like a flower to a probing bee, because the preacher said it would.

And then there were those who would follow any band of men, for what gain or comfort they could find; and those who would follow any voice that cried to them to follow, wherever it might lead.

And among them all—the worried and the warriors, the women and the weak—there was Blaise, who was one alone. Both worried and a warrior, neither woman nor weak and yet he felt so, he might as well be both for all the good he could accomplish here. Sent for a spy, he had foundered beyond rescue. The preacher spoke to no one when he was not preaching, and his disciples spoke to no one at all. What could a man uncover, in the face of such inhuman silence?

Nothing, nothing at all. Blaise had known and lived

under the strictures of the Ransomers' Rule, with its penalties for idle or inappropriate talking; he knew how young men kept such rules, and how they broke them also. Since he left the Order he had served on the borders of Elessi, he had fought raiders and been a raider himself. He could hear a voice's whisper in a wind; as the sergeant of a young troop, he had learned to read the movement of a finger or the twitch of an eye, to know when lads were sending messages under the uttermost silence of his glare.

There was none of that here, nothing at all. The disciples, the healed ones walked at a steady pace all day, behind the preacher who led them; they spoke not a word, they passed not a sign between them. Nor a mouthful to eat, nor to drink. They would eat at dawn and at day's end, but they showed no hint of need between. Even the hardest-trained army would sling waterskins along the line when the sun was high, and whatever dried meat or biscuit fell to hand, something to chew against the tedium of the road and the heat and the ache of wounds, perhaps, the bite of blisters. These, not. When they marched, they marched and did nothing other.

RELUCTANTLY, WHIPPED INTO something fearful by his greater fear of Magister Fulke, Blaise limped ahead of the murmuring crowd. He'd had to change his good soldier's boots for a poor man's sandals; the straps had rubbed his heels raw, the thin rope soles were no protection against the sharp stones of the road, and every step was a fresh reminder of futility.

He walked forward, to join the tail of the disciples' lines. For a while he made his way beside them, as silent as they were themselves; not a head lifted, not an eye turned aside to find him. He might have been invisible, a ghost in a parade of ghosts.

Eventually, he came up next to a boy whose name he knew. It happened sometimes that the disease they tracked would turn suddenly to snap at their heels; those who followed would wake in the morning to find one of their number weak and lethargic, unable to rise. Then the disciples would come, the preacher would work his abiding miracle in the dawnlight, and there would be one more to trail dumb and obedient in his wake.

No one ever fell sick in the daytime, on the march. Blaise couldn't decide if that was sinister or meaningless. He'd like it to mean something; he'd like to believe that the preacher gave poison to his victims and then stole their souls while they were weak and failing. That would be a thing to say to Magister Fulke. He couldn't make any sense of it, though, no matter how he strained. If the preacher came slipping through the camp at night, it would be known, however light his tread; if he sent one of his disciples, it would be the talk of all the company. And if he did either one—or if he sent his poison by the birds, if an earthworm carried it, a zephyr—there was still no reason in his choices. Man or woman, young or old: whether in the villages ahead of him or among the followers behind, the sickness struck at random, as a sickness should. Perhaps the man was a monster, perhaps he fed on souls and cared not if they were virgin and innocent or raddled with age and sin; but why drag their emptied bodies behind?

Fess was a boy of fourteen, who reminded Blaise painfully of himself at that same turn of life. Born to be big but born without a father, without name or place in the world, he'd scavenged for bread and begged for work since he was a child; that showed on his skin, tight-stretched over raw bones and muscles like bowstrings, no flesh at all. Too many years of short commons and short sleep, it would take years longer to mend, to fill him out to the man he should have been. Blaise knew.

Like Blaise before him, Fess had been waiting till he was old enough to be sworn a military man: for the God or for his local lord, no matter. But then the preacher had come, and Fess had seen a way to overleap his age, to be blooded young.

He'd followed the march with the light of that ambition in his eyes, a burning hunger when Blaise had spoken to him, and thrilling at the chance to make it happen. Thrilling at the food, too, surrendering a lifelong hunger, eating with both hands at every halt. The villagers were generous, with their storehouses full of that year's second crop; or else they were afraid, such a rabble dogging such a strange parade and camping in their fields or their lord's pastures. Fear could make anyone open-handed, however little they had to spare. If Fess fancied that a soldier always ate like this—well, he would learn. And regard the lesson lightly, no doubt. Even barrack fare would seem like feasting, after a diet of cabbage-water and scorched grains gleaned from others' fields. Blaise knew.

BLAISE HAD HELPED the boy to treat and dress a gash on his forehead, the result of a stone flung by a nervous goatherd; just a small cut, but it bled freely as scalp-wounds always do. After that they'd sat half the night over a glowing fire, while Fess talked and Blaise listened, sharing his memories in silence.

The following morning, the boy had lain stiff and still in his blanket, seemingly awake but unstirring, his eyes wide and blank as though his spirit were snared in horror. Blaise had struggled in vain to rouse him, finally had to be pulled away by others as the disciples gathered round. He'd been barely aware of the voices urgent in his ear, "Let the preacher have him, let him be healed, there's nothing you or any of us can do for him now." He'd wanted to fight with fists or knife, with whatever it took to keep Fess from a walking nightmare; better to let him die and bury him a stranger in a land where he'd never found a home.

Later, too late, he thought he might have put his knife to another use, to help Fess to a speedy death. Instead he'd stood slackly, uselessly, while the boy was snatched up and hurried off to where the preacher waited. He hadn't watched the healing. He'd seen too many of those tainted miracles already; he'd busied himself with sifting through Fess's few belongings, keeping the short sword and rolling the rest into the boy's ragged blanket, which he would carry himself in impotent fury at the preacher, at the world, above all at himself. Once more he'd failed, the boy had needed saving and Blaise had let him slip.

So now he walked beside Fess, or the semblance of Fess. The boy looked as well as ever he had, and yet he looked utterly different. He used to walk with an ungainly slouch, awkward yet in his growing body; now he carried himself on stiff, inexhaustible legs, almost like the soldier he'd yearned to be, except that it seemed to Blaise as though something else carried him. There was nothing boyish, little that was even human in his gait; his face was blank of any feeling, and his eyes were strangely dark where they had been blue before.

"Fess? How is it with you?"

Nothing, no response.

"Fess, speak to me, lad. It's me, Blaise, I have your things . . ."

Again, nothing. The rough bandage was gone from the boy's head, and only a pale scar showed where the skin had been so badly torn only two days before; the preacher's healing touched more than the sickness. But Blaise had known that already. Cripples walked when they were blessed by the saint's dead hand, the blind moved about without guidance, lepers lost their sores. Whether the power lay in the preacher or in his blessed relic, even that much Blaise had not yet contrived to learn. The only certainty—at least to Blaise's eyes—was that no power passed to the one healed, there was no true strengthening in this medicine.

He believed in miracles, he had to, he had seen them in all their swift brutality; but he was losing his faith in miracle cures. There was nothing holy here. Seized back from death, these bodies had been seized by another's will and marched to his desire. There was no healing in them, only the illusion of health. The preacher's cause might be sanctified, if he truly meant war against heretic Surayon, but what he had done in pursuit of it was pure wickedness.

Blaise tried again and yet again to speak to Fess, and won not the slightest reaction. In his frustration, he forgot to watch where he was treading; his foot came down on a sharp flint in the road. It cut through the ragged sole of his sandal and bit deeply into his instep. He cried out at the sharp stab of it, and still saw no reaction from Fess or any of the disciples. Hobbling, he lost his place, and was soon swept up in the following crowd. Someone there passed him a staff to lean on; even with that he could barely keep up, and was soon struggling in the dust at the rear of the march.

The road was roughly made, and it seemed that at every step his foot would come down on a stone, and hurt the more. At last he had to stop, to bind it up; he bound rags around the sandal, too, and then around the other to forestall another accident. With both feet lame, he'd lose touch altogether with the preacher and his band. As it was, he had to hasten after with a cripple's gait, using the staff to cover great stretches of ground, hop and swing, before he could catch them up again. He'd been on forced marches that were faster, but not by much. The mountains were a constant high shadow to the east; they'd already passed the border between Tallis and Less

Arvon, and another week or so should bring them to where the land was Folded, the impossible, impassable barrier that hid Surayon. What would happen there, Blaise couldn't conjecture. He was only sure that the preacher had an intent, a purpose that was equally hidden. There was something inexorable about their progress, something sinister and significant in the way that they could bypass settlements all day where the people were perfectly healthy; it was only in those villages where they stopped for the night that they found the sickness waiting.

As that night, when they came in the brief dusk to a small community of huts huddled in the foothills' lee, on the banks of a rushing stream. News of their coming had flown ahead of them, as it always did; they found a fire of welcome blazing in the open space between the huts, the village headman on his feet with an awkward speech prepared and three quiet bodies laid out at his back.

The preacher stepped forward, pushing back his hood. His disciples made a ring around him, the headman, the sick and the fire, encompassing all within their silence. Blaise and his companions pressed close at their backs, and the villagers came shyly, hopefully out to stand in their own quiet knot a little distance off. They were Catari, but that was not unusual; this disease discriminated, it struck largely at the poor, and the poor of Outremer were most of them Catari. Fess had been an exception. Unless it was that the disease picked its places rather than its victims: never a castle or a town, always those convenient settlements a day's hard march ahead, always close to the rising hills but never so close as to slow the preacher's progress. Blaise's people kept mostly to the towns, even after forty years of occupation; out here the lords and their servants kept to their manors, where a rabble like this would be closely watched and questioned. If Blaise had wanted to move a congregation quickly through the country, he would have picked this route or one much like it.

". . . Holy one, I have said enough. What more? There is only this: we are not of your faith, but our prayers have failed as our medicine has. Can you, will you save our children?"

"I can, and I will." The preacher's face looked at its finest, its strongest and most noble in this light, all glare and guttering shadows. By day he seemed weaker, more gaunt, half mad; tonight, though, Blaise knew exactly what these hopeful, hungry peasants would be seeing. The high brow and the backswept hair that hung to his shoulders; the eyes that glittered from the blackness of their sunken hollows; the thin lips that snapped at words and were overhung by the great hooked nose that was its own monument. Nameless and potent, he made a striking figure, terrifying in the way that those who hold power and hidden knowledge are always terrifying to the weak and ignorant. Blaise counted himself with the villagers in this; at such a moment he could forget even that Magister Fulke frightened him the more.

"Bring them to me," the preacher said, and the three still forms were carried forward by men who flinched back from the touch of his shadow but were still prepared to lay their children at his feet.

These really were children, Blaise saw, swathed in heavy blankets with only their faces showing, and those veiled by sickness and the uncertain light. Blaise thought he'd let any child of his go to death and paradise, sooner than to a Catari priest for a sacrilegious healing. But then, Blaise was not a father. Nor a husband, nor ever an acknowledged son; he knew that he didn't understand the kind of love that knotted families together. There were parents among the camp-followers who thought their healed children monsters, possessed, perverted, irredeemable. Blaise had heard them say so. And yet they followed where the preacher led, where the army marched, many miles from home towards a war that was nothing of theirs. It must be some tie of flesh that dragged them, a need that clung day after hopeless day, to keep gazing on a face they'd loved even when the spirit was long lost.

The preacher crouched above the children's silence. His long fingers reached to unpeel their coverings and the clothes they wore beneath, to show the dull grey slackness of their skin that even the fierce firelight couldn't enliven. Then he slipped a hand inside his own rough robes to pull forth the talisman that had brought them all this far, and would take them further yet.

A blessed relic, he said it was, the mummified hand of a long-dead saint that he had recovered from a cave in the wilderness. The instrument of his healing, he said it was, that also. Blaise had never seen it close; from this distance, from any distance it looked like a claw struck from some bird of myth and monstrosity. Black and twisted, glinting strangely, that dead thing caught the light and played with it.

There was nothing, almost nothing to the miracle itself. If this were true salvation—a life drawn back from the very mouth of hell, a soul's second chance gifted by the God's grace, the touch of a saint and the word and prayer of a preacher—then there ought to be ritual, Blaise thought, there ought to be ceremony and more. A sight of the God Himself, perhaps, his voice in the thunder and his eyes' glare in the lightning of a storm. Something so momentous ought to rive rocks and send birds wheeling, screaming under a sky ripped like silk to let the stars fall down . . .

Instead of which, the preacher simply bent above the slack and heedless bodies, one by one. He muttered something that Blaise had never yet been able to hear, for all the nights of trying; he stretched down to touch the children's lips with the desiccated fingers of his saintly, shrivelled hand; he stepped away.

And one by one, in the order of their touching, the children stirred. One by one they sat up, ungainly in their bodies; one by one they rose slowly to their feet to stand naked in the firelight and silence.

That was all there was to see, figures and movement and stillness among the ever-shifting shadows. Blaise listened more than he watched, trying even yet to learn something, anything that he could offer to his master. He listened hardest in the moments of healing, but there wasn't so much as a tightening of breath from the children, a sudden catch on slippery life or a gasp at the snatching of their souls.

As they rose up, the quiet was absolute. They didn't speak, and neither did the preacher; nor the disciples, of course, nor the camp-followers who had seen it all before, so often seen it all; nor the gaping villagers, crushed mute by the casual impact of a wonder.

At last something snapped in the fire's heart, breaking the silence and the stillness both. The villagers surged forward, voices rising, crying in their own tongue; the preacher flung his arms out, his hands upraised to halt them.

"Back, be still!"

His voice and gesture quelled their rush, as potent as sorcery. He turned his back and spoke to their children only.

"Dress yourselves," he said, and they did, in the patched and tattered robes they'd worn beneath their shrouding blankets.

Then, "What will you do?"

It took them a while, as it seemed, to find their voices. The words when they did come were slurred and tumbled across each other, though every child said the same and they were trying to speak together.

"We will follow you, preacher."

"You hear them?" He turned around slowly, arms stretched wide again. "They had been kissed by demon's breath, and they were lost to you. They came when I called, when I touched them with this holy relic; now they say they will follow me, although they do not know where I lead. That is faith, pure faith; they give themselves into my hands. How many of you will do the same . . .?"

BLAISE WISHED THAT once, just once someone would ask the question that burned always in the back of his own mind: how a ragtag band of dreamers such as this could hope to do what a generation of lords and their armies had failed at, time and again. Surayon was small, to be sure, just a fingernail's width torn from every map he'd seen. Even so, these few could never overrun it. The preacher had a faith that blazed, and Blaise himself believed devoutly in the power of the God; but he was a soldier yet, and he believed also in the simple power of the sword, the weight of men in battle.

While he was sure that justice must eventually come to Surayon, and that it must come with the God's blessing, Blaise could not see that blessing here. He looked at the disciples and saw the soul-stolen, empty shells. Nor was he alone in that; and yet people followed regardless, and no one questioned the preacher.

WHEN HE CAME to unbind his foot that night, he ripped scabs away with the rags, wincing at the sudden sting of it and then again at the sight of fresh blood oozing from the cut. A soldier needed his feet in good condition. So did a spy.

He bound the foot again, then wrapped himself up in

his blanket and in Fess's too. The mountains held back the Sands as a sea-wall holds the sea, but it seemed to him that desert air was slipping over, slopping over the brim, bringing the touch of desolation with it. The preacher was mad, that was all. Mad and gifted, but mad none the less; and his disciples were the echo of himself, mindless and stumbling towards they knew not what. No more did Blaise know; and Magister Fulke would ask him, ask him soon, and he would have no answer. He laid his head on good damp soil and smelled dry sand, and shivered. He closed his ears to the murmur of voices where he knew that mothers were speaking uselessly to their lost children, closed his mind to the future, tried to sleep.

AND FAILED, AS he had been certain that he would. His foot throbbed, his soul ached for sick children, deluded adults, himself. He lay on his back, on his side, on his belly; he gazed at the stars, at the dying fire, at nothing at all. Whichever way he lay, he could find no rest; whichever way he looked, he could see no path to glory, no hope for any one of his companions on this mad march. Only failure and death could lie ahead, just as death and failure were all that lay behind him, all his life.

Almost on the wings of that thought came a touch, a cold and clamping kiss on the sole of his foot. No natural cramp, no twinge of pain: he sat bolt upright, staring, and for a moment there seemed to be an eddy of mist around his blankets, that seemed to be sucked suddenly inward through the weave and through the rags he'd wrapped around his foot, as though the cut there had opened like a mouth to draw it in.

Demon's breath, he thought, as the chill of it surged up the bones of his leg, spreading in an instant through all his body. He opened his mouth to cry it aloud, to wake the sleepers all around him; and felt it reach his mind, clouding his sight and numbing his intelligence with a bitter lethargy.

Slowly, slowly he lay back down, as the strength ebbed from his muscles. His blankets had fallen away, when he sat up; he was so cold, he thought vaguely that he ought to reach out and pull them up to cover him again. His arm wouldn't respond, though, and he had no will to force it. He was aware yet, he knew who and what he was—*I am Blaise, I am a soldier and a spy*—but that was all, so little, he felt like a pale flame in a vast night, a spirit cut adrift from his body.

HE LOST ALL sense of time's passing. He could see the stars dimly, as though through a fog, and his eyes tracked their course as they wheeled above him. It signified nothing, he didn't understand that nor the gradual brightening in one quarter of the sky, the sudden swift uprising of the sun. He could find the word for it, he had its name but not its meaning now.

There were sounds all about him, as there always had been; they made no more sense than the moving lights did, stars and sun. What had been breathing, snores, the dry bark of a fox became words, voices, talking. He heard the words, but they could not reach him.

He saw faces, bodies, people leaning above him. These did not talk. He felt himself lifted by many hands. The blueing sky turned over him, or else he turned beneath it, he did not know; the sun glared at him but could not burn through the mist that cloaked his eyes. After a minute he was laid down again. The hands opened all his clothing, and then withdrew; a single figure loomed at his feet. His mind said *preacher*, but he did not understand it.

The figure stooped, reaching a thing towards him. It was black, it glistened like steel where the light struck; it was shaped like a claw, like a ravaged hand, fingers and thumb bent sharply. His mind said *relic*, though he did not know what that meant.

He felt one finger catch at his lip, tugging it downward; he felt something, a hint of nothing solid slide into his mouth. Not solid, but sharp regardless: it lay like a breath of ice against the coldness of his tongue, and was colder yet. His mind said *demon's breath*, and though it was only a name without significance, he still thought it was wrong.

It sank into his tongue and nested there, and seemed to draw everything that was chill in his body towards itself, and so grow still more chill. He felt the first warmth of the sun against his skin, but did not feel warmed by it, only that what hid in his tongue had stolen all the cold that was in him.

His eyes cleared; he could see precisely, the preacher's face with its sunken eyes and its beaked nose. *Beak and claw* he thought, and knew this time what he meant: how the preacher was a hawk, an eagle, fierce and predatory.

"Stand up," the preacher said, "and dress yourself."

He understood the words, and felt his body stirring to obey, though not at his own command. He watched his own fingers fumble with cloth and ties, slow and awkward like a child's hands at an unaccustomed task. He wanted to show them how easy it was, but could find no way to do so.

He'd have liked to say his own name, if only to hear it spoken one more time, just the once; but found that he couldn't quite remember it, as though it were freshly lost. He might have liked to say anything at all, he thought, only that his tongue was cold and heavy, a stone in the mouth and not for talking. Something else was heavy, a weight inside his robe, a duty that had been fearful once. There was a man in a hot land, where there was no sun. The weight was candle; he must light the candle and speak to the man. But there were words to speak first above the candle, and he could not pin them down.

Besides, there was no need to speak where no one listened. His body knew what to do. There were others of its kind all around him, turning now, leading, and it followed, it carried him away.

ALL DAY THEY marched in line and he with them, the disciples, one of them. He left his bedroll behind, and the boy Fess's too, and the sword also. He felt no pain, no weariness; he felt nothing, not even fear. He could see, he could hear, but he was drifting, unconnected, unconcerned.

That evening there was no village, no sick ones to be healed, to be drawn in. Only the preacher, standing on a rock where all could see him in the last of the light. The disciples were clustered close around him, but he spoke over their heads, to the others who packed behind.

"The demon that is in Surayon holds its breath," he said. "There will be no more sickness now. Now is the time to run, to be ready to strike when we may. We few will be enough; the God has promised me. Those among you who can keep up, you are welcome; for the rest, follow if you will, do what you can. By the time you reach Surayon, it will lie open before you. Do not be afraid to kill; evil must be burned out, corrupted flesh cut away, or the demon will breathe again."

He leaped down from the rock in a swirl of robes and began to run steadily into the gathering dark. His path no longer lay due south but south and east, towards the hills. The disciples followed, silent in their lines, their legs rising and falling, feet pounding all in time with the preacher's.

All through the dark they ran and on into the morning, while the land rose and rose beneath and around them. Sunlight showed them peaks and crags, bitter shadows. They ran on.

SIX

The First Meaning of Flight

IF THERE WERE three sides to every question, Elisande had never been particularly interested in discovering the other two. She knew where she stood, sometimes she even knew why she stood there. That had always seemed enough to her, and so it ought to have been enough for others, for everyone else.

When it wasn't—well, that was when the fights started.

WHERE SHE STOOD just now, there were three sides to everything, and she hated that. The place even had three names. She thought it stupid, demeaning, and never mind that she had a few herself and had used others freely when she'd needed them; never mind that she had one— her father's daughter, of course she bore his name—that she'd not used in years, that she liked to think of as lying rotted in a grave or in a garden, all overtangled with thorns and rooted through and through, never to be raised up whole again.

People were one thing, places something else. Places, she thought, should have just the one name, so that everyone knew where you meant and where you meant to go. This place was called Revanchard by the Patrics, for the castle they'd raised on the crag above; it was called Selussin by the Catari, for the ancient wisdom that it shared with all; its own people called it Torkha, and she had no idea what that meant.

Time was when the reputation of Selussin had brought princes across deserts, bearing gifts of gold in fee for the insights of the imam-scholars. Sometimes they brought their sons and left them here a year or two, to acquire religion and wisdom in equal measure. Religion and wisdom and diplomacy; everything here came in threes, and these people could rival Julianne's father in the celebration of manners without commitment. She thought them contemptible. Coren carried power behind his shifting veils, where they carried nothing at all. Empty hands and empty words: they were almost beneath contempt, living on past majesty, the dusty greedy ghosts of better men.

It was years, generations since they'd traded gold or wisdom. Once, convenience and curiosity had brought the caravan-masters here whatever their direction, north or south, west towards Ascariel or eastward to Rhabat. The Patrics' coming and the constant warfare since had broken all those silken ropes. Either side might raid a merchant's train, and why risk goods and men and profit when there is always another way to travel, at a slower but safer distance from the sword? The caravans had left Selussin and not returned; old trails blew themselves away across the sand, and far-flung princes sent gold-emblazoned letters but kept their sons at home.

Daughters were not to be thought of, not considered.

Elisande had passed this way once in her life already, when the world was bright and the future bountiful, except for the dark sucking well of bitterness that was her father. Her grandfather—who understood her waking or sleeping, whom she unconditionally adored—had sent her on the first great adventure of her life, to spend a year alone with the Sharai. *Away from Rudel* had been unspoken, implicit, a golden setting for the jewel. "Go to Rhabat," he'd told her, "and run wild with the children there, while you still have licence to be a child. Let them teach you the city, while their fathers teach you the desert. I have small hope of their mothers teaching you anything a woman ought to know, but they may try. Go to Rhabat, and show them this for surety," a ring too big for any finger that she owned, so she wore it on a thong around her neck. "Your way will take you through Selussin; linger there if you like it, but I don't suppose you will. Nor will it like you, unless there's been more change than I can guess at . . ."

He'd been right, both ways. There were many Catari who'd sought shelter in Surayon, before it had been Folded; she'd grown up with their children and was as comfortable with their ways as with those of her own people. There were Sharai, too, who came slipping in and out through the Fold. Those had intrigued her, and she'd always stolen what time she could to spend it in their company. Little girls could claim what was forbidden to those who were older; she'd understood that, and had expected to find the same among any people who followed the same religion.

Not so, she'd discovered, in Selussin. There were schools and libraries and temples, more than she'd ever dreamed to find anywhere outside Ascariel; but they were as closed to girls as they were to women. The priests would not speak to her, seemed not to see or hear her when she spoke to them. The little boys told her to tend the fields as their sisters did, and threw stones at her when she refused to go. One day had been enough to learn that this was no place for her; her Sharai guides had kept her there a week, to drive the lesson deeper in. One day she'd climbed the hill and wandered through the empty castle, but it had held only dust and walls and darkness, no adventure.

These days it held more, they'd learned that much, though not from the wise ones here. Esren said that it held Julianne.

Julianne and Morakh, naturally, and the 'ifrit. Everything here came in threes.

At least there were no doubts, no questions now. This close, Esren could be certain, or so it said. It didn't need to pick its way hesitantly through a dance of future possibilities, out of step amid forgotten music; what was here was laid out like a map, it said, clear and incontrovertible. Julianne was there, in that looming structure that hung above the township like a thundercloud, like an anvil, storm-grey even when the sun lay full upon it. She was there, and so were the Sand Dancer and the 'ifrit; and so was Esren's destruction, the djinni said, if it should try a rescue. And so was Coren's, and Marron's too. Separately or together, it said, they could not bring her out. It was a baited trap, where death waited; death was sure.

A trap for which of them, and why, it would or could not say. Could not, she thought; its silence was resentful. In its own terms, in its own strange world it staggered about like a drunken beggar, half-blinded and befuddled. That was the impression it gave, at any rate: of a once-proud creature brought low, disabled and disgraced. Even the great djinn were not omniscient, of course—though the one great djinni that she'd met allowed some room for doubt of that, and none for doubt of its abilities—but Esren felt itself stunted, crippled by its long separation from what it called the spirit-weft.

Julianne was there, and they were here and helpless, come so far to so little effect, blocked at every turn of the mind's eye, every leap of hope's imagination. It felt right, she thought, for Selussin: walls on all three sides, and an inaccessible darkness at the heart.

But she was not Selussin, and she refused to accept their count of what was possible, any more than she would accept Esren's. The 'ifrit could be no more certain than the djinn, of how any rescue attempt would turn out. She'd seen enough of those creatures die, to know that foreknowledge did not bring invulnerability. All they saw was possibilities, no more. If Esren saw three ways to try for Julianne, and each of them a failure—well, perhaps the 'ifrit could see no more. If she could find a fourth, she might surprise them both.

There was meant to be a fourth already on its way, what they were supposed to be waiting for, why they were wasting so much time and patience in this depressing town. Hasan was coming, with all the tribes of the Sharai. Necessarily he was slow, he lacked a djinni and had to carry water for so many men; it might take him another week to cross the Sands. He was coming, though, and like the others she pretended that he brought their hopes with him.

Like the others, she had small faith in armies. To be sure, such a force could overrun a castle, slay a Sand Dancer and an 'ifrit; but however swift it was, it would be too slow to save Julianne. There needed only moments to slit a girl's soft throat, or pierce her belly with a claw.

Why Julianne had been taken was a question to which Elisande could still find no answers. As bait, clearly—but bait for whom, and to what purpose? There was a fog in her mind, whenever she tried to think about it; even her curiosity didn't blaze bright enough to burn away the shadows. Answers could wait. The fire, the urgency lay in rescue. Rescue soon, rescue *now*, before Hasan came with his multitudes and his anger, to oversweep good sense and argument.

AND SO SHE was here in the dust and quiet of the morning, with half a plan in her head and small expectation. She'd left her companions in the little house they were renting by the southern gate; Coren had asked where she was going and she'd just said, "Out, for a walk." He had smiled and waved a permissive hand, "Try not to get into trouble." Marron had still been chewing slowly on his breakfast bread; his red eyes had watched her leave, but he'd said nothing. Jemel, brewing coffee on the fire in the yard, hadn't bothered even to look up from his scented steam and his simmering. A restless girl wasting energy while they simply wasted time in waiting, thinking, drifting—nothing unusual in that. It was the story of her life, she thought, and perhaps the story of life itself, that men would do what they wanted in defiance of what needed doing. Coren was more subtle than her father, more astute but no wiser when he should be, when she needed him to be, now. Marron was the opposite, more simple than her father, much wiser and more ignorant, hesitant to the point of immobility. Jemel simply followed Marron, who had no one to lead him; and her father—her blind, bull-stupid, blundering father, the epitome of all men, who could be absolutely relied upon to wait too long and then go roaring after shadows, as though noise and bluster could cover blood and waste—her father Rudel was not here yet but he was coming, with Hasan. He'd enjoy having an army to play with.

Which made it all the more urgent to forestall him, to snatch the bait but not to spring the trap; which was why she walked the streets of Selussin this early morning.

By an hour after dawn, Elisande knew, all the boys of Selussin would have been already in their schools, chanting together as they memorised their holy books under a teacher's stinging rod. The women and the girls would have been out in the fields, tending crops and harvesting the wiry grey-green reeds that flourished in what was marshland in the spring, when the rains ran down from the hills. Like everyone here Elisande had slept beneath the shelter of a reed-thatch roof last night, on a mat of woven reeds. The tough fibres of those same reeds could be beaten and twisted into cords and rope, plaited to make belts and sandals, knotted into nets or mixed with mud to give strength to bricks. They pervaded this dreary life more thoroughly even than the teachings of religion; the only surprise was that the Selussids didn't eat them too. Or perhaps—remembering the tasteless stringiness of last night's vegetable stew, the effort it demanded to chew and swallow—perhaps they did that, too, and simply didn't say so.

The women and children were accounted for, then, in schools and fields till noon. That left only the men. It was a man that Elisande was in search of: a priest, rather, an imam. Every man here was an imam, or seemed so: dressed in heavy formality with swinging chains and amulets above dark and decorated robes, bearded and remote, scowling normally, hurrying between school and temple, between lessons and prayer.

"Excuse me, sir—"

A glare, from beneath eyebrows like bushy crags; a quickened scurry of reed-soled sandals in the dust.

"Pardon me, holy father—"

A hiss of indrawn breath, a tightening of the hood that hid the beard, a back as swiftly turned to the importunate indecency of girl, even girl as politely veiled and swathed as she was. Perhaps she should throw off woman's dress and ape a boy again . . .

Instead she tried again and yet again, she had to: waylaying every man that passed, being rebuffed and spat upon but not yet giving up. Her hopeless pursuit led her from the tight twist of alleys to the wide and empty marketplace where there hardly seemed to be a market any more, and on into the shadow of the greatest temple of Selussin, a three-sided tower—of course, three-sided—built of mud reinforced by a framework of wooden beams, whose ends jutted irregularly from the heat-baked, crumbling walls.

There were more men here, coming and going through the low dark doorway, but still they dodged her or ignored her, importunate as she was.

At last, falling back yet again from the stiff outrage of a male back and trembling on the edge of acceptance, of defeat, she heard a soft chuckle from behind her.

And wheeled around in a fury—did they laugh at her, these silent men? they'd be sorry if they did—and found herself face to face with Jemel.

"Have you been *following* me?"

His hands waved in a calming gesture that could not gentle her, not while he was grinning so broadly.

"Only for a little, Lisan. I came to find what you were at."

"Well, you have seen." And had found it funny, seen a joke in her desperation, which amused her not in the least.

"Seen, but not understood. I cannot see your thoughts. What do you want, with these men who will not speak to you? You know they will not speak."

"Yes, I know. But it's such a small thing to them, so important to me, and they make me so angry . . ." She hesitated a moment longer, then confessed. "I want one of them to bless my knives for me, that's all."

"To bless your knives?"

"To make them effective, against 'ifrit." What else? She didn't need to say it, except that then he could say, "Are you expecting to meet 'ifrit, Elisande?" and she could say, "Were you expecting to meet 'ifrit at Rhabat, Jemel?" and he could smile and say, "Give me your blades, then, and I will ask. And lay my scimitar beside them, in case I too should unfortunately meet 'ifrit all unexpected. I wish you had told me your thought before you came out," he added, frowning.

"Why, so that you could have saved me this humiliation, begging in the street to no avail? So do I, then."

"No, I enjoyed that," with the flashing grin again, that came and went in moments. "But I could have brought Dard also, for the blessing."

"Marron doesn't need an enchantment on his sword, to slay an 'ifrit." He was skilled enough—she thought, she hoped—to do it with a bare blade unblessed, a straight thrust to a hot red eye; or else he had the Daughter, he always had the Daughter. "Besides, he doesn't like to kill."

"I know," Jemel said, his eyes briefly shadowed. "Not even 'ifrit. He may have to, though, before all this is over. Give me your knives."

There was no choice, but still she hesitated. "They're my blades. I want to see . . ."

He nodded. There was a bond between a weapon and its owner, of course there was, how not? Why else would so many give a name to steel? "It will be done in the temple here, if I can find a man to do it. Unbelievers are forbidden to enter, but women are not, and the veil hides your race. Follow us inside. There will be a screen in the eastern quarter; watch through the lattice. You'll see as much as I do. It will be brief, in any case. These are busy men, these imams."

There was a cynical note to his voice; she gazed at him curiously, remembering how many mornings she'd seen him leave even Marron and go off alone to say his prayers in the Sands. Mornings and evenings both, but it was the mornings she remembered: the pale light, the cool breeze and himself a silhouette against the new-made sun, all pride and purpose . . .

"Don't you mind?" she asked. "That I'm there, I mean, if it's forbidden to me?"

"It is for the God to mind, not me."

She slipped the knives from her belt and passed them to him, hilt-first. He took them respectfully, as though they had as proud a lineage as Dard; he stowed them in his own belt and stepped away.

A minute later, along came another of those ubiquitous imams, hustle hustle in his weighty robe. As he passed, Jemel gripped the man's arm and pulled him abruptly to a halt.

The priest was furious, all but muted with rage, spluttering incoherently; Jemel's voice cut easily across the gabble.

"Your pardon, holy brother, I do but ask a service of your wisdom. There is a fee . . ."

Whether it was the sight of silver coins in Jemel's left hand that stilled the imam's protest, Elisande couldn't say. It might have been what else that sight revealed, the missing little finger, coupled with what Jemel's clothes proclaimed, that he was Sharai but tribeless; no desert priest would offend a man who might be sworn to the Sand Dancers.

"What service? Brother?"

"Your blessing, on my blades."

A moment's pause, just long enough for those coins to be passed from one hand to another; then, "Come," and the imam ducked in through the temple door, with Jemel on his heels.

Elisande waited for the space of a few steadying breaths, before she followed.

*   *   *

IF SELUSSIN'S PRIME purpose was to teach, then its high temple was a lesson in itself, she thought, that the surface of a thing gave few clues to its innermost heart.

From the outside, the building was crudely made and eccentric, speaking more to the weakness of its people than the power of its priests. The difference inside was startling, all the more so because the materials remained the same.

The floor was pounded earth, and sandy near the door where the constant passage of feet dragged in the dirt of the town's streets. Further in, she saw a small boy with an aspergill sprinkling water where he walked: not enough to muddy the ground, just to dampen it and quell the dust. It kept the air cool too, and a little moist; she was reminded of the boys in the Sultan's gardens at Bar'ath Tazore, doing much the same out in the open to keep a jungle thriving under desert sun. The purpose here was subtly similar, she thought: to keep mysterious the place where power lived, to let no one pass from there to here without seeing, touching, breathing the change from that to this.

As Jemel had promised, there was a carved and pierced screen to her right, dividing the eastern angle from the body of the temple. She let her feet find their way unguided, while she stared upward: up and up into twisted height and darkness, while she thought of a candle's flame, the small hot glow at the heart of it where the wick burned, and then the rising column of light.

The temple-tower was a single vaulting chamber, undivided; and all that high-leaping space was criss-crossed by an intricate and eye-defeating maze of blackened wood. From outside she had seen the beam-ends and thought them strange enough, an irregular studding, a scaffold to give shape and strength to the friable mud of the walls. Here were the beams themselves. Tall trees they must have been to run as they did from wall to wall, clear across the temple at unpredictable angles, in no pattern or design that she could discern from the lights of many lamps and braziers. They made a baffling knotwork that drew the eye in and up and wanted never to release it.

Coming at last behind the women's screen, she dragged her gaze downward, found herself alone and so nudged her veil aside, hooked her fingers through the narrow piercings and set her eyes to the widest space that she could discover.

There were Jemel and the imam, kneeling before a rough block of black stone with a burning charcoal brazier set atop. Laid on the floor between the men and that simple altar were her knives, Jemel's scimitar, faintly gleaming in the smoky light.

The imam spread his hands above the blades and probably began a prayer, some well-used form of words. She couldn't hear, and had trouble believing that any blessing so lightly, so cheaply bought could truly prove effective. She'd seen sanctified weapons shear through where normal steel rebounded; that was more of a mystery to her than other, stronger magic that she'd met. She might not understand the Daughter, but it was real, she couldn't dispute its existence and she knew what it did. A priest's blessing on a blade, though, when she gave his god no credence—it challenged her true faith, that the world was well-made whoever it was that made it. She might have believed that a priest's wisdom could invest some power in what he touched; but this distracted man with his wispy beard and his crass self-satisfaction? Jemel had more wisdom in his missing finger, and yet Jemel could not make a sword bite through 'ifrit armour.

Perhaps the imam could not do it either, and this was wasted time . . .

"Lisan." A voice spoke suddenly, shockingly in her ear; she choked and twisted around.

And saw no one, though she wheeled in a circle to be sure. Good sense took a moment to catch up with her racing heart and make her look again, more closely.

Esren was a spinning shadow among shadows, a finger's length of dust and gleaming darkness amid the confusion of light as it fell through the complications of the screen.

Second nature now to bite back the hot and perilous question; *what are you doing here?* Instead she took a slow breath and then another, as much time as she needed; when she was ready, in a hissing whisper, she said, "Esren, I did not summon you."

"Indeed not. I came. I was curious."

About what, she wondered—the temple, the blessing, something else? No way to guess; if it wanted her to learn, then it would tell her. Obliquely, like as not.

"I don't suppose the djinn go often into church," she said, trying to be oblique in her turn.

"I go where I choose." *Now,* unspoken but ever there between them, that deep and ever-resented debt it owed to her, that it repaid with grudging and disputatious service. "The same is true of all my kind."

"But you don't worship this god, or any other; so . . ."

"Neither does this god or any other worship us. So far as we know. It may be a nonsense, a game of men to defeat the dark with lies and promises; but a blessed blade will still strike home, Lisan, as though it had the wrath of the God behind it."

"Tell me if those blades are truly blessed," she said. She had visions in her head, knives hurled at iron-black body, hurled and bouncing back.

"They are. Any hedge-priest can do this work; his touch will be as potent as a saint's," and the imam was touching the weapons now, she saw, one finger to each still blade. "Have a care with those knives, Lisan. They may slay more than an 'ifrit."

As ever, she looked for deeper meaning beneath its words; as ever, she ended up drowning in uncertainty. Would the knives be potent against other creatures of the spirit world—against the djinn themselves, maybe? Was it nervous for itself, could she cut the thread of its long life and send it spinning into dissolution? It was not immortal, that she knew; a djinni could be slain. And yet it seemed to have no solid body to attack, being made of wind and whispers. Perhaps a blade charged with power could seek out some inner core, unravel what was wound so tight; perhaps it was afraid of her . . .

More likely of her ignorance, she thought, and set that thought aside. Grimly, for later consideration.

"I suppose it must be magic, then. Like laying a spell on the metal." Or on a man's mind, such as she could do herself, laying a Fold in the pathway of his thoughts such that he could look directly at her and see her not at all.

"You use words that have no meaning. That is magic; your hidden home is magic; I am a creature of magic," it said with a rich contempt, as it spun and sparkled in the air. "It exists, Surayon exists, I exist; in that sense we are all alike, and so, yes, the imam's blessing is a kind of magic. But Lisan, so do you exist, and the mud floor that you stand on, and the flea that bites you."

"I don't have—ow!" She slapped at her leg and hissed, "If that's all the use of your foreknowledge, to tell me I'm going to get bitten an eye-blink before it happens, then you might as well keep it to yourself . . ."

Sand-soft as it was, sand-sharp as she had meant it, her voice died on her, as she realised that she was speaking to the empty air. The djinni had disappeared from her shoulder without warning, without another word. She was becoming used to that, but not used enough; she still wasted a moment in glancing around, to be sure.

And was still looking, still squinting into shifting shadows when all thoughts of it were driven from her head by a sudden, bewildering noise. A high-pitched squealing, so high that it was almost painful; she couldn't place it except that it came from above, it seemed to come from every upper corner of the roofspace, every angle of beam and wall.

And then it moved, it fell down towards her like sound turned solid, dark and demonic.

Towards her, towards everyone, all at once: she saw how all the men were staring up, transfixed and terrified. Some were crouching under the weight of it, grovelling almost on the floor, setting their voices against the noise in a rising prayer of desperation.

Her eyes were drawn inexorably back to the swirling darkness overhead. The living darkness—there were voices in that numbing scream, there was a pattern to the movement. She looked towards the poor protection of her knives where they lay before the altar and saw Jemel stooping to snatch up his own blade. *Good,* she thought, *but you leave mine for me . . .*

Something hurtled at her, and she ducked instinctively. It skimmed above her head, leaving a brief impression of gaping jaws, teeth, a red gullet—but small, so small, mouse-sized, no threat at all.

She gaped in her turn, stared after it, stared up, all the while choking down a churn of painful laughter in her gut. All of them, she wanted to laugh at them all, herself and those cowering priests with their abandoned self-regard and Jemel who stood so proud and warrior-like among them, gazing about him now in bafflement that was only slowly turning to understanding, to catching up with her.

They deserved all the laughter that she had, all the mockery she could raise. So many of them and so pleased with themselves they'd been, until a shriek and a shadow had punctured their overweening pomposity.

Bats whirled and circled among them now in hundreds, in thousands, enough to fill the air and block the light as though the mass of their dark bodies cast its own darkness like a net about them.

Bats, and nothing worse. Bats that must sleep the day out among the beams and rafters overhead, clustering together like kittens for warmth and safety; bats that had been suddenly disturbed and so erupted in alarm, all of them together like a flight of birds, startled and stupid and beating round and round the narrow compass of the temple rather than brave the sun's glare outside . . .

Bats that had been suddenly disturbed—and here was Esren back as unexpectedly as it had disappeared, silent at her shoulder and somehow smug in its silence, she thought, exactly as a capricious creature might be that had made so much mischief in a moment.

"That was you," she said, without a hint of a question in it.

"I did nothing."

"Liar."

"The djinn do not lie, Elisande."

She ducked another flight, a skirmish-party that had found its way behind the screen—to its great regret, judging by the way it screamed and veered wildly as it passed close to the djinni—and sighed extravagantly. "Tell me whether you went up into the roofspace."

"I did."

"Tell me why."

"I was curious."

"You knew that the bats were there."

"Yes. I could sense them sleeping."

"And you knew that your presence would wake them, and that they would be terrified by your presence as any animal is, and so you went up to see what would happen."

"As I said, I was curious."

"It is not amusing, Esren," in her sternest voice, "to use fear to satisfy curiosity."

"It is interesting, though. The bats are frightened by me, which is perhaps appropriate, although I mean them no harm; these men it seems are frightened by the bats, which is absurd."

"Not truly frightened," she said, struggling to defend her kind against the facts, "only startled and alarmed."

"I do not see the difference. They shrieked, they prayed for protection; listen, they are praying yet, against whatever evil spirit they believe has raised the bats."

They were; and actually it was amusing, although she refused to say so. They were right, after all, by their own lights. She wished briefly that she could take Esren's experiment further, to find what would scare a spirit.

Instead she stepped out from behind the screen and gestured across the temple floor. Jemel seemed to be looking for that exactly, her appearance, her impatience. He gave her a cautious, distracted wave amid the confusion of men and animals, shrieks and prayers. Even he wasn't immune to the mood, though he had sheathed his scimitar by now. He stooped to scoop up her knives from where they lay, blessed now and she hoped more potent than they had been before—and he stayed stooped, walking all but doubled over as he came towards her. He might want her to think that it was the pain of suppressed laughter that folded him so, but she could see how his eyes were alert, how his head jerked whenever he saw or thought he saw a stray bat or a school of bats coming gape-jawed towards him. Their own swerving always came late, at the last possible moment; so many flying so fast, and yet not one had struck a beam or a man, a hanging lantern-chain or even another bat. The dense clouds whirled and circled, split apart and melted together again as seamlessly as their individual voices knitted together to make that one endless, penetrating scream.

Knowledge was no substitute for instinct, though, and never had been. It would take a brave man or a blind one—blind and deaf—to walk through the maelstrom and not to flinch. More than brave, perhaps: Jemel had courage to spare, and was almost crawling under the intangible weight of those packed and circling bodies above.

And what of a girl, could she be braver? Or more deliberately blind, perhaps? Elisande eyed the way to the door, and thought about walking with her eyes closed. There were too many obstacles, though, too many men scuttling to the sun like crabs to the shelter of a rock. Or like 'ifrit, she thought, remembering the clawed black shapes scurrying up out of the water. Then, inevitably, she remembered Julianne, trapped under an 'ifrit's red gaze; and strode determinedly towards the bright summoning of the doorway, pulling her veil straight as she went and feeling glad almost for the first time in her life that she was so short. She could feel her headdress stirred by the wind from the bats' wings, she knew there was a living ceiling of them barely a hand's span above her; but if she kept her eyes down she couldn't see them, and if she just kept her feet moving she might not need to think how close they were, she didn't at all have to imagine how it would feel to get just one tangled in her clothing . . .

Then a small flight of them came swooping low, heading straight for her. She bit back a shriek, though it felt like swallowing a pebble, hard and painful in her throat; and that took all the will she had, she couldn't keep from ducking and twisting aside. Twisting into their own path, indeed, as they yawed, so that they had to turn swiftly, violently in mid-air to avoid her. The breeze they made in their passing pressed through her veil, bringing with it the rankness of their breath, the musty smell of their fur; one glimpse of yellow incisors and vivid throats and she did close her eyes after all, telling herself how small they were and how harmless to her, chanting it under her breath like a mantra against the way the image filled her mind.

She was still standing, still bent over like an old woman when she felt a hand grip her arm. Chanced a glance aside, and saw Jemel. Of course Jemel, who else would touch her? Here?

He was standing tall now, despite the blurring darkness all about his head; she could see the effort he made to keep his eyes on her, and not let them go darting after the bats as they flashed in and out of his sight. She gave him a mirthless grin he wouldn't see—*be brave then, now, when you know that I'm watching: too late, but you needn't know that*—and let him urge her back into movement, towards the illusion of safety and away from the illusion of risk.

Head down and feet hurrying, her free arm rising despite herself in a useless ward: at last they broke into sunshine and she could straighten up, draw a deep recovering breath—her first for a while, or so it seemed—and look up at the Sharai to see him blushing darkly, with an embarrassed grin.

Her own face would match his, she knew. The veil might hide that, if it didn't catch fire simply from the glow of her skin, which could outburn the sun; it couldn't hide the tremble in her arm where he was still holding it. She tossed her head defiantly against the world—or against her own malignant djinni, that could so humiliate her with a little casual curiosity—and said, "Give me my knives, then."

"Not here." His own head moved more purposefully, to indicate the swarm of men who filled the square around them. Men didn't yield weapons up to women.

So she followed Jemel meekly enough, away from the temple and its open square, into the tight tangle of alleyways that surrounded it. As soon as they were private, in a shadowy angle that was overlooked by no windows, he handed her knives across. She hoped to feel some tingle in the metal to say that they'd been changed, perhaps to see a new shimmer on the edge to show where power ran, and was disappointed; they seemed the same as before, sharp and finely balanced, nothing more. She knew that they were dangerous to mortal flesh, but whether they could hack or skewer the chitin of an 'ifrit—to learn that, she'd have to get closer than she liked, closer than she'd been yet.

Which must mean doing without Jemel's company or the djinni's, going alone against the world, the way she'd always liked to. She sheathed the knives invisibly within her robe and gave him a respectful bow that was less mocking than it might have looked, than he might have thought it. "Thank you, Jemel. Will you go back now, to seek Marron?"

She was out of practice at asking questions. Even to her own ears, that sounded more like a command, the rising inflection at the end only a meaningless courtesy.

He might have been angry, indignant, resentful, and was none of those. He stood before her, smiling as he said, "Will you go to seek Coren?"

"I—no. Not, not yet. I thought I might wander the town a little, learn its ways . . ."

"As you did yesterday and the day before, as we have all done since we came here? Or did you think that today perhaps you might go a little further, outside the walls—up to the castle, say, a nice distance for a day's exploring . . .?"

She was blushing again, and sure that he knew it again. She was becoming distressingly easy to read, or else simply too dangerously close to these few friends, who were stealing all her secrets from her one by one.

"Well then, yes," she said. "Yes, up to the castle, why

not? The gate is open, we know that; the 'ifrit watches Julianne, we know that. There's only Morakh left, then, and he can't watch everywhere at once . . ."

"The gate is open, and the trap is baited; will you walk inside?"

"The trap is baited for Coren, surely, not for me."

"We don't know that, it's a guess. Besides, a rat-trap may catch a mouse as easily. Morakh can't watch everywhere, but he can watch the gate; there's only one."

"So I'll climb the wall."

"And if you climb the wall and meet another Dancer, what then? Morakh may not be alone in there any longer."

"Esren says that he is, and the djinn do not lie."

"No, but they can be mistaken. They are dangerous creatures to put your faith in, Elisande."

"True; but I am a dangerous creature too. More so, now," touching the hafts of her daggers. "I am going, Jemel. Esren will not, nor will Coren, nor Marron; they are all afraid of the 'ifrit. With reason, perhaps, but their reasons don't apply to me. Julianne can't help herself, so one of us must help her."

"Two of us," he said flatly. "If you go, I am coming with you."

"Marron will be angry with you."

"He would be more angry, if I let you go alone."

That might be true. What was certain was that she was afraid, even without her companions' reasons. Her knives might be blessed, but they were still pitifully small weapons to set against a Sand Dancer and a spirit-monster. She hadn't looked for support from Jemel, hadn't dared to hope for it; to have it offered unexpectedly was a gift, a blessing in itself. Perhaps, if she really tried, she could see it even as an omen of success.

"Let's go, then," she said firmly. "Quickly, before Marron comes looking for you, or Coren for me." It would be that way round, it would have to be, but almost—almost!—she didn't care.

THERE WERE THREE sides to Selussin. The wall that gripped the town was shaped like an arrowhead, and the point of it faced the desert. Raiding Sharai would break like a wave around it; raiding Patrics would meet the opposing wall head-on, like a hammer. For both cultures, that seemed appropriate to Elisande.

Each wall had a curve to it, an inward bowing that would allow defenders to target any attacker along its length; each wall also had its gate at the centre, which must have allowed easy access for the traders who used to come in such numbers but would place any attacking force at the heart of the field of fire. For what good that would do. It looked well, she thought as she trailed Jemel out through the westerly gate—dogging his heels like the very picture of an obedient Catari girl, as Selussin was the very picture of a well-defended settlement—but she couldn't picture those priests and boys up on the walls and making any kind of fight to protect their schools and temples.

There had been no need in recent history, or at any rate no attempt. Sharai and Patric armies both had been intent on the castle; they'd simply absorbed the town into their temporary possession, riding like conquerors through wisely-opened gates in search of food but largely ignoring it else. Neither side had stationed a garrison there. The priests could count themselves lucky, perhaps, to have faced no Ransomer fanatics; the Duke of Ascariel was said to be a religious man, but not a foolish one. He'd let the temples stand and the schools survive, for the sake of peace.

*   *   *

ABANDONED AS THE landscape, empty as the Sands before it and the hills behind—abandoned long since save for birds and spiders, adventurous children, presumably now one girl, one zealot, one evil clad in chitin—the castle loured none the less above the town, a thundercloud of threat, and all the more so once they'd passed outside the shielding walls. It seemed almost to stoop from its height like a vulture on a crag, not so much guarding as inspecting what lay open and vulnerable below, picking over what might be worth scavenging.

A vulture with battered and dusty feathers it might be, and yet it stood out before the broken hills that made its backdrop, thrust itself forward indeed, made its declaration. *Mine! What you see from where you stand, all of this is mine,* and Selussin was only a morsel, it seemed to suggest, and might not abide there long.

And yet the town was ancient and the castle was newmade; the town thrived, where the castle stood forlorn; the town's walls were high and whole while the castle's were crumbling. Even from this distance, Elisande could see gaps in the parapet where stones had fallen in. Jemel must be right, that Morakh would watch the gate; she'd like to be proved right in her turn, that they could climb in over the wall and behind his back, now that her djinni had proved unreliable.

There were patches of cultivated ground all around the walls, where the women and children grew what food they could while their men studied and prayed the days away. Beyond the parched green of those fields lay another harvest, though it looked like nothing better than coils of grey-green wire, running in tangled, matted blankets to the first slope of the hills. Halfa-reeds: even the word seemed strange, to a mind grown accustomed to desert drought. But there were marshes here after the spring rains, where the mountain run-off pooled; the reeds grew tall, then wilted under the summer sun. Tough and fibrous but shallow-rooted, they could be pulled by the smallest child, then worked in a dozen different ways or else bound into bales and traded with what caravans still came this way.

Between the fields and the halfa-beds a road ran, dangerously below the castle's overlooking eye: Morakh's eye, if he were on the watch. Perhaps Elisande should have asked the djinni to carry them into the hills unseen; but Esren was so wary of the 'ifrit, it might have refused even so much help.

Well, too late now. If Morakh were watching, he would have seen them already. And could have seen nothing, after all, bar a man in local dress with a woman submissive at his heels. Not so unusual, surely. Except that no one else was moving or even visible, they were alone in the landscape; with the sun rising to its height, the fields had been abandoned. None who lived here was fool enough to carry water to the crops or sweat to pull halfa in the heat and glare of noon, why would they?

"I'm sorry, Jemel, I should have thought—we must stand out like ants on white linen down here, in our robes against this road . . ."

"Do you want to go back?"

"No."

"No, of course you don't. Well then, shall we go up and walk in at the open gates after all? We might as well."

And fight their way past a Dancer—at least one Dancer—only to be confronted by an 'ifrit that would know they were coming, that would be ready and waiting as the Dancer was? But then the 'ifrit would know anyway, however careful or clever they were. It was too much to wind her head around the complexities. Enemies that sensed the future were beyond all reason. Friends that did the same were as bad or worse; she thought evil things of Esren, and said, "Jemel, beat me."

"Do what?"

"Beat me," with a nod towards the stick that he carried in his belt like all true Sharai among settled folk, to show that they were camel-riders and no pastoralists, "as if I were a lazy girl who hadn't done her morning's work. Then stand over me, while I gather reeds; we'll make our way across the bed there and into that cleft, where we'll be out of sight of the castle. Then we can climb and find our way across the hill and around. If he is watching, it'll be the road that he watches."

"With good reason," Jemel murmured, surveying the rough crag. "It'll be a hard climb, and worse going after. And you'll be sore. Are you sure?"

"You don't have to beat me hard," she growled. "Just make it look good, from a distance. And yes, I'm sure." It was that or go back, there were no other options; and to go back meant failure, today and tomorrow. Jemel would tell Marron; Marron would tell Coren, those two were suddenly close as cousins; and Coren would look anxious and forbid her to try again, and never give her the chance anyway.

Jemel shrugged, and made great play of drawing his riding-stick as though it were his scimitar. She thought he made rather too much of it, indeed, flailing it through the air a few times before he gripped her shoulder and brought it whipping down across her back. She flinched as she heard its whistle; but the rod only stung when it struck her, and that lightly. She'd been beaten enough in her life, in various guises, to know the true cut of a cane. He must be holding his stroke at the last moment, doing all for effect.

Even so, half a dozen such strokes left her smarting, aching, having to bite down on her tongue to stop herself yelping; wishing almost for observers within earshot so that she could let go those yelps, sob and plead and play the beaten girl as vigorously as he played her husband, brother, whichever he'd decided in his arrogant male head.

"Enough," she muttered, glaring up at him over her shoulder as he raised the stick again. "Hit me again and you'll feel my blessed knife in your ribs, I swear it."

He grinned and let her go. "I said you'd be sore. Go on, then," with another great flourish of the stick, this time using it to point towards the reed-beds. "Go and gather, girl. I'll stroll behind, I need the rest. It's hard labour, disciplining a recalcitrant sister . . ."

Sister, was it? That would make better sense than wife, she supposed. To him at least, and maybe also to her. Well, she could play his browbeaten, back-beaten sister, for any eyes that watched their comedy.

And did: hunched over to emphasise her pain, cowering from his shadow, she scuttled to the edge of the reeds. Bent lower to claw her fingers into the dry, knotted mat, and tugged. Ripped up a poor handful, and felt a stinging in her palm; gaped down at it and saw blood, saw how the skin was sliced.

Cursed the superstition that forbade the reeds to be cut by any blade, blessed or otherwise, and showed her hand surreptitiously to Jemel.

"It's tough as wire, and as sharp. How do they ever make cloth out of this?"

"By dint of much soaking and beating. But have you tried wearing it? As well wear woven wire. That's why they trade for wool, this makes better rope than robes. Just pretend," he urged her, "make a show of it, that's all we need. And you'll want your hands whole, for climbing."

She would; she did. She made her bent way crabwise towards the crag and the cleft that would hide them, never quite facing the direction her feet were taking her; facing her feet, indeed, stooped over like a crone and swinging one arm like a monkey, down and up in great looping movements like a fool's imitation of a harvest. With luck, no one would see from any distance that her hand came up as empty as it fell, that the arm she held crooked in her body's shadow held no gathered crop.

Jemel paced slowly behind her, occasionally tapping shoulder or thigh with his stick like a man who drove a donkey; she thought she might turn and bite him soon, like a donkey driven too far.

"How do little children ever pull this stuff?" she murmured out loud, if for no other reason than to remind him that she had a voice, and a mind behind it. "The women here have hands like hide, as women everywhere; but children . . ."

"There'll be a trick to it, a twist of the wrist; but their grandfathers stitch them palm-guards out of camel-leather, haven't you seen? It's holy work, if it keeps the women busy and the little girls at their heels."

She had seen old men on their doorsteps plying needle and thread and had thought it more practical than praying, and the first useful work she'd seen any man do in Selussin. She'd just assumed they'd be making a piece of harness or mending a shoe, as men did in other towns.

"If we disappear into that cleft and don't come out again, Morakh's going to wonder what we're up to. Isn't he?"

"Not necessarily." There was a pause in the steady pace of Jemel's footfalls, the sudden pop of a cork; she glanced back to see him drink from a water-flask, making a great pantomime of being hot and weary. Then his stick urged her on again, as he said, "With luck, he'll think we're just resting in the shade. It'll be an hour or two before he starts to worry, if he doesn't forget about us altogether. By then we should be safely up and out of sight of the castle gate."

Somewhere round the back of the castle, indeed, and looking for a way in or over; it was an odd definition of safety, she thought. But Julianne's need was pressing against her thoughts again, urgent and imperative. She moved on until the walls of the cleft grew high around her, until cool black shadow cut off any chance of their being overlooked. Then she straightened slowly, easing her sore shoulders and stiff back while she gazed upward at the climb that awaited them.

Height held no fears for her, she'd climbed often in the quiet valleys of her home and again in the Sands, with the Sharai. Here on the desert's rim, though, in the shelter of the cleft, neither rains nor sandstorms had softened the sharp edges of the rock. She chewed her lip for a moment, looking at the holds, and said, "I wish you'd bought two pairs of those palm-guards, Jemel."

"I didn't know we'd need them."

She knew that, she'd only been talking for its own sake, to postpone the moment. Her one hand was cut already; the other would be leaving its own trail of blood before they'd hauled themselves out of the cleft and onto the broken ridge above.

SHE LED THE way, knowing that Jemel would follow; she stayed determinedly ahead of him all the way, although it was like climbing on knives. She tried not to think about her fingers, nor about how Esren could have lifted them both up in a moment. Instead she forced her mind to focus on Julianne, thinking how her friend would have hated and feared this climb but how her courage would have driven her to it despite that, if it had been Elisande who needed rescue; wondering how that courage was holding up after days of captivity, whether she still clung to hope or felt herself abandoned. Whether she might hope for abandonment, indeed, knowing herself to be bait in a trap . . .

Too bad, if so. The others might abandon her, but

Elisande not. She climbed until she could drag herself over the crag's edge and into the shelter of a massive boulder. She waited until Jemel had joined her there, then spent a little time and a little strength that she could ill afford to take his hands in hers and still the bleeding, knit torn flesh together. She heard him gasp softly at the warmth of her healing touch; all he said, though, was, "What of your own? They're worse than mine."

"Alas," she said with a thin smile, "that I can't do anything about. We may be witches, we Surayonnaise, but we cannot spell ourselves." Healing was a journey into another's body; if anyone had learned the art of journeying within themselves, she'd never heard it. Now that the strain of the climb was behind her, she could feel every gash in her throbbing, blood-slick hands. Nothing she could do, though, except allow Jemel to tear strips from his robe to wrap them crudely.

Above them lay a slope of loose boulder-strewn shale. Scrambling over that tested her again as stones turned and slid away beneath her feet, forcing her to grab for insecure holds with stinging palms, eventually to crawl like a spider. Resisting the impulse to look behind and see how Jemel was coping took her mind from her own gracelessness until she'd reached the top; once there, she fell gasping on her back and called it generosity to stay so until he joined her.

From this new vantage-point they could look down on the path that came up from Selussin, look up to see the castle, with its gate standing open as they'd been told. They kept flat to avoid being seen in their turn, watched for any sign of Morakh on the walls and saw none. Had it been wasted effort, then, that savage climb? She couldn't be sure, there was any number of places where a man could stand concealed behind an embrasure or an arrow-slit and still have a view of the town and the way up.

She was busy mapping the landscape in her mind, plotting a route that would lead them around in secrecy to the rear of the castle, when Jemel nudged her suddenly.

"Look . . ."

She followed the direction of his nod and saw movement on the road that came down from the mountains, from Outremer. Movement that resolved itself quickly into a line of people, dark against the dust. Briefly she thought it was an army, men on the march in defiance of the abiding truce.

Another minute's watching, though, and she was only confused. The people were organised like an army, running steadily in two long files behind a single man; but they were all afoot and there was no glitter of armour among them, barely the glint of a sword's blade where they ran in sunshine. And she could see women and children among their number . . .

"Who are they?"

"Your people," Jemel murmured, "not mine. You tell me."

That she couldn't do, but she wasn't sure that he was right in any case. Some, many looked to be Catari, even if none were dressed like the Sharai. The only certainty was that they were bound for the castle; she huddled low in the shade of a rock and watched as they turned in at the gate. Perhaps half of them were inside before she thought to count. There were more than a hundred, though, she was sure of that. And still no sign of Morakh. Could he have been expecting them, not an invasion but a reinforcement? These were not Sand Dancers, but still . . .

"This changes things," she said positively. "Coren needs to be told."

"Yes. We'll go back."

"No, not both of us. You go, Jemel. Julianne still needs our help; it may even be easier for me to sneak around in there, with so many others to confuse Morakh and the 'ifrit."

"I said before, I won't let you go in there alone."

"There isn't any choice now. If we go in together, how long will it be before Marron comes blundering in after us, looking for you? He'll be anxious already, you know that. And there's no telling who he might meet, or what might happen after. Or Coren might come, and stumble straight into trouble. They've got to be warned, Jemel; and I've got to go in. Remember, I've always got Esren to whisk me away if I get caught. You don't have that protection, you're not safe in the way that I am . . ."

That was a direct lie, but she thought, she hoped he wouldn't recognise it.

Nor did he; he only grunted unhappily, and said, "Be careful, then. Don't do anything stupid, don't fight Morakh and the 'ifrit by yourself. Just learn what you can, find out who these people are and what they want, and then come back."

She promised, lying again; and waited while he slid away on his belly, watched while he slid back down the slope, raising a cloud of dust and a small landslide as he went. Then she turned her eyes and mind back to the castle, to her quietest way in. It meant another climb with her hurting hands, but she was prepared for that. She tried to prepare herself too for what she might find inside, what further surprise awaited—and was none too surprised, not really surprised at all when she saw the gate swing shut against her, against the world.

SEVEN

Out of the Sands

MARRON STARED AT Jemel—blood on his hands and on his robe, sweat in his hair who almost never sweated, news that sounded like betrayal on his tongue—and felt anger rise to meet the Daughter who had risen already. Controlling that was nearly too much for him; controlling his temper too was too much altogether.

"Elisande went into the castle—and you left her, you let her do that? Alone?"

"Yes," he said quietly, sullenly, aware of its moment. "Would you have done otherwise, could you have stopped her? I could not."

"You could have tried."

"I did try."

"You could have tried harder."

"Marron, peace." That was Coren, pushing his way physically between them. "You cannot think rationally while Jemel is bleeding, the Daughter prevents you.

Jemel, change your robe and wash the blood from your hands. I have an ointment that will stem the flow, enough to quiet what burns inside Marron. Then we will talk, and decide what's best to do."

Marron knew already what was best to do. There had been altogether too much talking. Words had left Julianne in her captivity; they wouldn't do the same for Elisande.

Jemel unlaced his robe with awkward fingers, let it slip from his shoulders; Marron turned his back on that well-known and well-loved body and stormed out into the yard, first steps on a far longer journey—

—AND WAS STOPPED, was startled to find a djinni spinning strongly in the gateway, barring his access to the street.

"Ghost Walker, do not walk into foolishness. Think. I know where you mean to go, and what you mean to do there. If I can see this, who can see so little,"—it was Elisande's djinni, then, surely the only one that would brag of weakness—"of a certainty the 'ifrit can see it too. If you went to the castle, you would meet nothing there but death."

"Then so will Elisande."

"Then you would be too late to save her; she is within its walls already. But Lisan moves more quietly through the world than you, Ghost Walker. She slides between the threads and leaves them barely singing, while you tear wherever you touch. She is within the castle, and not dead yet. Believe me, I would know. The weight of my oath is a burden; her death would free me, and I am not free."

"So obey the terms of your oath, and help her!"

"What is true for you is equally true for me. We have spoken of this before. If I went to the castle, I would be destroyed. Lisan would not be helped by that. Be patient, and take counsel; there are wiser men than you among your party, and others coming."

Wisdom and delay walked hand in hand, he thought, or more often walked not at all, but sat still and contented. Even this little check, though, had cooled his lashing fury. He sighed and heard it say, "Now you are thinking clearly," high and clear as ever but somehow further off, although it was not moving. He saw it not fade but reduce to a shimmer, a whisper of wind, and wanted to call it back. He was not Elisande, though, to order its comings and goings.

He stood silent until it had disappeared entirely, until a cautious step forward confirmed that the way lay open to the street, although he would not take it now. He lingered a while in the yard, and then when he did go back inside, his feet lagged heavily against his will, as though the weight of a boy's dark gaze was enough almost to hold him still. His hand reached out nervously to touch cool clean robe and cooler skin beneath, still damp from a hard scrubbing; his fingers hesitated, tremulously uncertain, before they dared to circle Jemel's elbow, the most casual of touches.

"I'm sorry," he said; and was rewarded with a smile as anxious as his own.

"No, I. I should have followed her, perhaps. I thought I should; but she forbade me, and she is hard to ignore . . ."

That brought stronger, safer smiles to each of them, and a chuckle from Coren where he was wiping his hands in a corner.

"Hard? Impossible, I should have said. And no, you should not have followed. To lose Elisande would be bad for us, worse for her father; to lose both of you and not know how would have been worse for us all."

"The djinni says we have not lost her yet," Marron murmured, shifting his arm round Jemel's waist and feeling the jolt of that news, that double news snatch his friend breathless.

It was Coren who said, "Djinni? What djinni?"

"Hers, Esren Tachur. It came, it wouldn't let me go to her . . ." That was a confession, and it won him another hard stare from Jemel.

"Did it, indeed?" Coren went on, seemingly oblivious. "That's . . . interesting. Has it ever come to you before?"

"No, never. Why would it?" And then, quickly, before Coren could give him an answer he didn't want to hear, he turned to Jemel and said, "Let's walk in the sun a little."

"Patric madness. The wise man avoids the sun."

"The wise man sits in shadows all his life, for fear of being burned. Come, I want you." *Not Elisande, not her djinni, you I want.*

IN HONESTY, THE worst of the sun had passed. Even Jemel could be drawn to confess that at this time its warmth was almost pleasant, though he had to add that only in the true Sands did you meet the true sun, the God's hammer against the infidel.

Marron didn't argue. Born and raised under gentler skies, he was sure there was some touch of truth in Jemel's vision. If there were a god—any kind of god, Patric or Catari or otherwise—then surely this land of fierce light and heat must be his country.

They set their backs against the sun; that way lay the girls in their danger, the risk of blame rising again. Better to go the other way: to skirt the marketplace, to press through throngs of boys released from lessons—ignoring how they stared at a Patric face, how those stares were redoubled at their first sight of his eyes—and so to come at last to that high angle of the walls that faced due east, back to the Sands and Rhabat. Nothing was neutral in that direction either, but at least those memories were a story told.

There was a flight of steps leading up to the wall's height, and a man standing watch at the top. He glanced down as they climbed, but said nothing.

After murmuring a greeting that brought no response, Jemel led Marron to stand at a little distance.

"He thinks I am mad, no doubt, keeping company with a Patric who dresses like a Sharai and has the eyes of a devil. Mad or heretical, or both. Perhaps he is right, perhaps I am."

"Mad, or heretical?"

"Both. You have made me both, Marron. You have turned me from my good sense, so that I stand bareheaded in the sun; and you have turned me from my God also, so that I cannot remember when last I prayed and meant it."

"Do you regret either?"

"No." He might have said that with a laugh, but he did not. "I have one purpose left that you cannot turn me from, one oath that you will not make me break; so long as I have that, I am still Jemel. All else that I am is yours. If the God condemns me for it when I am dead, then perhaps will be the time for regrets."

His oath, of course, was to kill Sieur Anton d'Escrivey. Marron harboured his own secret oath, to prevent that by any means in his power. So long as Jemel was mad enough to follow him, he thought he could achieve it; his dream of travelling came back to him, the call of the far lands to the east. He gazed outward, trying to see past all the country he'd walked thus far, into the haze beyond— and was distracted suddenly by something closer, significantly close, a stirring twist of dust that hid dark figures at its heart.

"Look," he said softly. "There, do you see?"

"No, nothing. What is it?"

No dispute, no suggestion that perhaps there was nothing to be seen. Jemel had desert eyes, but Marron had the Daughter's.

"They are here."

At last, they were here. Marron hadn't realised until this moment just how much he'd been waiting for it, for them. Waiting more in hope than expectation, perhaps, but waiting none the less. A handful of people could sit quiet within a township's walls; an army not, and this should be an army. Coren could be patient, Coren could outsit a mountain; Hasan not, and this must be Hasan.

"Who, and how many?"

Marron smiled; even his eyes couldn't make out banners or numbers at this distance. "You could guess, better than I can see. These are your people. A small group of men, it's not a column, the dust is settling at their backs; and they're riding swiftly. Outriders, come to scout the land?"

"Of a sort. There will be two dozen men, and I could put a name to each of them. Will you wager?"

"Would I lose?"

"Oh, yes."

"Name your terms."

Jemel chuckled, and brushed the back of his hand lightly against Marron's arm as he shook his head. "Gambling is a sin, forbidden. But I will tell you, and you will see how well I know the tribes, and be impressed."

"Isn't vanity a sin too?"

A purse of the lips, a rocking motion of the head: "It is preached against. Does it offend the God, or simply courtesy? I am not sure. Ask an imam; I am a warrior. And this I am sure of, that Hasan leads those riders himself, and at his back you will find the sheikhs of every tribe that rides with him. Where else would they be but at the head, how else could they bring the tribes to follow?"

Marron nodded. Hasan, the sheikhs—and one other, sure to be riding in that party.

"One of us," he said neutrally, "is going to have to tell Rudel that his daughter has gone into the castle."

Jemel nodded. "That is mine to do. If there is a storm to come, it is mine to endure."

Not alone; Marron would stand beside him. But, "No storm. If there was a fault, it was Elisande's, in choosing to go."

"You did not think so when I told you. Perhaps her father will not think so either."

"I was wrong, Jemel, and I am sorry for it. And Rudel knows her better than any of us, he will not make the same mistake." *He knows her better and loves her less,* he might have added for his friend's comfort, except that he didn't believe that it was true.

"You think so? You may be right—but he is still her father. We should go and meet them."

"They'll be a while yet." Indeed, Jemel was still straining to see what was so clear to Marron, the distant figures and the dust-cloud of their passage; the watchman close by hadn't sighted them at all. "No point walking so far out that we have to run back at their stirrups." Marron could run all day, with the Daughter's strength allied to his own; Jemel only thought that he could. "Wait a little, and watch."

"If we wait much longer, he"—the watchman, indicated with a contemptuous jerk of the head—"will see them at last," for all the world as though Jemel saw them clearly himself, "and strike his alarm," an iron ring suspended from a tripod at his side.

"And then?"

"And then they will close the gates, and we will be prevented from leaving the city."

Only Jemel could call this little township a city; surely only Jemel could imagine that it would have fire enough

in its belly to defy an army of the Sharai. Marron smiled
and said, "Wait. If they will not let us out, then we will
wait until they let Hasan in. I do not think it will be long."

IT WAS LONG enough before the watchman spotted the
approaching riders—so long, indeed, that Marron was
tempted to go to him and point them out.

At last the man stiffened and stared, muttering nervously into his beard; then he snatched up a bar and be-
laboured his alarm-ring, crying out above its clatter.

Marron turned to watch the streets below, and saw the
panic that he'd been expecting: people spewing from
every house amid a rising babble of voices, men and boys
milling uncertainly, looking for leadership and finding
none, while the women came running in from the fields,
herding their daughters before them and trying vainly to
gather in their sons. Some of the men carried arms, and
some of those came to the walls, but more were hurrying
to the temples where their greater confidence lay.

"We should go to the gate," Jemel said urgently.

"If you think so."

It was easier to make their way along the wall than
through the streets. The men who had climbed this high
stood for the most part numbly clutching a useless scimitar or spear, or else gripping the parapet two-handed,
gazing at the plume of dust that foretold their greatest
fear. Some were silent, some spoke of the supposed truce,
of the faithlessness of the Sharai; more than once Marron
had to drag Jemel on, where he would have stopped to
dispute that.

When they reached the gates in this south-easterly
wall, they found them still standing wide, abandoned
even by their guards. Jemel exclaimed aloud; Marron
grinned, and led his friend down the steps to ground
level.

"Why slam a door, only to have it broken down? These people cannot stand against the Sharai, Jemel. They will welcome Hasan as they have welcomed my people before this, and yours again before them; they will starve themselves to feed his army, and pray only that he leaves or is driven back into the Sands before they starve indeed."

Even as he said it, here came the welcoming-party: a group of flustered elderly men in ornate robes, clutching talismans or plucking at their beards with fretful fingers. They arrayed themselves in the road below the gateway, jostling for precedence or seeking to deny it, some of them, pushing others forward in their stead. Jemel hissed in irritation; Marron swallowed a chuckle and pulled him into the shadow of the high gate.

The harsh, doleful tolling of the alarm stopped abruptly. The whole township seemed to be holding itself in stillness, all the clamour of the last minutes fallen to nothing. Marron gazed up at the baked mud of the arch above the gate and thought he could feel how ancient this place was, and how weary as it faced yet another force of men, yet another invasion. Weary but strong, strong in patience and in faith: and that faith would be rewarded, that patience would win in the end. This army would leave in the end, as every army before it. Selussin would remain.

Strength to endure, simple survival—it was a quality that Marron admired, envied, hungered for. Every living man is a survivor, of course; every man endures everything he meets until he fails, until he dies. Marron had endured more than many and survived it; he expected to endure more yet and to survive that too. But it wasn't his own strength that had brought him this far or would take him further. *The Ghost Walker is traditionally very hard to kill.*

The boy in him—what was left of the boy in him,

when he could find it—yearned for another kind of life, but could not speak of it even to Jemel, especially to Jemel. He was ashamed of his own dreams, because even if there could be a life for him without the Daughter, it still wasn't his own strength that he dreamed of. He still wanted to live in strength's shadow, sooner than be strong himself.

He'd seen many kinds of strength since he came to the Sanctuary Land. Here about Selussin was the simplest form, high walls that were undefended, that could do nothing but stand; and here came a couple of strong men who were anything but simple, who rode veiled against the dust they raised, whose hearts were as obscure as their deeds were daring.

Any man arriving so, out of the Sands with seasoned warriors at his back, any such must have caused the priests anxiety. When such a man threw back hood and veil, gazed down and said with quiet authority, "I am Hasan," pure terror showed for a moment on their faces. All the world knew that Hasan was hungry for war with Outremer. If he'd chosen this time and this place to fight it, they could see the final end to Selussin's long history played out in blood and destruction, their libraries burned and their temples ransacked, their people's lives and their own consumed in blood and pain.

The eldest among them, gaunt and white-bearded, recovered himself quickly. He took a slow pace forward, leaning on what might have been a staff of office or else simply a support for unsteady legs; he bowed his head lightly, a gesture of respect from priest to warrior but nothing more, no hint of a surrender; he said, "Hasan, our gates are open to you as they are to all, if you come in peace."

The gates were open in any case, however he came. Hasan bowed in his turn, though, and said, "Always in peace to you, most holy. I come to reclaim one who is most precious to me and has been stolen away; but she lies in the castle yonder," a gesture towards the high dark shadow that the Patrics called Revanchard, "not within your walls. The tribes will not disturb your teachings."

The old priest nodded his gratitude; Marron wondered if he could truly be so naïve. Having come so far with an army at his back, Hasan was unlikely to settle for Julianne's recovery. Outremer was too close, too tempting . . .

Selussin's best hope must be to see the Sharai overrun the castle and then march on across the mountains, to fight their war within the Kingdom's borders; its greatest fear would be defeat for Hasan, a swift retreat with his enemies harrying hard. His men would flood into castle and township both, lacking time to lose themselves in the Sands; the decisive battle of this generation would be fought out against Selussin's walls, and that spelled doom, dust and ashes for the generations following.

For the moment, though, all parties were prepared to pretend otherwise. After further exchanges of courtesy, the priests stepped back and Hasan rode in with the sheikhs following in a crush, crowding for position.

Rudel ceded place to them all. A jerk of his head for beckoning, and Jemel ran to his stirrup while Marron hung back, not to unsettle the camel.

"Someone must speak to the tribes," Rudel said, "which means me, since these are all too grand. Wait for me here, and be patient; it may take a deal of shouting."

"What will you tell them?" Marron called.

"Much the same—wait, and be patient. Otherwise the hotheads will ride up to investigate the castle while the old campaigners head for the town and make a liar of Hasan. I presume nothing's changed at the castle, Morakh is still there with Julianne?"

"And the 'ifrit, yes. But things have changed, Rudel, they're not alone any more . . ."

"How so?"

"Be quiet, Marron. It is mine to tell," Jemel insisted. "Rudel, we were watching the castle, Lisan and I, looking for a way in when people came, on foot, from across the mountains. About a hundred, not well armed, not warriors, women and children among them. They went in, and the gates were closed behind them. I came back, to tell Marron and Coren."

"And my daughter?"

"She climbed the walls and went inside."

Rudel sighed slowly. "Of course she did. And nothing you could say would stop her. Don't look so guilt-ridden, Jemel; there's only one person I know who could conceivably shift Elisande when her mind's made up, and I gather he wasn't there."

No, I was talking with Coren, doing nothing while my friends walked into danger without me. Rudel hadn't moved his eyes by so much as a fraction, but Marron understood him perfectly. So, he thought, did Jemel. Swiftly he said, "Djinni Tachur told me that she was well," which wasn't quite true but true enough.

"Did it?" Like Coren, Rudel was instantly interested. "What exactly did it say to you?"

"That she was inside the castle, and unhurt." Exactly, it had said *not dead yet,* but he wouldn't pass that on to her father. "It was seeking to stop me following her."

"Which it did, clearly. We must hope that it was right to do so. Unhurt does not necessarily mean uncaptured; she may be as much a prisoner as Julianne. If the djinni speaks to you again, Marron, you might ask it—or no, not ask, but try to find out. I must go to the tribes," with a glance over his shoulder that drew the boys' eyes after, and showed them all the dust of the army's approach. "Wait here."

He turned his camel almost savagely, beat it into a run; Jemel watched him go and said, "He is upset."

"Of course he's upset, she's his daughter. Never mind how bitter it is between them, she's still his daughter."

"Yes. Patrics are a strange people; they spit at each other in public, and where they love they conceal it."

"Not all of us," Marron said softly.

"No? Sometimes I think your heart is veiled and no more honest than your eyes."

"Jemel . . ."

"Then I remember that it would have to be so, or you would not be Marron, nor the Ghost Walker." A brilliant smile, entirely unexpected; a sudden kiss, all the more so; and then, "Let's go up and watch the tribes disperse. They will be hot and angry after a long day at the end of many long and hard days before this; and now Rudel will tell them that they cannot come into the town nor go up to the castle, and they will fight each other instead. Not much, perhaps, and not for long; nobody will die, they would not risk a blood-feud here, but there will be fighting. You will see."

MARRON DID INDEED see, better than Jemel, if more strangely. Through the red cast of the Daughter's eyes he saw a dozen sudden flurries, stabs of sunfire as the light caught a thrusting blade; he saw dark figures stumble and crouch wounded on the sandy ground, he could almost smell their blood from here. Each time Rudel was there at speed, wheeling on his mount and gesturing widely, speaking too soft to hear or else crying out loud enough to stir the dead in the dusty hills, doing whatever was needful to see knives sheathed and quarrels cooled. Each time he couched his camel and stepped into the brittle peace, to spend some little time with those who had been wounded.

"They will meet again to argue later, by the wells," Jemel prophesied, "but there will be no more weapons

drawn. We will fight for water rights but never by the
water, for fear that blood should taint it. It is a desert law,
but it will hold here. It would hold anywhere. That is why
your people pushed us back into the Sands, because there
is so much water beyond the mountains there and they
would poison it all to win the land, where we would not.
I have heard that they *drowned* all their Sharai prisoners,
sewed them into sacks and threw them into the water
until they died . . ."

That was an awesome death, clearly, terrible and
shocking and profound. Marron had heard that all prisoners had been treated with honour and ransomed back to
their tribes; he was inclined now to believe neither story.
There were men of virtue and there were men of cruelty,
and they could be found on either side. Some men could
be both at once, but he didn't want to think about Sieur
Anton.

"Morakh attacked you by the well, before we reached
Rhabat—when I brought Elisande back from the land of
the djinn, when I ran to fetch Hasan, remember?"

"I do not forget. Morakh fights by his own laws; he is
no longer of the Sharai, and so no longer of the desert."

"You are a Sand Dancer yourself, or so you keep pro-
claiming. Doubly outcaste, you, tribeless one. Does that
mean you are no longer of the Sharai, or of the desert?"

On some subjects, Jemel would not be teased. He
gazed levelly back and said, "You know what I am."

Not really, no. Servant, lover, follower, friend, all of
those; and Sharai, and of the desert, and so the sworn
enemy of Marron's people; and Sieur Anton's sworn
enemy too, which made him more complicated than
ever—but Marron knew where he was, here at his side,
and that was good enough. He would have kept the
thought close, but remembered what Jemel had said
about his veiled heart and tried to prove it untrue. "You
are with me," he said, "the Ghost Walker's companion."

"Indeed." Jemel didn't seem satisfied, and in honesty Marron couldn't blame him. His tongue was tied, though; another figure stood always between them, forbidding any deeper confession. His heart was as infected as his blood; he was tainted by two worlds, two lives, yearned for both and could trust himself with neither.

Jemel pulled his hood up then, *enough of this Patric madness*, and they stood in silence until they saw a single rider come wearily back towards the town.

They went down to meet Rudel where they had before, below the arch of the wall. This time he dismounted and went to pass the reins to Jemel with a sigh of exhaustion; but he checked himself, seeing the state of those torn hands.

"In the name of mercy, what have you been doing to yourself, lad? Losing one finger wasn't enough for you, but you had to try to take the rest off too?"

"I was climbing rocks that were edged like knives. Lisan healed me once, but I had to come back without her."

"Yes, so you said. And I said you are to take no blame to yourself for that. Well, give them here. I have followed my daughter across Outremer; tired as I am, I can follow her in this also."

Marron wondered briefly why Rudel should be suddenly so tired; then he remembered the wounded among the Sharai, all those stupid squabbles. Of course, he would have healed there also. Indeed, Marron had seen him doing it.

Jemel's hands were not so serious a hurt. Coren's unguent had been enough to stem the bleeding; Rudel needed only a moment's magic to knit ripped flesh and skin together. Jemel rubbed his thumbs across the pads of his fingers, where the deepest cuts had been, and said, "Lisan took longer, and her touch was not so hot . . ."

"There are some ways yet that I can best my daughter.

Not in wilfulness: she had that from her mother, though her stubbornness is my own. It's an unhappy combination. Tell me more about these other people who came to the castle, Jemel; them I confess I don't understand."

"No more do I. It is as I told you, they were not an army, not all men; they looked like peasants, Patrics and Catari mixed, but they followed one man, and they ran like wolves." Then, with a glance back over his shoulder, "They ran as Marron runs, as if they could run all day and all night too. Perhaps they had done so, all through the mountains. And they went in as though they were expected, and closed the gates behind them, as I said. I cannot think what they would do with Morakh, nor he with them."

"No. It is strange, but all of this is strange. We had guessed that Morakh waited there for something. I'd been looking for Sand Dancers, though, or more 'ifrit, perhaps an army of ghûls. Assumptions are dangerous; we must remember that and be careful. I could wish that Elisande had been more careful, but that is the story of her life, and mine. At least she has a gift for being overlooked, when she chooses to use it. Now, where are we going? I remember the shape of this place, but little more; it is a long time since I last brought books to Selussin, or good wine to Revanchard."

"You've been inside the castle?" Marron demanded, a beat ahead of Jemel.

"Yes, but years ago, and not so deep as my daughter. I was never let in past the bailey. It was garrisoned by the duke's men in those days and they were a suspicious breed, wouldn't trust anyone who traded with the town. Wouldn't trust anyone at all, if they hadn't grown up as neighbours. Outremer can be like that; and the closer you come to Ascariel, the worse it gets. It's not like being a stranger in the Sands, Jemel—the Sharai will either kill you or kill a goat to welcome you, but the Patrics will do neither. They will watch and guard, and never welcome.

"My wine, though—that was welcome enough, after the beer they brewed below. They loved me for my wine and took me in, but never beyond the first court. Little use that knowledge is; we must rely on my errant Elisande to find the way to Julianne. And then come back to tell us. Now," again, clapping his hands, "where are you taking me?"

"Uh, I'm not sure where Hasan has gone, with the chiefs . . ."

"Are you not? I am. Haven't you found the priests' house yet? I remember that, at least. The next building behind the great temple; every house hides its secrets here, but some at least reveal that they have great secrets to hide. This one has gates of bronze, etched with the words of the prophets. All the elders of all the temples live there in its safety, cut off from the sight of alluring women and the noise of those vexatious boys. That's where they'll take Hasan and his entourage, there's room enough; and I'd be no more let in there than you would, Marron, with your eyes on show. No, take me to Coren, wherever you've left him, and let us mourn together over our missing daughters."

WHEN THEY CAME to the house it took both Jemel and Rudel to force the foul-tempered camel through the narrow gateway and into the yard. Marron watched uselessly until Rudel went inside, leaving Jemel still struggling to settle the balking animal.

"I'll go to the market," he called out, "buy her some feed."

A wave of the hand was all the response he won, assuming that the curses that came with it were not also directed at him. He grinned and turned and walked away, accompanied for some distance by Jemel's opinions on the camel's birth and breeding.

AT ONE TIME, the marketplace at Selussin must have been a sight to rival any in the Ekhed empire. The great open area below the temple would have been like a confluence of many waters, where caravans came together from all over the known world; big as it was, it could barely have been big enough. It must have seethed with crowds, with colour, with merchants crying the value of their silks and jewels, their spices, their camels and slaves. Now the people traded only with themselves, and only what little they could spare. One family had killed a goat, perhaps, and couldn't eat all the meat before it turned, couldn't spare the salt to keep it good; another had a precious harvest of apricots from a pair of trees nurtured in the yard, but needed oil.

So the women would gather as the sun came down, setting out their stock on a blanket in one shaded corner of the wide and wasted space and haggling almost desperately with their neighbours, trying to eke any benefit they could from their meagre goods.

No one traded halfa-reeds, of course, when they were free to gather; besides, Marron wasn't sure that even a camel would eat that wiry stuff. But here was a woman with a sack of withered greens, the outer peelings of her harvest. Elsewhere they might have been thrown on a dung-heap to rot; on his uncle's land they might have been fed to the pigs, but never sent to market. Here they had value, they could be traded. No pigs to eat them in this town, of course; there were donkeys, though, as well as goats. Now, there was a camel.

She was an elderly woman, or looked it from what little Marron could see of her body, eyes and hands. One of the eyes had a cast in it and both were rheumy, crusted with dry yellow matter; the hands were twisted and their skin was loose and wrinkled, ridged with scars across the palms. The hunch of her back as she sat suggested that there'd be no straightness in her when she stood. Perhaps it wasn't age that had bent and shrivelled her, perhaps it was only hard years of work and hunger under the hot sun, children and disease and all the ill chances that come of being poor, for no god has ever loved a starveling; but Marron could deal with the world only as he saw it. Peering beneath the skin of things was a trick for subtle men, for Coren and Rudel and others. One other in particular, but this was no place nor time to be thinking of him.

The world was what it was, what he saw, no subtlety or deception. He crouched politely and said, "Old woman, I think I may have what you are seeking."

She snorted, showing him a mouthful of good hard teeth as she said, "Not so many years ago, boy, I might have had what you are seeking." *Not so old as all that,* she was saying; the world never was what he saw or thought it ought to be, however hard he tried to treat it so. "All I seek now is dung to make my fire, and I do not think you have so much of that."

"Actually," he said, "we have a camel, and you are welcome to the dung if you will feed the beast for us, as long as we are here." Which he hoped, he prayed would not be long at all now. "I'd meant to offer silver . . ."

He trailed that expectantly and watched her gape. Silver, for a mess of sun-shrivelled greens? She might not have touched a coin in months, in years; this was not a money mart. In truth he'd handled little enough himself, lifelong. The coins in his pouch had come from Coren and still seemed like an alien gift.

The woman recovered tongue and wits sooner than he'd expected. "Silver? And so you shall offer silver, boy. One camel's dung won't keep my fire, nor earn its food. Show me your silver . . ."

He fingered out a few small coins, wondering if they were too few or too many, willing to give her the whole pouch if she asked for it. As he leaned forward, he heard slow footfalls at his back. Three people stepping uncomfortably close, standing silent above him; his blood fizzed with the sense of danger, the Daughter waking to it, just a moment before the woman went entirely still before him. Briefly he thought he saw a faint shadow of smoke touch her sick eyes. Then she toppled over, to lie sprawled across her sack of greens.

Marron stood and turned. Two men and a woman, one Patric and two Catari and none of them a warrior, each of them simply dressed with that same lean look and weathered skin that spoke of a lifetime's labour for small reward. There was a blankness to their faces, though, that had nothing to say at all.

That emptiness seemed to suck at him, almost to sing to him, a greater danger than the blades they drew. None of them was a warrior, perhaps, but each of them had a knife. Well, so did he; and his vow not to kill was no hindrance here. With the strength and speed he borrowed from the Daughter, evading these slow strange creatures shouldn't be a problem. He was more worried about the woman unconscious at his back. He'd brought this trouble on her; if he ran, she'd be abandoned. She'd get no aid from her fellow Selussids. All about him, he could hear the cries and panic of the other women at the market as they snatched up their goods and fled at the sight of blades.

Besides, Marron had another, a better weapon than his knife, and he shouldn't need to use it. The threat should be enough to drive these hollow people back to whatever hole they'd crept from. He could guard himself and the woman both, if he just released the Daughter.

His blade was in his hand. A touch of the point to the ever-unhealing wound in his arm, blood and red smoke issued forth while pain coursed inward, through his bones. He had a momentary memory of another smoke, a black smoke insinuating itself into the woman's eyes; and then the Daughter shaped itself in the air between him and his three opponents.

They made no move, and neither did he. But there was a chill biting suddenly at his bleeding arm, different from the pain that he was used to; it sapped his strength, and his will also. He felt it strike deep into his body, numbing and draining where it passed; he dropped onto his knees, too heavy to stand any longer, and a grey fog clouded his sight. It clouded his thoughts, too. He was vaguely aware that the Daughter was losing its coherence, shifting into smoke and flowing back through his wound, into his blood again; it was hard to focus on how strange that was when he had not summoned it, harder to remember why it mattered.

And then it was within him, and the Daughter's heat met his cold invader; and had he thought that he knew pain before? He rolled on the ground, dimly aware that he was screaming; that hands were seizing him, lifting him, gripping with a strength that defied even his bucking struggles; that rags were stuffed into his mouth to silence him to the world as he was carried away.

EIGHT

An Exchange of Knives

IT WAS CHILDREN who came running to carry the news to Jemel. He was waiting at the open gateway, keeping a careful distance from the grumbling camel; he'd finally got her couched and tied, but any close approach brought her head whipping round and her teeth snapping. He had hopes that food might pacify her, but those hopes were not strong. Mostly he only wanted to have Marron safely back at his side. There was—or should be—little danger to the Ghost Walker within the walls of Selussin, but that didn't stop him worrying.

He looked for the familiar silhouette of his friend turning into the lane, burdened with any luck by a bale of fodder; instead he saw three small figures racing pell-mell around the corner. Just boys at a game, he thought at first. But they slowed as they came closer, and he saw how their eyes were wide and their skins flushed with more than exercise.

They came to a staggering, hesitant halt just a few paces from him; their leader, a scant finger taller than his fellows, said, "You are his man."

"Yes." No need for Jemel to pretend, *whose man?* or *I am no one's man*; no need for the boy to name him, *Ghost Walker* or *red-eyed whiteskin*. Of course the boys would know; of course Jemel would understand them. "What has happened, did he send you to me?"

"Strangers came to the market," the boy said, "and a woman fainted. He called a demon, a creature of smoke, we saw it; but then it turned on him, he was hurt by it, and the strangers took him away."

Jemel understood the demon, but nothing more: not why Marron would release it, nor how it could have hurt him. "What strangers were these?"

"Two men, and a woman; we had not seen them before," and that was strange too. They couldn't mean the Sharai chiefs, nor anyone from the tribes, if one had been a woman; if there were other strangers in Selussin, the children surely ought to know.

There was one other possibility. He said, "From the castle?"

The boy glanced at his companions and shrugged. "Perhaps." Children were natural spies; boys got everywhere, and sharp eyes saw it all. "They carried him off towards the western gate," the youngster added, confirmation enough. That way lay the castle, and nothing else but the road to Outremer.

"How long ago?"

"Not long, but they were swift. Will you come?"

"Show me." He ought to take a minute first, to tell Coren and Rudel; but a minute's delay might be one minute too long. And the old men would insist on coming too. He satisfied his conscience with a wordless bellow back into the yard, that started the camel roaring; that would alert them to trouble. They'd come out to find him gone, but perhaps they could follow his trail in the dust, or his scent in the air. If not, there would doubtless be other boys to guide them.

THESE BOYS WERE already on the move, throwing little summoning glances back at him. He ran after, working his scimitar in its sheath as he went. No need to draw it yet, but he wanted it loose. He wanted swordplay, he realised suddenly, he wanted the heat and fury of battle to quell the chill of his fear; he wanted to spill the blood of those who had frightened him so, who were trying to steal Marron from him. He pressed on faster, dragging the boys in his wake as he charged through the winding, narrow ways, turning always towards the setting sun. They might have known a quicker way—*show me*, he had said, and gave them no chance to do so—but his legs were longer and his urgency burned his soul; he couldn't wait for them, for anything.

Even so, he came too late. His first sight of the walls showed him the wide and open archway, a few men standing, staring out. As he came closer, he could make out a distant moving shadow in the sudden dusk, running figures on the road.

They'd gone too far, with too good a start. He could chase them all the way to the castle and not catch up. He let himself stagger to a halt, gulped down a cry of promise and despair; his voice would never carry to Marron, and he wouldn't so disgrace them both in front of strangers.

The boys had gathered in a pack at his back. He fumbled in the pouch at his belt, drew out a few coins and let them fall from nerveless fingers; then he started running again. Retracing his steps, heading back to the old men, the wise ones, those who would tell him what to do.

He came pounding down the lane and into the yard,

startling the camel once more. Ignoring her, he plunged into the house—and found it abandoned, both men missing and no message, no hint left behind to say where they were gone.

For a moment he stood irresolute, before he turned and ran once more. Driving against aching legs and a pounding heart, whipped on by fear and determination in equal measure, he went up to the marketplace. That wide space was deserted now except for a few abandoned blankets and some scattered, trampled produce. Men were gathering in the long shadow of the temple tower, agitation showing in their jabbing hands and their raised voices, but they held no interest for Jemel.

Instead he trotted past the temple, to find where the imams' house stood behind its high wall. The bronze gates were shut; he stifled a momentary yearning that the town's watchmen could have been as careful of what they were sworn to protect. If they'd closed all the gates when Hasan and his army had appeared, the strangers from the castle could never have come within the walls, and Marron would be safe now, the camel would be fed and quiet, all would be as it ought to have been with only the girls to rescue . . .

Pointless to dream; this town welcomed its enemies as eagerly as its friends. Rudel would call that good sense, Coren politics; to Jemel it was cowardice, no more. Better to fight and die than to be overrun. Here they had been overrun so often they had slave souls, it seemed to him, always looking for a master.

He tested the gates to be sure that they were locked, which they were; he hammered his fists against the heavy patterns of their decoration to be sure that the booming summons would go unanswered, which it did. Then he took a dozen paces back, steadied his breathing and his body, and threw himself forward.

As he reached the gates he leaped up, arms stretching

as high as he could reach above his head. He just managed to curl the fingers of one hand over the sharp edge
of bronze; briefly he hung there, feeling his grip start to
slip as he cut himself once more and blood welled out.
He swung his other hand up, for a doubled hold; his bare
toes scrabbled for purchase and found it in the deep in-
dentations of the design; he scrambled up and hauled his
body over, dropped down into the half-dark of the courtyard beyond.

Dark where he stood, crouched against the gates; light
elsewhere, light spilling from the doors and windows of
the house, more lights moving in his direction as men
came with lamps to see who dared disturb their holy masters' peace.

Jemel straightened slowly, tugged his robe into the
best state he could manage—not good, stained as it was
with camel-spit and now again with blood—and walked
boldly out to meet them.

They came with weapons drawn, of course. He kept
his hand a careful distance from his scimitar, far enough
to say *I mean no violence to you or yours* yet near enough
to say also *I am not afraid of you*, ready to draw in a moment if he needed to.

"I am called Jemel," he said, his voice carrying clear
and grim throughout the courtyard. "I have an urgent
message for Hasan."

One man stepped forward, confident in the weight and
authority of his office. "Hasan is in conference and may
not be disturbed. This house is closed."

"I said my news is urgent. Hasan will not thank you
for delaying me; it touches on his friends."

"Hasan will not hear of this. It is our laws that you offend, and all the laws of hospitality besides. I would not
pass you through if you bore letters from a prince."

"No? I bear something sharper than a letter," and now
he did draw his scimitar, "and will use it if I must. One

way or another, I will see Hasan. Go to him, tell him
Jemel is here; he will come."

"There are six of us, boy, and none will carry your
message. Do not add stupidity to your offences."

"Six indeed, and I am alone; but I am Sharai, of the
deep desert. And I am a Sand Dancer, see my hand?" as
he held it up palm out against the house's lights. "And
more than all of these, I am the chosen companion of the
Ghost Walker, of whom you may have heard. I have
killed men, Sand Dancers like myself; I have killed
ghûls; I have killed 'ifrit. I would not willingly harm one
of you, but I will kill all six if I must. My news concerns
the Ghost Walker, who is my friend and Hasan's; it is not
I who is being stupid here. Will you go, or must we
fight?"

At last there was some doubt among the men he faced,
some uneasy shuffling and sidelong glances. It was like
such men, he thought, to be afraid of words where they
hadn't the sense to be afraid of a blade.

Their leader said, "Those are not words or names to
bandy with at a time like this. We will take you before the
council, and let them judge; Hasan may speak for you, if
he will. But if you are playing with us, your punishment
will be severe."

"Trust me," Jemel said, trying to sound grateful, "this
is no game."

He went to sheathe his blade, but the man checked
him. "You must give up your weapon. I will not take you
armed before my council or your own, if you are as dangerous as you say."

And there, of course, lay the penalty of boasting, and
being taken at one's word. Jemel had lost too much time
already, in argument; he laughed and reversed the scimitar in his hand, presenting its haft as he walked forward.
The man took it warily, his own blade still upraised.

He didn't know much about the Sharai, if he thought

Jemel disarmed. There was a knife hanging in plain view from his belt-rope, which was neither ceremonial nor used solely for eating. Jemel stepped closer to the man, to distract his eyes from dropping so low, and said, "If you hold my blade, you should hold my name alongside. That you have, but I do not know yours. How am I to find you, after I leave the chiefs?"

"Ask for Limen, if you still have a tongue to ask with. I cannot speak for the Sharai, but the elders of Selussin will silence a man who speaks against their wisdom. Nor would I count on your own lords to protect you. They may ride over our lands, but they will make a show at least of respect towards our laws."

"No doubt they will, and I have no lords in any case, among the Sharai; I am outcast, tribeless," which Limen should have known, Jemel wore his condition so loudly. Any Catari should be able to read it from his dress. "Some of the chiefs would sooner kill me than hear me," he went on cheerfully. "There is only Hasan to speak for me, and him I once swore a blood-oath against, which is why we are so dear to each other now."

Limen could find nothing to say to that. He only beckoned with a jerk of his head and led the way into the house.

AT LEAST, THEY called it a house; to Jemel, it was a palace. This was the first glimpse he'd had, perhaps the only surviving memory of Selussin's fabled wealth. His bare feet walked on cool and coloured tiles, while the walls were richly hung to hide their simple brickwork; jewels sparkled in tapestries that were faded with age, but still vivid within their folds. One room was lined from floor to ceiling with more books than he had ever seen in his life before, more than he had imagined to be within the world. Reading was a slow and a difficult art to him, but he did understand its power; he gave a snort that was pure Sharai and pure deception also—*of what use or conceivable interest is so much dry and dusty paper, to a man whose life is given to the Sands?*—and went on without a glance back, trying to hurry the men around him where they would not be hurried.

At last they brought him to a pair of high, massive doors, closed doors. They were bronze as the gate had been, made and decorated he thought by the same craftsmen. Limen paused before them, seeming to summon his courage before he pushed them open.

THE DOORS SWUNG apart slowly and silently, at the first pressure from Limen's hands. Their interwoven patterns glimmered and shifted in the changing light, speaking of mutability in permanence—like the Sands, Jemel thought, that changed daily and were never changed—while their imperious movement spoke of weight, of balance, perhaps of the God. And, of course, of expense beyond measure, beyond any man's needs for a lifetime. Jemel—who liked to count wealth only in camels and had none at the moment, had never had more than he needed for bare survival, which was not wealth at all—felt himself staring and could do nothing about it, caught up as he was in their vast dull indifference. He gazed in fascination at the steady sweep of their lower edges over priceless rugs, the brazen lustre of their exposed hinges, the perfect moment of their halting.

Only when they were still again could he pull eyes and wits together, as he needed. Show him something he could neither eat nor carry, something that in the desert could have only cost and no value, and he gaped and drooled like a baby. Too much time spent with Patrics had infected him, perhaps, with their own watery vision of the world . . .

No matter. He turned his eyes to the chamber beyond those wonderful doors; he straightened his back and lifted his head and walked alone into a silence as heavy, as intractable as stone, and about as welcoming.

He walked boldly to the centre of the room, which was the centre of a circle of seated men. With each step he felt the silky softness of ancient carpets beneath his soles, the lulling smokiness of perfumed air against his throat, the height of the ceiling above him. Over all, though, he felt the weight of the eyes that watched him come, the pent breath of those who waited to hear him.

Only that one would not wait or did not care. Not Hasan who rose, and no words of welcome or enquiry: rather a hiss of fury, a dagger drawn and flung so that it bit deep into the piled carpets and stood erect, barely a hand's span before his feet.

And this was so like it had been before, when he had been brought before the council in Rhabat and had been met by a dagger tossed to greet him; and it was the same knife, he thought, and certainly the same man who threw it, who faced him now with a hint of triumph underlying his contempt.

"You are a fool to break in upon us, boy."

"Maybe so, but I am a fool with news. Hasan—"

"Hasan cannot help you here." And indeed Hasan stayed where he sat, cross-legged on the rugs, and made only a small gesture of regret. War-leader he might be, but this was a council of chiefs and imams, and he was neither. "Nor will the King's Shadow come wandering in this time to save your worthless skin. You have affronted our hosts, and for that alone you stand condemned; but you were condemned already, your very existence is an affront to me. I have waited, and I see no reason to wait longer. You gift me my excuse."

It was true, Jemel supposed. The man was sheikh of the Saren, who had once been Jemel's own tribe. If any man wanted his death, this was the one, in payment for oaths of fealty broken. He could pick up the knife and throw it back, and so accept the challenge; he could ignore it, and so be shamed before all the chiefs and the imams of Selussin also. This was no time to be fighting, but . . .

"It would seem a shame," he said softly, "to stain this beauty with blood, yours or mine."

"Yours, renegade, it would all be yours." Likely it would, too. The Saren was younger than most tribal chiefs, barely in his middle years, and broader than most Sharai, heavier and stronger far than Jemel. "I will kill you in the courtyard if you prefer it, as a courtesy to our hosts. Unless you have your fellow creature in wait for me outside, that abomination you call the Ghost Walker, that should have been killed in Rhabat along with you. I will not walk into a trap."

"Neither would I lay one. Marron is sick, in pain and captured; he has been taken to the castle. I don't know why." There, at least he had said what he came to say; he saw Hasan receive the news.

"All the better. We can hope that he will die there."

"If he dies in the castle," Jemel said, "Morakh the Sand Dancer will be the new Ghost Walker. Is that what you want?"

"Better a Sand Dancer than a Patric heretic." *Better war than a corrupted peace,* he meant, and none here would dispute that. Not even Hasan; especially not Hasan, who had led the tribes at last towards his war. If Marron's death was the price of it, Jemel thought their friend would pay it.

His own death was still the price of the message. He fingered the livid scar on his neck, where Morakh had so nearly claimed that death already, and said, "The Sand Dancer sides with the 'ifrit, who killed so many of your people—all your peoples, sheikhs—at Rhabat. Will you join with him, with them now? Any of you? Will the Saren ride with demons and do their bidding?"

"They will not—and you are damned again, for saying so."

"I am damned in any case, if I return your knife. If I slew you, the Saren would not rest until they had my blood for it."

"If you do not return my knife, I will kill you anyway, for the coward that you are. Choose, tribeless—but swiftly. You rub my patience thin."

"Oh, I will fight you, sheikh—but not here, and not yet. I have other battles first, that I deem more important." And he stooped, pulled the sheikh's dagger from the carpets and thrust it into his belt, drawing his own knife instead and tossing that to the sheikh's feet. "Do you keep my blade, and I yours. We'll exchange them later, once Hasan's wife is free and the insult to all Sharai has been redeemed. Then let our blades decide."

Trying to sound as casual as his words and trying to look entirely uninterested after, striving to remember how to breathe as he waited. At length—and it seemed a long, long wait—the man who had once been his sheikh and would now be his executioner stooped to pick up the knife. He examined it scornfully, then slipped it inside his robe.

"Very well, I will let you live a little longer—but do not try to run, or I will hunt you like a hare and drag your naked body on a rope at my saddle's bow."

"I will not run from you, or any man," Jemel said flatly. He turned his back on the sheikh—*another insult, another cause to fight me, let him add it to the list; he can only kill me once*—and found Hasan at last rising to his feet.

"Jemel, where did you take Rudel?"

"To speak with Coren."

"And where is Coren?"

"I don't know. Not in the house now, either of them. They didn't come here, they didn't follow me to the gate, to the castle road . . ."

"There is another way for those men, to the castle or anywhere. Coren can walk his friends through shadow-paths."

Not so shadowy, more golden and alight; besides, "If he wouldn't do so to bring his own daughter out, nor Rudel's, why would he go for Marron?"

"Perhaps if he thought the Ghost Walker more important than my wife, or her friend?"

It was possible. Jemel held the other's gaze with a surging hope—then crushed it, with a slow and deliberate shake of his head. "No. The 'ifrit would know and be ready for them, whoever they went for. That's why they've left the girls, because they cannot help them. The same must be true for Marron. It's something else they're doing . . ."

"Then go and find them, Jemel. Don't bring them here; we'll rally by the western gate. I hadn't meant to move tonight, but I'll let Morakh know we're here at the least, that he can't bring any further of his friends inside, nor steal any more of us. Before you go, though, tell me how it was with Marron. I don't understand how he can be hurt, he's the Ghost Walker . . ."

"He can still be hurt," Jemel said, who had seen the truth of that too often. "But I don't understand this either. Not hurt, sick, the children said. I didn't see what happened, but they said that what he carries—his demon, they called it—turned on him . . ."

JEMEL WASN'T SURE where to look, where to start looking for the old men. As he left the imams' house, though—through the gate this time rather than over it, with a silent Limen swinging one leaf open for him, handing back his

blade—he found the boys who'd brought him news of
Marron lingering outside. He hadn't realised that they'd
followed him this far, but of course they would have
done; he'd probably given them the most excitement
they'd known in their young lives, and certainly the most
money.

Well, he still had coins, and they were welcome to
those also. He touched a suggestive hand to the pouch, all
the hint they'd need, and said, "The old man, the father
of my house, and the guest who came today—where can
I find them, do you know? Or can you learn?"

"Wait here," was all they said before they scampered
off in three different directions, sending strange high
calls to each other as they vanished into the dark. Jemel
recognised the tone, if not the meaning: he and his cohorts had had a similar language when they were small,
designed to carry across the cliff-face of his home.

He waited long enough for the gates to swing wide at
his back, and all the chiefs to come riding out. Even
Hasan passed without a word; he rode straight towards
the western wall, while the others turned south to find the
camps of their own tribes and stir their men to unexpected action.

Jemel waited, immersed in gloomy imaginings and
barely aware of the occasional eerie cry rising from the
darkness of the town around him. Soon they were louder,
shriller, coming closer; he peered into the night, and saw
first one and then the other boys come racing back.

"The men you seek are in the woman Holet's house,"
the eldest said triumphantly.

"Will you take me there?"

"We will."

They didn't move, though. Jemel grinned, and worked
his pouch open with sore fingers.

He couldn't see and wouldn't really have known the
value of the coins he handed across. The boys knew,

though, and were more than content, to judge by the flashing white of their smiles.

"Come, this way. It is not far. The widow Holet is sick, and your fathers are tending to her."

It seemed a curious priority at such a time. Jemel asked no questions, though. He only followed the small figures through a bewildering network of lanes until they brought him to a ramshackle house, little more than a hut crammed in among its neighbours. A low door opened directly onto the filthy alley. A dim light burned within; as he ducked beneath the lintel he saw a globe of witchlight hanging below the ceiling.

Coren and Rudel were both there, as he had been promised. The man from Surayon was crouched over a bed of rags; Jemel had to look twice before he saw the dark shadow of a woman lying on the bed. Coren was crushing herbs into a bowl of warm water, scenting the air with a sweet savour. He glanced up and said, "Jemel. What's afoot in the town?"

"More to the point, where's Marron?" Rudel grunted, without looking round.

"You don't know?"

"We heard stories. I'd sooner hear them from you, they'll be less garbled."

Not much so, if at all; he could tell them only what he'd been told himself by the children, and then what bare glimpse he'd had of figures hurrying away up the road to the castle. He added that he'd been to the imams' house and told Hasan; he didn't mention what had passed between him and the sheikh.

Coren asked what Hasan meant to do.

"He will lead some men up to invest the castle tonight. He asked you two to meet him by the western gate."

"Well, we will go," Rudel said, his voice as grim as Jemel had ever heard it, "but not before I have tried once more here."

"What are you doing?"

"Failing to save this woman's life, I think. I cannot find the beat of her mind, the paths of her body nor the cause of her sickness. She confounds me; and I confess, that terrifies me every time I lay hands against her skin. But I must try. Once more, I will try once more before we abandon her."

Jemel leaned forward to peer over Rudel's broad shoulder and saw that all her skin was grey, true grey between her wrinkles, and the shape of her bones showed beneath it as though her muscles had lost any lingering touch of life. He watched, and couldn't see her breathing.

"Is she not dead already?"

"She might as well be, for all the good I can do her."

"Who is she?"

"A woman, from the marketplace. When you cried out and left us, we went there, not knowing which way you had gone; and found the market deserted and her lying there, while her neighbours watched from a distance. They gabbled of a demon, as your children did. We assumed that Marron had been there and that her sickness was in some measure due to him. There was nothing we could do to his benefit, and we couldn't simply leave her to her death. I persuaded some of those watching to bring her home"—whether with coin or a sword, he didn't say and Jemel didn't ask—"and have been trying to cure her since, but she has defeated me. Or rather, what has possessed her is defeating me. Be quiet now."

He drew a slow breath, and Jemel wondered at the trembling in his hands as he reached to lay them on the woman's scrawny chest.

Jemel had seen Rudel's daughter heal him of a wound that should have killed him; he had heard her confess that her father's gift was stronger than her own. Despite Rudel's protestations and Coren's silence, he waited to see the woman stir and rise.

Waited and waited, and saw only the sweat that gleamed on Rudel's brow, the vacant stare of his eyes that was worse somehow than the vacant stare of the woman's. It was a moment out of time, a moment that stretched almost beyond his bearing. Coren sat over his aromatic water and did nothing but stir it lightly with a finger; Jemel stood and did nothing at all; Rudel hunched above the woman and seemed also to be doing nothing, at least in his own body.

The witchfire light faded slowly, but that was all one with the woman's slow and irredeemable dying, Rudel's failing struggle to save her. Coren's finger fell still in the water.

Eventually, Rudel blinked.

Blinked and sighed, unless he was only breathing and it was because no one had done that for so long that it sounded so loud; and lifted his hands from the woman with a soft gasp, as though it hurt like tearing a clotted bandage from a wound, and pressed them to his sweat-slick face and seemed not to be able to stop himself from shaking.

The other two went on waiting. Even Jemel's urgency fell back from him a little, in the face of Rudel's extreme distress.

At length the Surayonnaise dropped his hands into his lap, or let them fall, rather, as though he lacked the strength to hold them up longer. His head he could lift and turn, seemingly, into the perfumed air, and appeared to take some relief from it; the witchlight flared brighter suddenly. All he said, though, was, "I don't think your taranth-water will do her any good, Coren, where my touch does nothing."

"This is for you, Rudel. Bend over the bowl here and breathe the steam, while I find a cloth that's not so rancid as to destroy all its virtue."

In the end it was Coren's own sleeve that provided the

cloth, although Jemel offered his own. Perhaps that was too rancid with camel-spit.

He waited while Coren wiped Rudel's face and hands, while he talked too soft to hear; waited until the one man was sure that the other was sufficiently restored to make a move. By then Jemel was at the door, fidgeting and fretful, though he was conscious yet of the old woman on the bed in the corner. Not dead yet but snared within her dying, beyond all help that any of them could offer except perhaps the swift kiss of a knife to send her on her way; and none of them could offer that, bar Rudel who had tried so hard to save her, and he would not. Even now his head kept turning back, and there was a mute despair on his face.

"I was like a man abroad in a blizzard," he murmured, "searching for another where I knew there was no hope, and only my own death promised if I stayed. Almost I lost the way back, I went so far . . ."

"That I had been afraid of," Coren said. "If she's gone or going, then let her go. Death is not so terrible."

"Hers might be. It was terrible to come even as close as I did, and that not close enough to find her. I've never known a feeling like it . . ." And he shuddered again, and needed to grip both hands tightly together to still their trembling.

"We should go," Jemel whispered, half-hoping that they would not hear; he felt like a child on the fringes of an adult world, mystified and demanding. Of course death was terrible, how not? And Marron might be dying even now, and still they only talked over the dying of a woman they couldn't even put a name to.

Coren reached to help Rudel to his feet, swaying a little under the other man's weight. "We should go back to your house, Jemel, so that Rudel may ride. Can you find the way from here?"

No need for that, his loyal servants attended him still

outside the door, and he had coins left to buy their services. He thought that Rudel might be better walking than fighting his camel's wilfulness, but kept that private. He wanted to be moving, that was all: moving towards Hasan and ultimately Marron, however slowly they must go.

THEY WENT AT last, although they had almost to pull Rudel through the doorway and he would not leave until the woman had been covered over, though she was so cold to the touch that her rags were useless to her; and they did indeed go slowly, behind their persistent guides. Rudel recovered a little in the night air, but not enough to quiet Coren's anxiety. Neither Jemel's, though his had a different source: childlike again, he burst out, "If Marron's sickness is like the widow's—"

"Widow, was she?" Rudel interrupted in a broken mutter. "I didn't know. What was her name?"

"Holet, the boys said. But *listen*, if Marron is sick as she was, and you could not help her . . ."

"If so, then you are right, I cannot help him either. Failure has taught me nothing except how to fail. I expect I shall fail faster, next time."

Try less hard and less often, he meant; try hardly at all, perhaps, for Marron. Rudel would still far sooner see him dead than flying loose.

Jemel wanted to seize the man, to shake him, to drive his own intense spirit into that flagging body and that bitter mind. Coren was ahead of him, though, and wiser.

"You are too tired to see clearly, Rudel. You have found the path to failure, yes, and it has exhausted you; rest and reconsideration may show you the path to success. A night's sleep will restore you."

Rudel snorted. "You think I or any of us will sleep tonight?"

"You will, yes. I will insist on it—and make it happen, if I must. Do you know where we are now, Jemel?"

"What? Oh, yes. Yes, I do. But . . ."

"Pay off these boys, then, and send them home. Otherwise they will follow us to the gate, and maybe further. Let's see them safe, at least."

ANOTHER FEW MINUTES brought them to the house. They found the camel sleeping; as he'd guessed, she was vicious when she woke, and he doubted any man's ability to stay on her back.

Coren soothed her, though, with a hand on her muzzle and a few words spoken into her ear. Magic again, Jemel thought; all the Sharai fancied themselves to be camel-masters, and he'd known a few who seemed to have a genuine charm in touch and voice, but none that worked so swiftly or so well.

He fetched saddle and harness and riding-stick, and saw Rudel mounted before he unhitched the hobble to let the beast stand. Still suspicious of her sudden docility and wary of her rider's weakness, he offered to lead her to the gate, but received a contemptuous snort for his pains.

"I may be weary, Jemel, but I'm not helpless. Besides, you can see, she's dozier than I am, thanks to Coren whispering her into a maze. She'll sleep on her feet all the way. You walk behind, and poke her if she starts to snore . . ."

"It'll be you that snores first," Coren said, falsely cheerful. "We'd be better off walking one either side, to catch you when you fall. Now come, we've wasted too much time already."

In fact it was he who led the way, with Rudel urging the camel on behind him. Jemel did walk a little while watchfully beside the beast, till he was sure Coren had been joking; then as an antidote to his own impatience, to keep his feet from racing ahead of his companions he forced himself to lag behind, glancing back a time or two to be sure that those curious and acquisitive boys weren't still following him.

The western gate should have been closed since nightfall, and was not; in the open ground beyond there was a mill of men and camels, bright torches blazing. He let out a huff of relief, and now could and did run on past Rudel, past Coren to seek Hasan.

He found him where he'd expected, out on the road and furthest from the gate, with only a few trusted men about him. Hasan would give precedence to the chiefs in council, but not on the field of battle, not where it was his own presence that had brought the tribes this far.

Besides, this was his own battle, for his own wife and friends. Of course he would lead; of course they would follow, if only because Hasan could not be allowed to ride alone or die alone for his own private reasons when he had all his people to die for . . .

"Where are they, Jemel?" The question snapped at him like a lash.

"They are here," with the jerk of a thumb back over his shoulder.

"We ride, then. There are spare mounts among the men; seek them out, and bring Coren and Rudel to join me."

Then he wheeled and cried out, loud and strong, drawing all men's eyes to him; he raised his riding-stick and gestured forward, up the road; he kicked his camel into a run and rode away without a backward glance. Jemel stood and watched for a minute, caught up in the thrill of it as the gathered chiefs swept past him with their retinues.

He saw the Saren sheikh pass by, snared like so many by Hasan's personality or else obedient to an idea that

drove them both, a vision of a world restored. Then he remembered his own obedience and dived back into the
churning multitude, in search of riderless camels and the
old men who were his own particular charge.

WHEN BOTH WERE found and brought together, he
tried at first to lead them up the narrow road at a camel-
canter. Rudel's beast was still stupid, though, and
couldn't match his pace.

"Can't you rouse her now?" he yelled at Coren, more
agitated than politic. "Hasan said—"

"Hasan has not seen. Rudel would fall, and only slow
us further. I thought patience was a virtue of the Sharai?"

So it was, ordinarily, but Hasan had shown little sign
of it tonight. And the thought of Marron burned in
Jemel's blood, so that he had none to call on; and then
there were the girls, and he didn't, couldn't believe that
Coren was truly so calm, or Rudel so weak.

Nothing he could do, though, but rein back. Lisan's
father swayed in the saddle as their way steepened, and
did look in genuine danger of falling. Jemel thought he
might have left him or sent him back to sleep the night in
Selussin: *if* he had been Hasan, *if* he had seen, *if* Rudel
was the kind of man who'd listen and obey any such
command . . .

None of those applied, and so they came last and lag-
gardly to the plateau where the castle stood, its great
rough walls looming high against the stars and its gates
closed hard against them.

THE SHARAI HAD spread themselves already, men from
each tribe watching a portion of the walls and raising
tents, building fires while they watched. There was
barely space enough, with their camps set uncomfortably

close. Hasan might have been wiser to have brought only his own tribe, the Beni Rus—except that then he might have lost the others, all the tribes else. Why should they wait down by the town, while the Beni Rus stole the fun of battle and the chance of loot? What were they here for, to dance attendance and applaud? They might, might well, almost certainly would have packed and mounted and departed to the Sands, and most likely Hasan would never have been able to bring them together again. This way they would all stay, though this way there was the constant risk of arguments and bloodshed before ever they faced what lay behind the gates. Where the sheikhs went, there went the tribes: into battle for Hasan or with each other, or possibly over the mountains and on into Outremer. Possibly, probably—certainly it was what the men left below tonight would be urging tomorrow, the only real argument for their having come this far. Hasan had never needed such an army to win back his wife, they'd all of them always known that. Whether Julianne lived or died—and Elisande and Marron and himself, whether any of them lived or died—that issue would be decided by these comparative few who coiled like a serpent around the castle walls.

And would be decided soon, Jemel thought. If there'd been a Patric army mewed up in there, the Sharai would have been willing to stay for a long siege and months of bloody fighting, as they had before to deny the infidel a foothold on the margins of the Sands. As it was only a stolen wife and a renegade Sand Dancer who held her, they'd expect Hasan to settle the matter swiftly, by parley or by force.

The Sand Dancer was the one who counted, in Jemel's mind and he was sure in the minds of all the Sharai. It was the Sand Dancer who had stolen Julianne, he was known and named. The other people in there were Patrics or Catari out of Outremer, farmers and peasants, not worth dwelling on. Though they had stolen Marron, or so it seemed, and done so with a power that could silence or turn his Daughter: it wasn't, it couldn't be their own power to do such a thing, no mortal magic, and so he could still dismiss them. And then there was the 'ifrit, and that was curiously hard to think about at all. It shifted shape in his mind, fluid as a cat and insubstantial as its shadow, he could get no kind of grip on it. How could you think about a creature that might know what you were thinking, and so change . . . ?

So when he thought about what might happen beyond those concealing gates, he thought about killing Morakh, all the many ways he wanted to kill Morakh. Let older heads and wiser minds consider the 'ifrit and how to defeat it when it knew your plans and all your moves already, let them consider the strangeness of the band from Outremer. He would kill Morakh, then kill anyone else who came between him and Marron; he would kill everyone in the castle if he had to, if that was the only way to break the spell that gripped his friend.

Or see them dead, at least. He couldn't kill them all alone, which was why he needed Hasan and his troops. Hasan, it seemed, needed old wise heads; Hasan had snapped at him already for being slow of delivery, and now was turning and twisting his camel before the gates, heedless of the chance of arrows from above as he called to Jemel's companions in a fret, almost a frenzy of impatience.

"Where have you *been?* I sent for you to meet me at the gates of Selussin—"

"—And so we did, but there was all your army between us—"

"—And then to join me at the head, did the boy not say?"

"There would have been no point in his saying; we

could not have reached you with Rudel. Better to travel carefully, and to arrive."

"What is the matter with Rudel?" The warlord seemed suddenly to register how quietly the older man sat his quiet camel, and how unusual that was. "Is he sick too?"

"Sick of a great sickness," Rudel said himself, surprising Jemel as much as Hasan; they were the first words he'd uttered in a while, and the voice at least was stronger than it had been in the town. "I have met a darkness tonight, and all but lost myself in it. I need to think . . ."

"He needs to sleep," Coren said flatly. "Let him seek a bed among your men, and take your counsel with me tonight, Hasan, for what good it will do either one of us. I am tired myself, and devoid of ideas."

Hasan grunted and turned his back to the castle. "Come then. Rudel shall rest, and think until he sleeps; you and I, Coren, we will eat and speak together. I do not believe that the King's Shadow is helpless, here on the borders of the King's country . . ."

Jemel sat still on his camel and watched them go, thinking that the King's Shadow was not helpless, no, only outplayed and defeated, his powers blocked by a greater. Hasan would learn tonight, Coren would teach him; an army was no more use than a magician, if you did not dare to use it. So long as the 'ifrit watched her, Julianne's life was forfeit however they approached the castle. And Elisande was somewhere, doing something, he had no way to find out where or what; and Marron . . .

Wondering how he should pass the night, sure that there was no point in his trying to sleep, he turned to gaze at the prohibiting gates again; and would do so unrelentingly while other watchers came and went around him, while they ate and talked and slept perhaps a little, and so would be the first to see them open.

NINE

Out of All Shelter

NO SUNLIGHT EVER broke into the cell through that single slit of a window, high though it was to her. Out in the yard, Julianne thought, it would lie at ground level, and the height of the castle's walls must keep it in perpetual shadow. All her days were grey and her nights were black dark, punctuated only by the ceaseless glare of the 'ifrit's eyes which cast no light but seemed rather to suck it in, to make both day and night darker.

Terror had abated long since, under the dragging weariness of time. She knew herself to be bait and nothing more; neither Morakh nor the monster had any interest in her, except to keep her here and well guarded. Once a day the door would be opened and she would be brought food, hard bread and dull flat-tasting water. Until now it had always been the Dancer himself who brought it. Today, though . . .

Today she'd been playing games in her head, dreaming rescue. She didn't need to close her eyes to dream; it was better not, indeed. Sometimes in that private darkness she thought that the 'ifrit was looming over her, its patience at last exhausted, its jaws already reaching for her throat. Then her eyes would snap open and she would be shaken and scared again, small comfort in the sight of the creature still crouched where it always was crouched, quite unmoving and unmoved, only watching and watching.

So she dreamed awake when she could, she dreamed alert; and today she had dreamed of the door swinging wide and a hero striding in to stay the monster and whisk her off to freedom. She couldn't do it by herself, she needed rescue, and so she dreamed of heroes.

Hero-fathers, hero-husbands, hero-friends: she didn't care, she wasn't choosy. Any or all would be welcome. She was past worrying about them now, long past praying that they not come after all.

She had gazed at the door and seen it shatter, seen the twisting fury of Elisande's djinni in its frame and the small solid figure of Elisande herself in the passage beyond, her hand cocked ready to cast a knife that would transfix the 'ifrit's eye and kill its glow, drive deep into its skull to kill the creature entirely.

She had gazed at the door and seen it shine with gold, bright enough to dim even the fierce red of the 'ifrit's glare; she had seen the spectral figure of her father walking through it, holding out his hand and drawing her into his mystery, leading her away before monster or Morakh could find any answer to him.

She had gazed at the door and seen it outlined with dim red fire, Marron opening a gateway that she could dive through into the land of the djinn, fast and easy and the way closed instantly behind her so that she would be safe with him in that strange and sunless country.

She had gazed at the door and heard its bolts drawn

back, had seen it open to her friend Jemel, his scimitar
bloody in his hand and his eyes alight with battle; or else
to Rudel, his clever fingers signing her to be silent, to be
swift; or else to her husband Hasan with his warriors at
his back; or else wonderfully to her husband Imber in all
his panoply of war, his laughing cousin at his side . . .

AT LAST, SHE had gazed at the door and truly heard its
bolts drawn back, had seen it swing open for real; and
then she had gaped, gasped, reached to rub at her eyes to
assure herself that this time she actually wasn't dreaming.

There was light out in the passage, bright enough to
dazzle. She needed a moment to blink her eyes clear, and
a moment more to realise that the man who stood out
there was neither Morakh nor any of her imagined rescuers.

Realising that she knew him regardless, recognising
his silhouette even before she saw his face—that was an
act stolen utterly out of time. How long he waited, how
long she stared—that was beyond counting, as the fact of
it was beyond wonder.

Then, slowly, forcing her mouth to shape his name
and her voice to utter it, she said, "*Blaise . . .?*"

He stepped into the cell, she took an equal pace back;
shadow engulfed him.

"Blaise, what are you doing here?" He wasn't dressed
as an Elessan sergeant now, rather as a peasant. Why
Morakh should have let any peasant into the castle, she
couldn't understand. Nor why it should be Blaise who
came to rescue her, when she'd thought him long since
fallen out of her story, left behind at Roq de Rançon several adventures since . . .

Both his hands were full; he held them out, and she
took bread and water uncertainly. She was close enough

to read his face in the dimness, and it might as well have been carved from wood. No wink or smile, not the slightest hint of a message, no recognition at all.

Neither did he speak. His duty done, he turned and walked away. Julianne reached out to stay him, then drew her hand back. She'd seen the shift of a shadow out in the passage: Morakh, perhaps, watching his new and bewildering servant, ready to snare her if she tried to slip away?

NOW SHE NEED not dream of rescue. She didn't give much thought to how Blaise might steal her from the cell, under the unending watch of the 'ifrit. If he were here—and he was, no fever-dream; she'd smelled his breath, she'd touched his fingers taking this goblet from him, she could still feel the warmth of his grip in the wood—then she had her miracle already, and the rest was mere detail. Any man, any god who could conjure someone so unlikely into such a place could conjure the pair of them out as easily; no man, no god would go this far and then betray her when she'd been so helpless.

So she had sat and dreamed herself outside the cell, her hand clasped securely in Blaise's as he guided her to the wall where a rope lay coiled and ready, or else to the gate that he'd left unbarred and open. She had dreamed of stars and wind, of freedom, and not at all of Morakh's rising from the shadows to prevent them.

And later, when the cell door was opened in the dark, she'd risen to her feet, heedless of the motionless 'ifrit, and Blaise's name had been half on her lips already when not he but two other men had come in, with a body slung unconscious between them.

*   *   *

HER MIND REELED under a crushing disappointment, all dreams forsworn. These men were as silent as Blaise had been, and they paid her as little attention, less. They simply laid their burden on the floor and departed.

Confused, distressed, she heard the bolts slammed shut and still stood where she was, hands and back pressed against cold stone, shuddering against the loss of hope. It took a while before she could move at all, a while longer before she was certain that the 'ifrit would not. At last, though, a few short, stumbling paces took her to where the newcomer lay sprawled on the floor. Unconscious, dead: she dropped to her knees beside him and reached out nervously to let her fingers discover what her eyes could not.

It was a man, a young man to judge by his slimness, the smoothness of his face. Not Blaise, then, at least there was that to cling to. She might have thought him a Patric, except that he wore the robe of a Sharai . . .

Those two thoughts joined together. She gasped, fumbled for his left arm and found what she had suddenly dreaded to find, twisting ridges of half-healed flesh.

It was Marron, then, but Marron in a desperate condition. Not dead, no, she could feel the faint stir of his breath and a fluttering pulse in the depth of his unhealing wound; close to death, though, that she was sure of, and she'd never thought the Daughter would let him go so far.

His hair was matted with a stinking sweat, his robe was soaked with it, and yet his skin was dry where she touched it, as though there were no more water left in him to be sweated out. It felt both cold and hot alternately beneath her palm, and stretched drum-tight across his bones. He'd always been brutally thin, but this was different. She thought his body was a battleground, with sickness surging through his blood, fever and chill at war; she wondered which one was the enemy. Unless they both were, and he was doubly infected . . .?

That made a sudden sense to her, thinking of the Daughter and how it lived its strange half-life inside him. It was like a fever, an infection, a burning that did not belong; and if he fell sick otherwise, of course it would fight that new invasion. If the sickness fought back—well, here was the consequence, and she thought Marron could not survive it. He needed more than an ordinary healer, he needed wisdom and magic both, Rudel or Elisande, and she was far past hoping for miracles now. She did what little she could, moistening the hem of her robe in what remained of her water and wiping his face with it, but when she touched his brow a moment later she found it baked dry again.

She might have cried then from frustration at her helplessness, from the dread of having him die under her hands and the fear of what might follow with the Daughter; but a sound intruded from the passage, the soft scrape of bolts being carefully drawn back.

She lifted her head, almost daring to hope once more, thinking that Blaise could carry Marron if he could only find a way out of this suddenly populated castle. For the second time that night she was certain of the sergeant's coming; for the second time she was deceived.

The door opened barely a shadow's width and a figure slipped through. Not Blaise, that much was clear even in the dark; this was someone slender, light-footed, a young lad or a girl. But who, and why . . .?

"Julianne?"

The voice was her answer, and her second miracle of the day.

"Elisande!" It came out in a breathless hiss, almost in a sob. A moment later her friend had found her; strong arms wrapped themselves around her and dragged her unexpectedly back into a corner. She grunted in puzzlement, then understood as she heard the whisper of steel

drawn, as she felt Elisande set herself between her and
the 'ifrit.

"Don't, don't worry. It doesn't do anything, it just sits
there, waiting . . ."

"Maybe it's been waiting for me."

Maybe so; if it could see anything of the future, it
should have known that she was coming. There was no
movement from the creature, though, only the steady
burning of its eyes.

"I thought it was waiting for your djinni," Julianne
said weakly, and was astonished again to hear Elisande
chuckle tightly.

"So did Esren. That's why it didn't come to pull you
out of here, sweetheart; nor Marron, nor your father.
They're all scared of that accursed thing. That's why I
had to come myself."

And for a moment, for one blessed moment Julianne
fancied that her coming was enough, that the two of them
could slip out as cautiously as Elisande had slipped in.
An hour ago, they might have tried it. But, "Marron did
come, he's here."

"Oh, what?"

"On the floor there. Elisande, he's dreadfully ill . . ."

A cold instant later she was squinting and covering her
eyes against a flare of light, bright enough to scorch the
inside of her skull.

Elisande swore, and the blaze faded to a glimmer;
when Julianne risked a glance, she saw a globe of witchlight hanging in the air above Marron's body. Elisande
had dropped her knife and was huddled down beside him,
touching with gentle, questing fingers.

Nothing Julianne could do there. She stooped to pick
up the discarded blade, eyeing the 'ifrit warily. She didn't
think it had moved, though, and certainly it wasn't moving now. It might even have retreated a little, from that

sudden eruption of light; she thought its eyes seemed duller against the glow.

Soon, too soon Elisande sighed, and turned her head to find her. "I can do nothing for him like this. I never could, when he had the Daughter in him. It resists, it won't let me in."

Julianne nodded. "I think that's what's happening now, something has got in and the Daughter's fighting it. But it's killing him, Elisande."

"I know." Two short syllables should not be able to contain so much grief.

"What can we do? Blaise is here, I saw him, but he may not be able to come tonight . . ."

"Blaise will not come at all. He's with them, Julianne, I've seen him too and his spirit is snared somehow. We have to get Marron out ourselves, somewhere safe where we can release the Daughter and work on him. We should take him to Rudel, he's stronger than I am. We can carry him between us, he weighs nothing."

"Call the djinni, and it could carry us all."

"It would not come. I said, it's afraid of the 'ifrit."

"So am I. Do you think it will let us leave? It's watched me so long, I'm the bait in its trap, and the trap's not yet sprung. It wasn't set for you, at least." She waited, had no response, at last said, "Elisande?"

"My blades have been blessed," her friend replied at last, "but two short knives would never be enough, against that monster. And no, I don't think it would let us leave. But listen. I was wondering earlier, what would frighten a djinni."

"The 'ifrit, you said."

"Yes—but there's something more. You know how Esren was trapped in the Dead Waters, by a stone brought over from the other world. I think it would be terrified of being caught again. The 'ifrit use the same trick to control their ghûls, so we know it works on other spirit creatures; and the djinn and the 'ifrit are close kin, even if the djinn deny it . . ."

"I don't understand."

"No, but trust me. In a minute, I'll ask you to do a thing; do it boldly, sweetheart. If you get the chance. It may be the only chance that Marron has."

And then she drew her other knife and touched it lightly to Marron's wounded arm, letting out a drop of blood, letting out the Daughter.

"Elisande, what are you *doing?*"

"I can't work on him while that's inside him; if it's loose, I can perhaps rouse him just a little. Besides, I need it free. Stand ready, Julianne—and watch the 'ifrit . . ."

She was doing that already. It had stirred, in the moment of that first wisp's smoking up from Marron's arm; it was stirring yet, shifting claws and pincer-feet and the plates of its distorted body in countless, constant motions that still kept it exactly where it was, crowded into its corner. She'd have said it looked scared already. Hoping to scare it further, she tightened her grip on Elisande's knife.

She was scared enough herself: scared for herself, and for Elisande, and especially for Marron. With the Daughter free—and more than that, free of his control—they might all be in danger. If she was right, though, his sickness would be free too to rampage through his body. Whatever sickness it was, that could fight back against the Daughter's strength . . .

It had Elisande to face now, a different kind of daughter. The light dimmed further, as she focused; she had her hands clamped on either side of Marron's head, and a terrible determination on her face.

A determination that seemed to falter suddenly, seemed almost to fail altogether. Julianne saw her forehead suddenly slick with sweat, heard a groan escape her

lips. But she set her jaw, closed her eyes, rallied to try
again. Marron's eyelids fluttered open, he gazed about
him vaguely, tried to speak.

"Marron." That was Elisande's voice as Julianne had
never heard it before, high and tight and demanding.
"Take control of the Daughter, make it open a gateway to
the land of the djinn."

He mumbled something that Julianne couldn't catch.
Elisande heard it, though, and replied.

"You can, and you must. For your life, and ours. Only
for a little while; Julianne will go through and bring back
a stone. With that, we can win our freedom and take you
out of here. Do it, Marron, do it now . . ."

And astonishingly, almost miraculously—because
perhaps there was not yet an end to miracles after all,
when a boy so wracked could even understand what she
was saying, let alone find the will and the strength to
obey her—Marron did it.

It was a poor, weak job that he made of it, reminding
Julianne forcefully of his early efforts to control the
Daughter: a twisted, shifting frame and the smoky red of
it a sullen crimson glare. Julianne gazed at the narrow
gleam of gold at the centre, the portal to the other world.
Elisande wanted her to go through there; and she would,
of course she would, because her one friend asked her to
and her other friend needed her to, and either one of those
would have been enough. The two together were imperative.

And yet she couldn't help remembering those early
days, when desert creatures had died and died again, as
Marron failed and failed again to hold the gateway open
against the wild nature of the Daughter. Just to touch the
rim of it was deadly; could she trust him to hold it wide
and steady while she went and returned, not to lose it
while she was in the land of the djinn, or—worse—when

she was halfway through and would die as those desert rats had died, in screaming terror?

No. One glance at his face confirmed that she couldn't trust him so far, she couldn't trust him at all. Elisande was struggling against whatever had infected him; Marron seemed to have given up already. Even his blood was sluggish as it dribbled from his arm.

Elisande had her head down beside Marron's now, her mouth at his ear, whispering, whispering. His eyes opened, his gaze seemed to focus—and abruptly there it was, a strong and solid gateway and all Julianne need do was step through into that golden summoning light . . .

Except that the 'ifrit moved first, and moved fast. It half scuttled and half flowed, losing its insect shape even before it reached the Daughter, pouring through the portal like a long thick sinuous ribbon of smoke.

Julianne stared in wonder, in amazement, once more astonished beyond words; distantly she heard Elisande's voice, exhausted and triumphant and still demanding more.

"Close the gateway, Marron. Quickly, let it go, it wants to anyway. Good," as the frame dissolved and the Daughter assumed its more natural shape, a veiled monstrosity not so very different from the 'ifrit, only so much harder to see or understand. "Good boy, you've been wonderful, you've saved us all. Now, one thing more. I can't keep you awake much longer, and I don't think you should sleep while that thing's free, it needs you keeping an eye on it. Besides, you've bled too much already, you need all your strength if you're going to get well again. Will you take it back for me, Marron?"

"It hurts," he said, clear enough this time, his voice sharp with dread.

"I know it does, love—but it keeps you alive, I think. It stops you sinking. You have to do it, Marron, you have to take it back. Just for a while now, till we can get you to Rudel. He'll be able to help, better than I can. I promise . . ."

Slowly the half-seen monster shifted to smoke and slipped back into Marron's blood. He writhed, and his mouth gaped open in a soundless scream; Elisande bent low above his head, and Julianne thought she was weeping even as she struggled to soothe him.

At last he lay still and she looked up again, dragging her sleeve across her face. "He's gone again," she said. "It was all I could do, to help him into unconsciousness. We have to get him to Rudel."

"What if the 'ifrit comes back?"

Elisande laughed harshly. "It won't. I don't think it can, they can't move between the worlds the way the djinn do, they need a gateway. That's why I did this, to give it an opportunity to flee."

"I don't understand, I thought you wanted me to go, you said so . . ."

"I was lying, sweet. I hoped it would be scared by the threat of a stone, scared enough to run. Just as well that it was, I wouldn't have known what to do with the stone if you'd brought one. You had to be ready, though, it had to sense a real danger."

"It didn't happen, though, I didn't go . . ."

"Because the 'ifrit fled, it didn't happen. They don't see the future exactly, only possible courses. It saw what I wanted it to see, a future where it would be at risk; that was enough. Now come on, let's get out of here."

"How? We can carry Marron between us, but there's still Morakh and all those other people. And Blaise, shouldn't we look for him . . .?"

"No. I told you, Julianne, Blaise is one of them. But leaving isn't a problem, now the 'ifrit has gone. Esren!"

She called out and the djinni was instantly there, shimmering brightly in the haze.

"Esren, take us to Rudel. Through the gate or over the

wall, I don't care. Whichever's faster. You'll be all right, won't you, Julianne? If we meet Morakh on the way, we've each got a knife for him."

Julianne was less troubled by Morakh than by the ride, but she'd endured worse these last weeks, with friends and enemies both. She swallowed, nodded, said, "I'll cope. Let's hurry."

✠   ✠   ✠

HE HAD FORGOTTEN his name and any sense of purpose, until the prisoner gave them back to him. He had forgotten almost everything, including how to think or why he should.

Until he had been told to take bread and water to the cell and give it to the girl there. That he'd done; but as he did it she had said a word, *Blaise*, and he'd remembered it to be his name.

I am Blaise, he'd thought; and that thought had stayed with him even after he'd bolted the cell door and come away.

Before it had had time to fade and lose itself in silence, he'd caught a glimpse of his face reflected in a barrel of water as he stooped to drink.

I am Blaise, and I am a man.

There were others behind him, waiting their turn at the water; he looked at them and saw that they were not Blaise, not him. Some were men, like him but not the same; others were women and others children, boys and girls. He didn't know their names, only that they were not Blaise, not him. Nor did they know that he was Blaise; neither did he tell them.

The prisoner in the cell had been a girl. He remembered that, though it was past now. She had gifted him his name, she had known and remembered it. Perhaps he might remember hers if he tried, if he had reason to try.

He thought that he might remember her face, as she had remembered his.

He was sent to climb steps, to stand upon a height and watch. As he climbed, he saw walls and towers all around and knew that he was in a castle. He had been in other castles before this. He remembered one in particular, a greater castle than this was, and he thought the girl had been there also. She had been in his charge; he was Blaise and she had called him *Sergeant* then, and he had called her *my lady*, although her name was Julianne.

I am Blaise, and I am a man; I was a sergeant, and I had charge of the lady Julianne . . .

He stood on the wall above the gate and watched the road below as he had been ordered. For a while, nothing moved. Then as the sun set he saw distant figures coming up from the town, a small cluster, three people carrying a fourth. They came to the gate and no one followed them.

I am Blaise, and I am on guard here, as I have been elsewhere; though I do not serve now those that I served before. I do not serve the lady Julianne. She is a prisoner here, and I serve those who have imprisoned her.

They had imprisoned her with a demon. He had seen it in the cell, but at the time he could not recall what manner of thing it was. Now he knew. It was black and shaped of cruelty, with eyes of fire.

He remembered fear, but not how it felt; he could not feel it.

In the dark, he saw many points of light that glittered and moved together outside the town. He had seen such things before. They would be torches, carried by men. When they began to stream along the road, he knew that an army rode against the castle.

He watched as he had been told to, and saw the army come; he saw its fires leap to life around the walls, he saw shadows of men at every fire and tents set up beyond. He remembered the word for this; it was called a siege.

WHEN HE WAS called down, he went in obedience, because he could remember no other way to act.

There were many people in the yard behind the gates. The lady Julianne was not among them. She was in her cell, he remembered, with the demon. He remembered pity but not how it felt, he could not feel it.

These were all the people who had followed the man to the castle. Blaise had been one among them then; now he thought he was not, because he was remembering so much.

The man who had led them here—they had called him the Preacher, he remembered, when they had had voices they could use and words to fill them—that man stood close to the gates, facing the gathered people. He did not speak at all; he had no need to. His will was their will. It might as well have been the will of the world, and perhaps it was.

It made no difference how much Blaise was remembering; he couldn't remember how not to follow the Preacher's will.

I am Blaise, I was a sergeant, I served the lady Julianne because it was my duty; now I am Blaise and it doesn't matter, I serve the Preacher because . . . because I serve the Preacher, because I do.

He walked to the first of the people where they stood together, because it was the Preacher's will that he should do so. He was vaguely aware of another man on the other side of the group doing the same as he did, pressing his lips against the lips of the person he faced.

This one was a woman. He remembered kissing in homage, as a sign of fealty; he remembered kissing in desire, in passion, though he could not remember how that felt. This was neither the one thing nor the other, not a kiss at all. Their open mouths met, and he felt not warm breath but the touch of something cold, a chill pass from her to him.

The woman screamed.

Blaise remembered pain, though not how it felt; he thought the woman was remembering now, and feeling too. He watched her subside, he watched her roll and thresh on the ground and remembered another word, re-membered agony.

Then he moved on, to the next in line. This was a man, an old man; after Blaise had done that thing that was not kissing, after the slip of cold had passed between them, the man stared, choked, collapsed in silence.

Blaise moved on.

Men and women, and children: for those Blaise had to bend low to touch his mouth to theirs. From each he claimed a chilly breath, and each one fell when that was done. Some screamed, some bled; most did neither.

Fess did neither, when Blaise came to him and knew his face, and remembered his name but could not speak it.

He remembered another word, which was death. He left Fess among the dead and moved on.

The sense of coldness grew beneath his tongue like a swelling, chilling tumour—unless it was within his tongue, he wasn't sure. He was conscious of the weight, the strength of it in his mouth as though it were solid, hard-shelled, and each sliver that he took wrapped an-other skin around it.

He thought it was good that there were two of them reaping this harvest, claiming souls for the Preacher. One man might never bear so many. He had been sick, he had been drunk, he had been overburdened and exhausted; once he had smoked a herb that had kept him erect and urgent throughout the night, for all that two separate women could do about it. He remembered all of those, and none had been like this. The chill was in his mouth, but the power of it filled his body from skin to skin, throughout. Filled and almost overfilled; one more, two more and he thought he might split entirely, like a blood pudding badly cooked and erupted from its casing. He thought he was a vessel, a jug top-full and fit to spill.

He walked, and could barely believe that he was doing that; like a storm that must break, he thought that he would pour and thunder across the land, not step with these impossible legs, one pace and then another and balance in between.

He took another soul, and there was only one left, and the other man took that one.

All the yard was crowded with dead and dying, or so he thought them, all those people who had been carriers. And what he held was only half of what they'd brought between them; and he thought it could rive the world if it were let loose, and he had no way to contain it.

He remembered dread, but not how it felt; he could not feel it.

He and the other went to the gates, where the Preacher wished them to be. They slid the beam aside and drew them open—high heavy gates, he could have moved them with a finger, he did move his leaf with a single, casual wrench that hauled it almost off its hinges—and then fell in behind the Preacher as he walked forward, out of the castle's dark and into the gaze, the glare, the bristling suspicion of the enemy.

HE REMEMBERED FEAR but not how it felt, he couldn't feel it. Magister Fulke had frightened him, he remembered suddenly; he thought that this should frighten him too, at least as much. If he'd ever been closer to death, he hadn't remembered it yet.

There were men all about him, men of the desert, those he had fought all his life. They were hostile and watchful; scimitar-points and arrow-points tracked from every side, following the Preacher, the other man, himself every step of their way from the castle gates to the tent of their enemy.

I am Blaise, I was a sergeant and I served the lady Julianne. This I remember. Now I serve the Preacher, and I cannot remember why . . .

Neither did he understand how, exactly: only that he carried something in his mouth that was not himself, nor any part of the Preacher. It lived, he thought, in its own cold way; it had lived in all those people and now it lived in himself and in another, and soon perhaps it would be whole and free.

He did think of it as one thing, however many fragments it had made. Not like a nest of bees or a school of fish that swarm or swim together but are still separate creatures, rather something mythical and monstrous that could shatter at will and reform, like ice-shards melting and running into a single pool of water.

All the people he had drawn it from were dead now. It would be drawn out of him soon, he thought, and then he would die also. That was something else that ought to frighten him, and did not. He couldn't find the place where fear lived inside him, though he had been a fearful man.

He remembered how frightened he had been in that strange land that Magister Fulke had sent him to. He thought of it as the heart of the sun. Everything had been hot and golden, even the water, and there was no other sun in the sky, so where else could it be?

He remembered how he had got there, by means of a lighted candle and a few muttered words that he thought were a demon-spell, that the Magister said were a prayer. Now that he was remembering so much, the words burned in his mind, in the Magister's voice, repeating them over and over.

He still had the candle, too. He'd carried that beneath his robe for safety; he could feel it now, pressing against his belly. The taste of terror was gone, but he could still remember the fact of it. It had overwhelmed him then, and he thought it ought to be doing the same now as he followed the Preacher into the enemy's camp with death in his tongue, death threatened on all sides and treachery to come. He was sure of very little, but he was sure of that. He remembered truce, he remembered parley, but this was something entirely other.

He might have cried a warning even to his enemies— *do not trust the Preacher*—but his mouth was full of evil and he could not speak.

THEY WERE TAKEN to a tent behind the ring of fires. The tent was large and bright with lamps, warmed by a brazier. It was furnished simply, rugs and a wood-framed cot, no more.

Half a dozen men stood to greet them as they entered, as their guard dispersed around the tent walls, still with arrows nocked and scimitars drawn.

He stood shoulder to shoulder with the other man, the two of them a little behind the Preacher. They faced the men whom they had come to see, and Blaise looked at their faces and knew two of them as he had known himself and the lady Julianne, and Fess.

There was the King's Shadow, father to the lady Julianne, who had left them by magic on a road long ago, and so all Blaise's troubles had begun; and there at his side was Rudel, who had claimed to be a jongleur at the great castle but was not, though he sang very prettily.

Both men were gazing at him. Their faces were very still, but he thought that their minds were not.

He knew Rudel, he knew the King's Shadow as they knew him, which was distantly. The other men in the tent were strangers all, and all of the desert. He remembered their own name for themselves, which was Sharai: Elessans used it, Ransomers used it, he'd known it and used it all his life. It was their blood-kin the Catari who worked the land in Outremer, defeated and tamed and seldom even defiant. *The Sharai are Catari,* he remembered, *but to be Catari is not to be Sharai.* Many of those dead in the courtyard had been Catari, by their dress and skin; he thought not one of them would have been Sharai.

"I am Hasan," one of the Sharai said then, and Blaise remembered more: the night raid on the castle when he was not allowed to fight, the bodies in the morning sun. Hasan had led that raid, and failed, and been driven back into the badlands. He remembered the sourness of triumph, though not how it had tasted.

"I am Hasan, and I do not know whether I welcome a friend or an enemy to my tent; but you are welcome none the less. You need have no fear for your safety. The guards are . . . precautionary, because there is an 'ifrit in the castle, and they are devious beasts. Should it come to meet us, we are ready. Allow me to name my companions to you: here are the lords of several tribes, and princes also from Outremer . . ."

Blaise remembered the word *'ifrit* from childhood stories, from the warnings of his elder brethren when he had been a Ransomer, from campfire tales when he had been a sergeant of Elessi. There had been other words, other creatures spoken of; he remembered that he had never truly believed in any of them, until he saw a djinni on the road to Roq de Rançon. Today he had seen a demon, in the lady Julianne's cell; he supposed that was the 'ifrit, though he would still use his own name for it. There was another demon in his tongue, for which he had no name at all.

The Sharai Hasan named the men who stood with him, one by one; then he waited, to hear the Preacher name himself and the two who stood behind him. He waited in vain; the Preacher said nothing.

After a time, Hasan took a breath and asked directly. "Will you tell us your name? It is the custom, at a parley."

"My name is unimportant; I have not come to parley."

"Have you not? To what end, then? My wife is captive in that castle, and if those who hold her will not parley, they will die. Do you speak for Morakh the Sand Dancer, or for the 'ifrit, or for all those who came later, or for whom?"

"I speak for the God I serve, and for none other."

Blaise didn't understand or believe either man, though it didn't matter. The lady Julianne was married to the Baron Imber, Blaise had seen that marriage made himself. And the Preacher surely did not serve the God that he proclaimed, a hundred corpses demon-slain could testify to that.

"If you want free passage out of the castle for you and your followers, you may have it, so long as you have done no harm to my woman."

"I have done no harm to anyone," which was a lie direct, though Blaise could not speak to denounce it. "I am a healer, blessed by the God and by the relic of a saint. See, I will show you." He reached inside his robe to produce the black and twisted hand, and held it out in plain view. Light glistened on its glossy skin; Rudel took half a pace forward, only to be stayed by the King's Shadow with a touch on his sleeve and a murmured word.

"There is a sickness abroad in the Sanctuary Land," the Preacher went on, "which I have named the King's Evil. It is sent by the God as a reprimand, because the King has allowed heresy and false teachings to thrive. Only my prayers and the touch of this relic will cure it. Those I have healed follow me; I led them here that we may strike together against the greater sickness, which is Surayon."

"Surayon is hidden," Hasan said mildly, "and you are not many, to make war against a state."

"It will be opened to us, and the God's strength is in our arm. Nor will we be alone. I have seen this, and it is sure."

"What would you have me do? I have my own quarrel with Outremer, but I am here for my wife, who has been taken by one of our people. I have said that I will let you pass, if you can bring your followers out of the castle; though I am curious to know why the Sand Dancer let you in."

"The gates were open, and he welcomed us as you have. Perhaps he is not the enemy you think. Or there may be a greater reason than his own, why he has drawn you here. He too is a servant of the God, though he may not know it. And you are an army, poised above Surayon and sworn against the Kingdom; if the Folded Land should open . . ."

If the Folded Land should open, Blaise thought, not Hasan himself could hold his army back; the glint in his eye said that he would not try. He might consort with a Surayonnaise sorcerer, but he would still lay waste to Rudel's land on his way to Ascariel.

He said nothing, though, and neither did Rudel. It was the King's Shadow who spoke, who said, "However that may be, you and your people are free within the castle. Could you bring my daughter out, among your number?"

"There is no need," the Preacher said. "Look, where she comes . . ."

And indeed she did come, the lady Julianne blundering in through the doorway of the tent, and talking already as she came.

"Rudel! Rudel, are you here? Oh, Rudel, come quickly! Esren would bring us no closer, I don't know why, but we need you, Marron is dreadfully sick, Elisande is with him but she cannot help, she says she needs your strength . . ."

Not Rudel, but Hasan who reacted first: Hasan who strode forward to claim the girl he spoke of as his wife, while the rest were simply staring. Hasan who had been so careful with his doubtful guest, who forgot all that care in a moment; who passed within a hand's span of the Preacher in his urgency.

And as he passed, the Preacher struck. Not with a blade, not with a fist: with the distorted black claw that he called a relic.

He used it like a weapon, not a hand of healing. He slashed it across Hasan's face and the hooked fingers dug deep, leaving long red weals where the blood rose.

Briefly, everything was very still within the tent. Even the lady Julianne's pleading voice fell into silence.

Then three bows sang, and the Preacher wheeled once before he dropped.

Hasan raised a puzzled hand to his cheek, touched the blood there, made a choking sound and collapsed.

The lady Julianne cried out incoherently, hurtled forward and dropped to her knees above the fallen Sharai.

Her father's voice was louder as he called, "No!" and ran to seize her shoulders, to drag her away.

She resisted; he said, "*Look,* Julianne! Use your eyes, use your mind . . .!"

Her gaze followed his pointing finger; so did every man's in the tent. So did Blaise's.

THE RELIC, THE saint's hand lay where it had fallen on the rug, where the pierced Preacher had dropped it as he died.

It lay there, and it moved.

As though the life had passed from man to thing, it

flexed and squirmed, began to stretch upward. It never had looked much like a hand, so bent the fingers were, so withered the palm; now it seemed more like a blackened plant in hasty growth, reaching for the sun.

At the same time, a wispy smoke stole from the Preacher's mouth and twined itself around that sprouting darkness, and was absorbed. The thing swelled outward and grew more vigorous.

The lady Julianne gasped sharply and flung herself full-length across Hasan's stillness. "It has eyes!"

"Indeed." The King's Shadow confirmed calmly what Blaise too had seen already, red points glowing against the black. No doubt the eyes had always been there even in its shrunken state, though they must have been hidden behind a fold of chitin. "It's an 'ifrit, daughter—and as far as I'm aware, you're lying on top of the only blessed weapon in the tent."

Blaise watched all this dispassionately, as he must; but then his own mouth opened as the dead Preacher's had, and he felt the ice in his tongue uncurl.

He saw it issue from his mouth, not ice but smoke, black smoke rushing to feed the demon, the 'ifrit. The same was happening to and from the other man at his side, nameless and doomed.

Blaise remembered terror, agony, despair, he remembered how they felt; he felt them all. The pain started in his feet and crept upward, a rotting, consuming fire. He fell quickly, wanting to roll and thresh against the searing; but despair was a lethargy that engulfed him entirely and far more quickly. Screaming was a waste of precious air, struggling was purposeless; better to lie still and suffer, and so die . . .

Except that he was lying on his belly in an enemy's tent, with treachery all around him. Here was neither honour nor justice, and he did not want these people to have the disposal of his body.

He had no care for any of the chaos above and about his head. He could feel the candle that he carried, pressed against his stomach; despite his pain—or because of his pain, perhaps, a whip to use against black melancholy— he could work his hand in to draw it out.

And when he held it, he could drag himself on his el- bows the little distance that he needed, he could hold the wick of it in a puddle of burning oil from a lamp that had tumbled from its tripod and would burn all the rugs and the tent besides if it were not attended to; he could cup his hands around the flame and whisper the words that Magister Fulke had branded into his brain. No matter that his breath came in shudders and his voice too. The soft hiss of it was meant not for mortal ears, but for the God.

And the God heard. There was a glimmer of gold in the eye-dazzling light, a taste of gold in the air, a touch of gold in the warmth soaking up into his pain-wracked body, and he was quite alone and could die so, and would be glad to do so even here where he had been so scared before.

✝   ✝   ✝

ELISANDE WAS SO in dread for Marron's life, she couldn't understand why the djinni had left them here, still a distance short of Hasan's tent. Surely it had under- stood her urgency, her order . . .

Stranded close and yet not close enough, she'd sent Julianne to run into the tent while she waited as patiently as she could, cradling Marron's head in her arms and glaring at the Sharai who gathered uselessly around her, muttering to each other but saying nothing to the point, nothing at all to her. Peering between their pressing bod- ies, she watched the door of the tent, waiting to see Ju- lianne come racing out with Rudel on her heels—and waited longer than she'd wanted, longer than she'd ex-

pected, far longer than she thought Marron could afford.
His skin was shifting constantly beneath her touch, ice-
cold one minute and burning hot the next, as the Daughter struggled against his strange invader.

She thought she could hear shouting in the tent; she
saw the light shift strangely. Something emerged at
last—but not the human figures she'd been watching for.

Something black and long, so long: its body was
snake-like, she thought, except that it moved on twig-thin
legs. And moved fast, whatever it was, gone into the dark
before she could raise an arm to point it out; and left her
in terror for what new tragedy they would come to tell
her of while she knelt helpless, nursing a boy she could
not heal.

Too late, there was a yell from the castle gates and a
figure racing out, sprinting after the creature. That was
Jemel, inevitably—cocksure in his own courage, determined to be first to prove it. Unless the creature waited
for him, though, he couldn't hope to match that insect
scuttling.

For a minute, Elisande was torn desperately between
desires. She wanted to watch for him and also watch the
tent with the sudden crush of frantic men outside it,
shouting and gesticulating and almost coming to knives,
and she still didn't know why, what the monster had
wrought inside; she wanted to run to discover, to find her
friends—and, yes, even her father—to be sure that they
were safe, at the same time as she wanted to run after
Jemel. Julianne had one of her blades but Elisande still
kept the other, she could help. And she wanted also to
stay just exactly where she was, Marron's head in her lap;
she couldn't leave him, not possibly, so she wanted
everyone to come to her with news and comfort and suc-
cour for the grievously ill, all at once and now . . .

Her eyes flitted from side to side, seeking friends,
seeking reassurance, finding none. She thought seriously

about screaming, loud as she could. Almost, she took a breath to do it; but then there was movement beyond the firelight, and there came at least one of her desires, outrun and defeated.

"Jemel! Over here, I have Marron . . ."

That was safe to fetch him, and it did. He stood staring down at his unconscious friend, and even with his back to the firelight she could see how his complexion changed; even through the hard panting of a young man who had run too far and too fast, she could hear his sudden breathlessness.

"Sit down, Jemel," she ordered roughly.

Somewhat to her surprise, the tough young Sharai obeyed her: of necessity, she thought, his legs giving way entirely beneath the weight of his distress.

"I have been searching for him, in the castle."

"I thought you must have been. Esren brought us out," and she could almost have smiled at the absurdity of it— Jemel running in at one door, no doubt, while they flew out of another—if Marron hadn't been so ill and both of them so anxious, if the memory of that swift flight to freedom hadn't been overlaid by the sight of heaped bodies in the castle forecourt.

"Will he live?" The voice was gruff, the question brusque, the truth of his feelings entirely betrayed by the way one hand reached out and lay hesitantly in the air above Marron's face, just a fingertip short of touching.

"I don't know," she answered honestly. "He's lived this long," rather against her expectations, "so there must be hope. I can't help him; I sent Julianne to fetch Rudel, but something's happened in that tent. You saw the 'ifrit come out," and she couldn't think how that had come about, as she was sure no 'ifrit had been seen to go in, "and there's been no sign of anyone since." Not that anyone else had had a chance, with that great scrum of men around the doorway, but her heart was full of misgiving.

That at least she wasn't afraid to admit to. "I'm scared, Jemel. I want to know what went on in there, but I couldn't leave Marron . . ."

"Go now," he said. "I will stay. But send Rudel, as swiftly as you can."

"I will," she promised. *If he still lives . . .*

She pushed herself to her feet and ran, a harder effort than she'd imagined; her own legs were none too steady.

Being small was useful for once, as she squeezed through the pack of excited Sharai at the tent's mouth; so was having sharp elbows and a woman's voice. The guards at the doorway might perhaps have remembered that she had a djinni at her beck and call; they made no move to stop her, as she ducked beneath their drawn blades and stepped inside.

She'd been dreading what she might find here, how many dead. There was a moment's sheer relief as she saw only one man down and Coren, Rudel, Julianne all unharmed; she thought she ought to feel relief too for her country's sake when she realised that the figure slumped on the carpet was Hasan.

For her friend's sake, though, she couldn't do it. Julianne held her husband's head nestled in her lap, much as Elisande had held Marron's a short minute earlier; her own face was bowed and hidden, but Elisande could see black gashes on Hasan's cheek. Even clotted blood should never look so dark, she thought. Nor should such trivial wounds leave a man looking as Hasan looked now, sick unto death, again much like Marron; nor should they have left a powerful healer like Rudel looking so defeated.

He acknowledged her first, with a glance and a few quick words that stole her breath away.

"Elisande. I'm glad you're here, we need you."

She gaped, she couldn't help it; then, recovering her

voice, she demanded, "What happened here, where did that 'ifrit come from, what has it done to Hasan?"

"Hasn't that djinni of yours taught you not to ask questions yet?" He sounded exhausted and troubled in equal measure. "I'll tell it all, but not now. Hasan is beyond me; he would be beyond you too, or the both of us together, so don't suggest it. Call up your djinni. The only hope that I can see is to take him to your grandfather, as fast as that spirit can carry us, if it will."

"Oh, it will." Her grandfather could work miracles, she'd always been confident of that. Seeking him meant Surayon, and home; for a moment her soul rejoiced. Then, "There's Marron too, he has something of the same sickness, I'd guess . . ."

"Can the djinni carry them both, and us too?"

"Esren carried all the Dead Waters at once, don't you remember?"

"Then we will take them both. Why not? The two greatest threats our homeland faces, and we will carry them to the heart of it to save them if we can. Never tell me that the gods have no sense of humour. Swiftly now, Elisande. Minutes matter."

Not as much as he thought, perhaps; but just then Julianne lifted her head like a blind creature seeking the sun. One glance at her face, tear-stained and racked with grief, and Elisande dropped to her friend's side, put both arms around her and said, "Don't mourn the living, sweet. Save your tears for where they're needed."

Julianne gave her a wry glance—*and you've shed none for Marron?*—but her voice was sour barrens as she said, "He's as dead as need be, if Rudel cannot wake him. The 'ifrit might have killed him utterly, just as easily; it left him this way, I think, to make me suffer the more."

"Then it made a mistake. Two mistakes. One, to think you so weak; and again, to think Hasan as good as dead. Whatever it's done to him, my grandfer will undo it.

Trust him, if you don't trust me. And hold tight, we're going to hurry."

Julianne clenched her hands tight in Hasan's robe, but then straightened suddenly, as if she'd only just realised what was meant. "Your grandfather—but he's in Surayon, isn't he? And Surayon is . . . gone. Closed, Folded . . ."

"There's always a way in, love, for those who know it. We'll be with him in an hour. Esren!"

The djinni was there at her call, silent for once; she said, "Take us along the road, to the border with Surayon. Me, Hasan, Julianne, Rudel. Marron too, we must collect him. And probably Jemel with him. Coren?"

"Yes. I will go with my daughter."

"All of us, then." And with an idea of making the ride a little easier for Julianne this time, that she not have to ride on empty air, "Esren, take us on the carpet."

"As you command."

The rug beneath them rippled and rose, began to move towards the tent's doorway. The other men not named, all those haughty and useless sheikhs crowded hastily back to give it room; the crowd outside fell over itself to make way. There would be more quarrels shortly, Elisande thought, unless the wonder of a flying carpet were balm enough to soothe the humiliation of crawling in the dust. Somehow, she doubted that it would be.

MARRON AND JEMEL: and of course they couldn't have one without the other, and she wasn't even resentful any more. She could even yield up her place at Marron's head to the Sharai boy, and do it with a good grace, though it meant her sitting instead beside her father.

As she had nothing to accuse him of, they both sat in silence. She poked experimentally at the rug she sat on, feeling how it was not stiff in itself like a boat's boards, nor was it laid over solidity like a rug laid over boards; it gave just a little beneath her finger as it did beneath her weight, as though it floated on something more sustaining than water. As it did: it wasn't the rug that flew, Esren simply carried that as it carried them, on a soft firm cushion of nothing at all. It would help Julianne, that was all, not to see the ground rushing by below them. That girl had her head bent low above Hasan's again; she wouldn't be seeing anything just now, bar his ruined face, but she'd look up sometime, look around. Better, Elisande thought, if she couldn't also look down.

Darkness would help also, and it was entirely dark now except for the stars and the horizon's hint of a moon to rise shortly. She glanced back and saw the fires of the Sharai dwindling behind them.

"What will they do?"

"The tribes? Come after us, of course. We have Hasan; they followed him this far, they'll follow him a little further. Besides, there's no point their watching an empty castle."

"Morakh," she objected, remembering him for the first time in a while. "It's not empty, Morakh's there . . ."

"You think so? Still? Use your mind, Elisande."

That stung, as it was meant to. She thought briefly, bitterly, and said, "No. He would not linger. Either he has what he wanted"—Hasan not dead but sick unto death, and Marron the same, perhaps—"or he has abandoned his plans. Either way, the tribes will not find him in the castle."

"They won't even look. Hasan hunted Morakh for Julianne's sake; they followed Hasan for his sake, and their own, and perhaps for Outremer. The sheikhs will follow immediately, with their retinues. The army will come after, as quickly as it may. All the way to the Surayon border they will come, more than have ever been massed against us before."

"They can't get in," she said, trying to sound certain, to believe herself.

"No, probably not. But they will see all the rest of Outremer spread before them, and no army there to hold them back. What do you think they will do, Elisande? When we fought them tribe by tribe forty years ago, we barely defeated them; they know that. They are together now, if not exactly united. Even without Hasan, they can hold together a few days longer. Long enough to march on Ascariel, at least."

She told herself firmly that she ought not to care, that Ascariel was her enemy also; but that was impossible to sustain. "Should we have left him, then, and let him die? Let Julianne be a widow, for Outremer?"

"Julianne can still be a wife if she chooses, to the Baron Imber. And many would say that we should have done exactly that." He sighed and went on, "I might say it myself, I'm afraid we will all have cause to say it in the days ahead. I couldn't have done it, though, any more than you."

"There must be some hope," she said stubbornly, "some way to stop them."

"Must there? Well, then, maybe there is. There's Coren."

"Coren? But—"

Her eyes shifted, she couldn't help it, across the carpet to where that venerable old man sat beyond Marron, beyond Hasan but still not far away, not far enough. Of course he had heard; his eyes twinkled at her, though he didn't speak.

"When fathers follow their daughters into some mad or foolish adventure," Rudel went on blandly, "it's not always or entirely for the girl's benefit." He might have been watching her closely, to see if she blushed; she determinedly didn't look at him, for fear that catching his eye might make her do so. "Coren could have stayed with the sheikhs and tried to argue against their riding after us; he would have lost that argument. On the other hand, if they have a long and tiring ride on a difficult road, and round the final corner to find him there waiting for them, perhaps with news of Hasan, they may be more inclined to listen. He is the King's Shadow, and that commands respect among the Sharai, especially on the border of the King's country. That's so, is it not, Coren?"

"I have hopes," he agreed quietly.

And what of Julianne, then, who has hopes of her father's support as she takes her ailing husband into a strange land and gives him over to strangers? There was no point even putting the question into words, she knew the answer already. But Julianne should not be the only one to worry over Hasan; Elisande was struck with a brilliant notion, bright enough to touch her face with a brief smile.

Rudel noticed it, of course. "What was that thought, then?"

"An idea, that's all. Something to do, after we're home. Nothing mad or foolish," and she could almost have smiled again, if it hadn't been him she would have smiled at. "I won't even leave Grandfer's house."

"You've made me that promise before. And broken it."

"I made *him* that promise," and broke it, yes. How else had they all come here? She was no Julianne, to sit obedient beneath her father's commandments. "Under compulsion," if that made any difference. Between the two of them she thought not, where everything was under compulsion. "This time it isn't a promise. I'm simply saying it. I wouldn't want to go anywhere, anyway. I wouldn't leave Julianne." Nor Marron; she'd let Jemel claim the nursing of him, but she wouldn't wander far.

"No," Rudel said, "I don't believe you would."

And then she did blush, fearful that he might have

added mind-reading to his many talents; and quickly said, "Tell me what happened in the tent. I don't understand where that 'ifrit came from, nor what it did, why it didn't kill you all . . ."

"No more do I. We'll trade stories, Elisande; you tell me how you escaped your own 'ifrit, and I'll tell you what I saw. You may make better sense of it than I can."

THAT SHE COULDN'T do, though she puzzled over it even while she told her own tale, and so took less pleasure than she felt she owed herself from her description of how she'd tricked the 'ifrit into flight, faking a future it could fear. Rudel was complimentary, but there was little pleasure in that either. After half a lifetime of setting herself against him at every opportunity, she wasn't about to warm to his congratulations now. Absolutely not.

Instead she stared out and away, looking perhaps as though she were deep in thought; she hoped so. The truth was that she was simply staring, and seeing less even than dark and speed could show her.

She had made this journey twice before, going and coming home, and the first of those had been the better. Much as she loved her grandfather and the land he governed, she had loved her freedom more; being away from Rudel had been her definition of freedom even then, and coming back had inevitably revoked it.

She'd never ridden this way at night, though. Even by daylight it had been shadowed and dangerous, barely more than a goat-track at times for all that they called it a road, little used and not at all maintained. The surface had crumbled constantly, she remembered, beneath her pony's hooves; occasional overhangs of visibly loose rock had had her wishing that the beast could tiptoe, for fear that a noise might bring them down.

She was glad to be flying now, for the safety and silence of their passage as much as for the speed. On horses or camels or on foot, she thought, this would be a terrifying path at night, worst for Julianne but bad enough for her; she didn't envy the sheikhs who would follow. Good sense should tell them to wait till the morning, though she doubted that they'd listen.

The djinni was a little pillar of flickering light at her shoulder. She'd told it to take them along the road and it obeyed literally, deliberately hurling them around every twist and turn in the winding way. The wind grew bitterly cold as they climbed high into the mountains; she drew her hood up and almost, almost huddled against the strong solidity of her father, did hunch into the lee of his stocky body for what slight protection it offered.

Julianne moved too, for the first time, when she felt the wind's bite; but she lifted her head into it and shook her hair free, so that she sat erect and silent and utterly still, her hands folded on Hasan's chest and her eyes wide and wild. She had always been promised Outremer, and had seen only the fringes of it in all her life thus far. She could never have thought to come to the living heart of the land—to hidden Surayon, no less, anathematised and cast out—like this: twice married and never widowed yet, wed now to the country's greatest enemy and on a desperate mission to save his life, riding a carpet carried by a spirit-creature out of myth and stories. It seemed unlikely that she was seeing anything of what her eyes were looking at, the great crags and crevasses of the high mountains, the way the road clung to sheer cliffs as it snaked between unclimbable peaks. Elisande wondered what her friend might be thinking, and decided it was better not to know. Marron snagged as ever at her own mind, Marron and Jemel together snagged at the corner of her sight, and all she had as shield was Rudel who had never, never been a figure of comfort; her own thoughts were bleak enough for anyone.

*   *   *

FOR A SHORT time, at the road's height, it seemed as though the mountains had been ripped fresh from the earth beneath, stark black shadows of what she remembered as stark black rock, like a wall erected between Outremer and the Sands. Too weak a wall, she thought, for all its massive strength: no wall could be stronger than the doors set within it. This was perhaps the hardest of the passes, and they could cross it in an hour, by the djinni's grace. The sheikhs who followed would need the night, no longer, and their army would catch them in the morning. If Coren could not stop them at the border, the Sharai would have an easy ride down to Ascariel, and there would be blood enough to drown the city before the war was done . . .

Perhaps it was the darkness and the chill that drove her thoughts so blackly, coldly deep. If so, perhaps it was the first hint of warmth in the wind that drew them up again and her with them, back into the immediacy of the world.

They had come over the mountains, faster she thought than any human ever had before them. Now as they descended there were other, lesser peaks to north and south, a spur of the great range that declined into gentler hills as it ran westward almost to the sea. Ahead and below them lay her own home, hidden but present none the less and compounded in her mind of bitterness and joy together, the uncountable memories that had made her what she was.

The air smelled rich and damp, to senses long used to the desert's dryness; summer's heat lingered here even at night, cupped as it was within mountain walls. Elisande felt her anxieties stilled by hope. Surayon would stay safe within its Folding, her grandfather would work his reliable magic on Marron and Hasan both, Coren would hold the Sharai army back until its commander returned. And surely then simple gratitude would demand that Hasan lead it back to the Sands, and Outremer too would survive at least a while longer, whether or not it deserved to . . .

She breathed deeply, hungry for the smells of home. The road was wider here as they came to the valley's mouth, if in no better repair. At length it forked, one branch running away southward towards Ascariel. Esren needed no telling; the carpet with its riders swept on along the northern branch.

Soon it slowed, though, soon it settled to lie flat on the stony road. Elisande stirred at the sudden unfamiliarity of hard ground beneath her; she got to her feet a little awkwardly, stretched and stamped like a sailor come to land, testing the solidity of earth.

Others rose around her, Coren and Rudel. Jemel and Julianne stayed predictably where they were, with the two sick men. Julianne turned her head, though, with that same unseeing gaze.

"Why have we stopped?"

"We've reached the border, sweet. We have to stop, to open a way through the Folding."

Directly ahead of them was a strange discontinuity, like a rippling veil drawn across the road. There seemed to be more starlight than there ought to be on the other side of that invisible curtain, less shadow: soft rolling hills to north and south rather than the height of mountains, an open aspect ahead. Elisande almost fancied that she could hear the sea, almost expected to scent it on the warmth of the breeze.

Between where she stood and what she saw lay a whole country, wrapped in magic and concealed from view. If she tried to walk forward through the barrier, she knew that she would feel dizzy and sick for a few moments, she'd lose all sense of balance or direction before suddenly she found herself in that scene she could so impossibly see from here, some thirty miles from where she stood. If she tried to ride, horse or camel would panic and she'd likely be thrown off.

Far more than a simple illusion, the Folding was a powerful defence: a necessary defence for Surayon against the forces on either side, the Patric dukedoms that denied all brotherhood and would crush her country if they could. Still, it was a wall with doorways for those who knew how they could be opened. Elisande knew, and had used that knowledge when she'd felt it needful, though it had been a difficult and draining exercise for a girl working alone. No need for her to face that strain again. This time she had her father with her.

Rudel had already walked forward, to stand within touching distance of the boundary. He glanced at her, all the summoning she needed. She told Esren to be ready, to whisk the carpet through as soon as the way was opened; then she went to join him.

It felt strange, so strange to be doing this with him, father and daughter working as one as though there were no ghost unlaid between them. It was an old ghost, though, and seemed to be retreating; sometimes she had to struggle to remember the taste of what had tainted everything so many years before.

Just now, it was almost meaningless. She shrugged it aside, surprised to find how easy that could be, and focused her attention on Rudel.

Even with two, this would be no simple task. Surayon had been Folded, slipped aside from mortal eyes or understanding, but it was still fixed as it must be, still rooted in the everyday world. Her grandfather and his fellow savants who had achieved the Folding had laid bonds of power all across it, from one border to the other in every direction, tethering north to south and east to west like a needlewoman stitching and gathering a fold into a sheet. Their task now, hers and Rudel's, was to cut some few of those stitches, to make a breach large enough to pass all their companions through. The difficulty lay in remaking the stitches afterwards, to seal the boundary again; the greater danger was that if they lost control of their cutting, the whole intricate network of the bond might unravel, to leave Surayon utterly exposed.

Another glance between them, and both Surayonnaise reached out their hands to touch the insubstantial curtain. It was like healing, Elisande thought, looking below the skin of the world to see the reality beneath. Here were threads and cords of power like woven music, chords rather than ropes; she could hear their throb and pulse, if she closed her eyes she could see them like lines of light against the darkness of her lids, wrapping around her fingers as she probed the mesh. She could feel the suck of them as they sought to pull her far, far away; it took concentration to deny them.

Rudel, she thought, would not have closed his eyes. Older and stronger and far more experienced, he would stand foursquare and demand that they yield, that they part to his touch. She heard his voice now, through the subtle insistence of the web: "I have begun, Elisande. Do likewise, but remember to keep hold of the threads, we must knot them after."

She knew that, of course she knew that; for a moment the age-old resentment rose like bile in her throat. She swallowed it down hastily, fighting to keep her mind on what her fingers did. This was no time to play the sullen child.

The beat of the music was the beat of her blood. She had the right and the power to do this; besides, she had done it before, and alone. Not so great a tear, nor holding it for so long a time, only the moment that it took a slender and agile body to slither through the smallest gap she could create; but she had done it then, and mended it after.

Her fingers unpicked the strings, like a musician plucking her instrument and snapping where she plucked; but she sang her own song in silence as she worked, and so held the mesh together. It was like having other hands, hands of the mind that seized the threads as they broke and wouldn't let them fly. She could grip this many and more, this one and that, more yet; she felt them strain against her control but would not let go, simply refused to allow it. And her father was at her side, he could lend his strength to hers if she should need it, though she would not ask for it yet.

But then suddenly there was another body between herself and her father, she felt it loom beside her and she didn't understand it at all. Only Coren was up and about, not settled still on the carpet; and he wouldn't come so close to disturb them, he if anyone must know the delicacy and danger of their work. Besides, the smell was wrong: the mustiness of unwashed wool with the dry spicy smell of a man from the Sands underlying all, that was certainly not Coren . . .

Her eyes opened despite herself, so that she struggled to keep her mental grip on all the threads she held; and she saw Morakh close enough to touch except that her hands were vitally busy already, and he was facing her father and had his scimitar drawn.

Rudel was staring at him, his own hands caught in the barrier's weave, helpless to defend himself. There was the touch of a smile on Morakh's face as he raised his curved scimitar and brought it down.

One swift stroke, it seemed almost too casual, too small a thing to end any man's life, let alone such a man, such a life.

Coren was shouting something, but he sounded a long way off and Elisande wasn't listening in any case. Elisande was screaming, wrenching her hands free of the intangible web that held them, forgetful of everything except the knife in her belt and the sight that filled her eyes, her father fallen in a gout of blood with his head half severed from his neck.

Morakh seemed slow somehow, so slow to turn. Her fumbling fingers had time to find the knife and draw it, time to thrust it deep into the Dancer's belly before his sword came up again. She was screaming still, she could hear herself, as though she'd forgotten how to stop; he made no sound at all, only sagged heavily against her so that she staggered backwards and almost fell herself beneath his weight.

He took her knife with him as he slumped to the ground. She didn't care, she was transfixed, seeing a strange smoke rise from Morakh's slack mouth; but then there was the 'ifrit scurrying out of the moonshadow, still shaped long and stick-like on slender legs except that it had claws now, and the smoke twined around its body and was absorbed even as those claws reached towards her.

She had just time to remember that her knife was blessed, and then to remember that it was out of her reach now, lost beneath Morakh's body, and so she was as dead as her father or would be in another moment.

The 'ifrit seemed to lose sight of her, though, even as it poised to strike. Its head turned, blindly questing; its claws flailed at the air. She stood frozen yet, lacking the wit to run, the sense to do anything at all. Someone else was running, she heard his steps and couldn't so much as look around to find him; and then Coren was there at her side with Hasan's great curved scimitar in his hand. He hewed and the blade cut, he thrust and the point drove through the 'ifrit's gleaming chitin and deep into its body, and it died and dissipated like dust on the wind.

And still she stood there, staring at her father's brutal corpse; and it was only when Coren said her name, "Elisande," with a terrible sadness that she remembered what was worse, what was the greatest horror of this dreadful, suddenly more than dreadful night.

NOW SHE COULD move, although she didn't want to. She moved only her head, and that only a little: just far enough to see what no one had seen for thirty years, Surayon her homeland unFolded and unsafe, open and exposed, where all her grandfather's careful protective magic had frayed to nothing and was gone because she and Rudel had let the web unravel.

TEN

Into the UnFolded Land

ANTON WOULDN'T SAY that he lit the candle in all innocence, no, he couldn't conceivably claim that. None the less, he declined absolutely to accept any guilt in the matter. Guilt for what offence? Marshal Fulke was sought, and could not be discovered; there was one in the company, one Sieur Anton d'Escrivey who knew where the marshal might be found, and how to reach him there. There could be no objection if that same Sieur Anton went to seek his master commander . . .

There had been no hesitation in him when the moment came. He'd been on watch half the night, and making his way towards his bed when he was overtaken by a runner with an urgent summons for Marshal Fulke. They'd gone together to the marshal's tent and found it deserted. On a simple camp table had been an oil-lamp burning, a linen roll unfolded to show a number of candles, black and white tapers intricately plaited together. For Anton, that

had been better than a clue to his commander's where-
abouts.

He'd dismissed the runner, "Get you back to your
post, lad; say that the marshal is coming, I'll fetch him to
you," and scooped up one of the candles on his way out
of the tent.

At the camp's southern perimeter lay the mysterious,
intangible border where Surayon ought to be and was
not. Marshal Fulke was known to spend a lot of his time
on that front, watching and praying; but the lad and
Anton both had come from there.

Anton had turned the other way, towards the rear of
the camp. He'd walked through lines of horse-pickets
and groups of sleeping men; he'd found guards on watch
and questioned them, and yes, the marshal had come
through the lines alone and only a few minutes ahead of
him.

Anton had walked on until his eyes adjusted to the
moonlight. Then he'd stood still, scanning the slopes of
the hills that closed in around the road there. He might
not have spotted a black-clad figure moving through the
darkness, but after a minute he'd seen a momentary
spark, another, and then a flickering point of light to his
left and above him.

He'd stepped softly over the stony ground, slipping
between thorns and scrub while he slipped the candle
from his robe and his own flint and tinder from a pouch
at his belt.

Soon he'd been close enough to see Marshal Fulke's
silhouette, stark against a guttering light; close enough
also to hear the marshal's voice, chanting quietly. He'd
heard the words before, and this single repetition was
enough; he'd always prided himself on a sharp memory.

Shielding the candle with his body against both wind
and the marshal's eyes, he struck sparks until the tinder
caught, then lit all four of the candle's wicks. Straighten-

ing slowly and already murmuring the chant, he turned to
see the marshal weaving cords of light, stepping into a
golden nimbus. For a moment it hurt to watch, but the
glow faded quickly, and the man was gone.

Anton followed swiftly but not hastily, guarding the
candle's light with a cupped hand and speaking the words
clearly now, trying to be confident both in his actions and
in his intent.

In the one at least, he was successful; the flames of the
candle were suddenly white and still as glass, brilliantly
flaring. Anton touched them, bent them with his fingers
as the other had before him; they seemed to cut a doorway in the dark, and he felt only a moment's lack of
courage before his determination took him through.

THIS WAS NOT like the last time: no vision of the country spread out below him, no sense of flight or falling. Instead he was snatched instantly, urgently from one place
to another, stepping into a new landscape, other hills.

The ground was dry beneath his feet, walls of rock
were dry around him, even the air felt dry and strangely
lifeless in his lungs; nothing grew, nothing could grow
here. There was no sun in the pearly sky, and all the land
gleamed dully gold; he wondered if night could ever
come to such a place, and felt briefly glad not to see it.

The marshal was standing a little distance ahead of
him, just where the gully opened out onto a plateau. Beyond that still figure Anton could see another, a man
lying fallen on the ground; his clothes, his bulk and the
unlikelihood of chance made that man Sergeant Blaise.

Anton thought that he could maybe see something
more, a slight disturbance of the air above Blaise, some
twist of wind and light that seemed to sparkle faintly. In
his own world he would have dismissed that as a mirage;
here he was less sure.

Fulke walked forward less briskly, less confidently than was normal. He was still a few paces short of the body when a voice spoke, thin and silvery and seemingly out of the dead air—but it came, Anton thought, from that air that seemed not dead at all, that had a little spin to it, a touch of shine.

"Stay back, human. He is not dead, and I can prevent his dying, though he will be dead to you. It would be as well if you did not touch him."

"He is my man," Fulke said, quite calmly.

"He was, perhaps. No longer, and not for a while now. He has been a man of the 'ifrit; soon he will be nothing at all, unless I make him mine. Which I will do."

"If he is injured, we have medicine of our own."

"He is not injured."

"Well then, what ails him?"

It seemed to Anton that there was an extra hum to the voice suddenly, as though the creature—whatever it was—had been pleased by the question.

"You have asked, and I will tell you—though you will owe me a debt for the answer, and I will claim it later. The 'ifrit do not breathe and this is not a poison, but you might say that the man has been first poisoned by the breath of an 'ifrit, and then possessed by a fragment of its body. When it abandoned him, the poison remained. Or you might say that the 'ifrit cast a shadow in your world as a snake casts its skin, and that shadow has fallen over him, and he has breathed within it, breathed it in. It is a cold thing, and eats at the will of creatures such as yourself. This one is strong, he did well to make the journey here, though it has drained him now; most would not succeed so far. The djinn do not breathe either, but my own breath, if you would call it that—or else my own shadow, even here in my own world—will rouse him, if only to my service. He is lost to you. Accept that, and go back."

"I will stay, and see if he recovers as you say. And hear

what he says, after. The deceits of demons are legion, and he is a servant of the God."

"I am a djinni; we do not lie. Perhaps he will serve your God, in serving me. That I do not know. You would be wise not to speak to him; if you ask him questions when he is mine, you will only increase your debt to me. But stay if you will, both of you. I do not forbid it."

Now Anton could stand back no longer; he walked out onto the plateau and saw Fulke's brief surprise.

"You, Sieur Anton? You followed me?"

"There was a message," though the excuse sounded ridiculously thin, here and now. "Besides," more honestly, "I was curious . . ."

"Well. Curiosity can work to the good; we are both in a new world tonight, where we face new revelations. Though I did not know that the King's Eye would shield creatures of the underworld."

"Creatures of spirit," the voice, the djinni corrected. "The King's Eye sees far, and it sees deeper than you can, human. Do not rush to judgement in your ignorance. You stand in my world now, and it is not less than yours."

"If you would save Blaise," Anton said neutrally, thinking that this was an argument that could run forever, "it would be as well to do it soon."

"Patience. Mortal flesh is not as weak as you suppose, though a simple scratch opened his body to the 'ifrit. He might live here for days before he died. I do not plan to linger so long, however."

The djinni fell silent then and seemed to contract a fraction, insubstantial though it was. Aston thought that the coil of its spinning had grown tighter, like a spring compressed; he thought that perhaps there was a difference to the quality of the air between the djinni and the man, a stronger dust of gold; he saw a stir in Blaise's hood, as though a bellows had blown that hot and glittering air down upon him, directly into his face. He supposed that you could call that breathing, if you were a djinni.

Then there was other movement, this time in the man himself, a little shift of muscle that became an inch-slow squirm, a cautious stretch—like a snake flowing back into its skin, Aston thought, or a man rediscovering the limits of his own body—and then at last Blaise gathered himself together and stood up.

His hood fell back, and they saw his face for the first time. It was Blaise, and yet not quite. All the features were right—the bull brow and the once-broken nose, the jaw that could outstubborn an ass—but they had once all been animated by a spirit both men could recognise, and they saw no hint of it here. Blaise's face, yes, but occupied by a stranger: that was as close as Anton could come.

"Blaise!" the marshal said, apparently disregarding all the djinni's advice, though it had sounded good to Anton.

The man turned, slowly, from where he had been regarding the floating column of the djinni's intangible body.

"If you would call me so."

"It is your name, Blaise. You have been far from it, perhaps, but you own it yet. As you do your rank of sergeant. Come back and all your life awaits you, as it was; serve this creature and you imperil all, as well as your immortal soul."

"It has touched me, it has claimed me; there is no life that can compare with that. I will go with it—"

"—And betray your masters once again, and betray the God. Blaise, you once asked, no, you *begged* to call me Magister. I granted that as a sign of your redemption, your returning to the wider brotherhood of faith. If you denied me now, I should be sorry."

"I cannot help your sorrow."

Anton almost had to choke down a laugh at that, so apt a reply from a man who had never been quick-witted till now. The humour lasted only a moment, though, as the implications of the thought sunk in. This was not Blaise—not quite? not at all, more like, another spirit entirely, just clothed in Blaise's body—and he was afraid that Marshal Fulke would forget that.

The marshal surprised him, though, and not for the first time. He showed no sign of temper; there was only reason in his voice as he said, "You could dismiss it entirely, if you chose to come with me. Back to your own world, Blaise, even if your old life holds no attractions. You cannot live here; this place was never made for mortal man."

"I can live in a djinni's shadow, until it chooses to let me die."

"That is no life for a man—and I think this is no man's true voice that I am hearing, djinni. His mouth, your words, I fancy."

"That is not as true as you think. The choice is his, to stay or to leave; he would live in either case, but he will choose to stay. Just as those who are touched by the 'ifrit will choose to die. Perhaps you would have had me let him be."

"Perhaps I would. Better to die than to trade this half-life for his immortal soul. That is a deadly bargain."

"I do not see how serving me will cost the man his soul, if he should have one. But I will not argue theology with a Marshal Commander of the Order of Ransom; that is a fruitless occupation."

"Begone then, demon—but leave my man, I conjure you, by the power of the God!"

That was bluster only, Anton thought; and the djinni thought so too, he guessed. At least it surprised him, it surprised them both by laughing, a sound like a high-tuned peal of bells.

"Oh, I will leave you your man, Marshal Fulke. But I will take my own."

"We will meet again, Marshal Fulke," Blaise said un-expectedly; and to Anton's ears it was much like hearing the djinni speak through the sergeant's voice, with just the same cadence to it.

Before Fulke could draw breath to reply, the man was moving away across the plateau—moving but not walk-ing, not running, seeming to glide rather as though the djinni were sweeping him away on an invisible cushion of air.

The two Ransomers, marshal and knight stood and watched, fascinated and helpless as the spirit-creature and its captive—or its convert, perhaps?—dwindled into the distance. It was hard to be sure, but Anton thought that they reached the edge of the plateau and simply car-ried on, not falling but truly flying now.

When they were utterly gone from sight, when he could no longer make out even a dot against the horizon, he stirred and rubbed his strained eyes and looked about him. There was a sign left behind, he saw, to show that this had not all been some fantastic illusion; Anton was almost grateful for it, as he stepped forward and stooped to pick up the broken candle.

"Blaise must have fallen on it, in his sickness."

"Indeed." Fulke's voice was cold and distant; his eyes had still not left the far horizon, and it seemed that nei-ther had his thoughts. "I had heard tales, of course, before I came to this country, but I never thought to meet any of the demon-kind. I was never sure till now that the tales were even true."

"Sergeant Blaise reported meeting a djinni, on his way to the Roq."

"Yes. I thought it merely a heat-dream, no more than that. Blaise was the type to insist, against all logic . . . But no matter. We know the truth now, or some little of it, and Blaise is enslaved to that creature. Remember,

Sieur Anton, that all demon-spawn are the children of lies."

"The djinn do not lie, according to all the stories I ever heard. It said so itself . . ."

"Precisely so. It said so; it was lying. That is axiomatic."

Well, maybe so. Anton wouldn't argue the point. He was both wonderstruck and exhausted; he wanted nothing but to get back to the encampment, and to bed.

Fulke had another matter on his mind, though. "Explain to me how it was, Sieur Anton, that you followed me to this place."

Anton sighed and offered his prepared excuse again, the undeniable summons; and then confessed his curiosity again, as a good and obedient Ransomer should.

Fulke made an impatient sound. "I did not mean your motives; those I understand and even applaud, although I do not condone your stealing the candle from my tent. I mean how you contrived to follow me through the King's Eye to this spot. I looked into the Eye and saw where Blaise would be, and came to him; but you lack that skill. If you'd simply lit the candle and said the prayer, you should have stayed on the site of the encampment."

"That I cannot explain, Magister. I lit the candle and recited the words, much as Blaise did, I expect, knowing nothing of their meaning; and the way opened, and I stepped through here. Perhaps I was so close behind you that the wind of your passage carried me in your wake?"

"Perhaps," though the marshal sounded quite unsatisfied. "Or perhaps we should not enquire too deeply into mystery. It is not named the King's Eye for nothing; he watches all of us within his Kingdom, and he may have had his reasons to send you after me. This message, for example. It may be important . . ."

Important, surely, to have the commander of the guard send for the marshal in the deepest hour of the night,

when even Fulke might have been sleeping. But important enough to have the King in his far palace twist the
nature of the world to send a discredited knight across a
magical realm in pursuit of his superior officer, simply to
ensure its prompt delivery? Anton said nothing, but his
mind balked.

"Blow out your candle, Sieur Anton, and we will go to
investigate."

Startled, Anton glanced down at his hands, to confirm
that he was indeed still holding the candle. Its flame
burned quite normally now, pale in the opalescent light of
this place. He drew a breath in obedience, but then hesitated, struck by a wandering thought.

"Why didn't Blaise go back to the world we know,
when he fell on his candle and extinguished it?"

"That I cannot say either. Perhaps the King required
his presence too, for what reasons we cannot guess; or
perhaps that—creature—worked some casting of its own,
to hold him here. You must let go of Blaise, Sieur Anton,
as I have already. A man lost is a man mourned, but no
more than that. Blow out your candle."

Anton hesitated no longer, but did as he was bidden;
and found himself abruptly back on the hillside above the
road, and blinking against the dark.

A moment later, there was a transitory gleam of gold
and Marshal Fulke stood once again at his side.

THEY WALKED BACK to the encampment in silence,
through the sleeping soldiery and the horse-lines, past the
officers' tents and on, till they came at last to the guard-
fires that marked the border.

It was the attitude of the guards that first alerted Anton
to some great change. They stood in unaccustomed hud-
dles, speaking in nervous murmurs; as the two men
passed they fell silent, and some abandoned their posts to

drift along behind. Anton waited to hear their sergeants call them back, and heard nothing; he waited then for Fulke to snap an order, and again waited in vain.

The man in command of this watch came running, as soon as he saw the marshal's familiar figure in the fire's light.

"Magister, I am so glad that you have come . . ."

"You sent for me?"

"Yes, but that was before . . . There was a voice, a creature, spirit or demon I know not, I could see nothing but a flickering light, like a marsh-phantom; but it spoke to me and said to send for you, and so I did. But—"

"But what?"

"Look, Magister. See what has happened since . . ."

Like Fulke, Anton looked where the desperate man was pointing, across the border. Even in the dark, with only the faintest line of light in the east to promise a new dawn rising, he could see now what it was that had changed.

The border had been a terrible thing but a constant, immaterial and yet dreadfully real, a line torn across the natural world. By daylight or at night, it had been equally clear: a rift in the hills' march, a shift in the fall of sunlight, a break even in the unending pattern of the stars.

Now there was nothing, it was gone. Now they stood on the road and saw that road follow its proper course, running onward along the bank of a stream that they had not dared to drink from, because it flowed from an invisible and accursed source. Now they could see its path glinting beneath the restored sky, they could see where it met the road and how before that it came plunging down a high hill that had simply not been there when Anton left his place of duty a bare hour since.

They could see how the road wound on around the base of the hill and vanished into shadow—and they knew what lay beyond that shadow, and that even so much shadow could not linger now, would be burned away with the rising of the sun.

In short, they could see the way to Surayon, that they had waited for and prayed for all this time.

"Rouse the men," Fulke said, after a swift murmur of blessing, gratitude to the God which should also be proof against any lingering, leaking corruption from the cesspool that was Surayon. "See them fed, and then break camp. We ride at sun-up."

Not knowing what they rode into, except that it was accursed; none in their ranks could remember—or would admit to—passing through Surayon in the years before it was Folded. Not knowing what would result either, except that there would be a cleansing, a great scouring of the poison that oozed from Surayon to infect all of Outremer.

Poisoned flesh must be cut out, the doctors taught; Anton had seen the truth of that, time and again. Trying to save a rotten limb could kill a man. Better to seem harsh than kind; better to strike, swift and sure.

The land lay before them, the breeze was fresh and the night was paling; there would be blood and death before this new day was over.

Anton couldn't wait.

☧   ☧   ☧

COREN HAD BEEN here before, of course. He was the King's Shadow, and the King bestrode this land from northern march to southern sand, from western sea to eastern height where Coren was standing now. The King sat in Ascariel and never left his palace, but his Shadow fell wherever his will might glance; in forty years that will had pried into every secret corner of this country, and much that lay outside its borders too.

But Coren had known this pass even before he was the

King's Shadow, even before there was a King. At that time it had been a killing-ground, where they had hounded the Sharai through the mountains and back into the desert.

Ten years later it had been a way of trade, a constant passage between Surayon and the Sands. By then, though, Surayon was already anathema to its neighbour states, and its dealings with the Sharai only further evidence of its debasement. All of Outremer traded across its borders, but the other states traded only goods, what could be bought and sold from camel trains. Surayon traded in knowledge, the arcane wisdom of its Princip and his court for the witchcraft and indecent practices of the Sharai. That was heresy and should have been forbidden, only that the King was silent on the subject. There had been worse rumours too, even that the lords of Surayon traded in people also: not the slavery that was common throughout the country, but their own children sold to sorcerers deep in the desert, apprenticed to the blackest of the arts.

And then Surayon had Folded itself away before the other states could bring the God's clean justice down upon it, and like every path across the border, this road had passed into nothingness and out the other side of Surayon.

And so Coren had seen it for the past thirty years, like every traveller who came this way. As the King's Shadow he could come and go throughout this land, no work of man could bar him, but his eyes still saw what other mortals saw.

He'd always hoped to see it again as the God had made it, the high pass running down into the broad, deep cleft of the valley principality. He'd never truly expected it, though; he was too wise in the ways of his people. Mistrust and bigotry fed off each other and could thrive for generations, building higher and stronger walls even

than these mountains. He hadn't dared to hope that
Surayon would unFold itself in his lifetime, and he'd
been sure that no outside force could break in through the
Folding.

He'd been sure, and he'd been wrong.

For all the King's insight and his own, for all their
knowledge and their great anticipation, he could never
have imagined that he'd find himself here like this, in the
road with the Folding dissolved and gone, an army from
the Sands marching towards him and the body of his
friend laid out in the dust at his side.

He'd insisted on that, against Julianne's tearful pleading and Elisande's tight silence. "I'll bring him home,"
he'd said, "as soon as I may. That I promise. But the
Sharai respected Rudel while he lived, and they respect
the dead who died bravely. If I cannot persuade them to
turn back, it may be that Rudel can. Without Hasan's determination to drive them on, they might choose not to
pass his body; it could win us a few days' grace, if nothing more."

Privately he thought that the opposite was more likely,
that finding the road open and having pursued Hasan this
far, the Sharai would pursue him further, all the way to
Surayon town and the Princip's palace. This was a desperate cast of a die that was weighted against him,
against them all; but he'd still seize any slight chance that
he could. The sheikhs might at least honour Rudel's
memory far enough to turn back to the fork in the road
and ride for Ascariel instead. That would be a small, if a
bitter victory; Ascariel at least mounted an army, which
Surayon did not. Perhaps the tribes' love of battle would
draw them that way. Perhaps in Hasan's absence, the
sheikhs would yearn to show that he was not needed, that
they could achieve what he had not. Sharai ambition had
won many a fight for the Patrics.

Coren stood foursquare in the road beside the body of

his friend and waited while the outriders of the Sharai army came slowly down the defile from the mountains. It would be past dawn on the Sands, he knew, but not yet in Surayon; there were still stars to be seen above him, though they were fading now. Light was creeping into the sky, but matters here would still be decided in the dark.

It was as ever the sheikhs themselves who led the line of march. He knew them all by more than name and reputation. He knew their tempers and their temperaments, their pride and ambition, their quarrelsome natures and every quarrel that lay between them. Under other circumstances, he would have been confident in playing one against another until their unity was shattered and the best that they could hope for was a chaotic withdrawal, the worst a pitched battle between their tribes. Here, though, on the very borders of the country that was as holy to them as to his own people, he felt himself weak and helpless. Now would be a good time for the King to guard his realm with an earthquake or a vision of fire, something to terrify or tear apart these long files of desert men, rip the courage from their hearts or the ground from beneath their camels' feet . . .

He did not, and Coren had not expected him to. The leading sheikhs rode up and reined in, three abreast; Coren read their mood on their faces—exhaustion, anticipation, exaltation—and almost stepped aside without a word, almost bowed and waved them on their way. The smoothest voice in Outremer, which was his, would do him no good here. He held his ground, though, scrabbling after every little minute he could buy for Surayon; he folded his arms passively, impassively, and awaited their questions.

"What has happened here?"

"Rudel has been murdered, by Morakh the Sand Dancer, while he was working us a passage into Surayon. As you see, that has undone the Folding. Also, we were

attacked by an 'ifrit. We slew them both, spirit and
Dancer; Morakh's body is over yonder," a casual wave of
his arm towards the rocks beyond the road's limit, "if you
wish to bury your man before you continue on your
way."

A general hissing, hands touched to scimitar-hilts,
and, "Morakh was not our man!" from several throats at
once.

"No? Strange, then, that he was so eager to ease your
path for you. Honourable men would refuse to accept this
gift he has left you," a bare movement of his eyes to show
what gift he meant, the death of a man they knew well.
"Honourable men would turn back and wait word from
Hasan, whom we are seeking to heal."

This was the crux, confrontation the only tool he had
where diplomacy was bound to fail; he did not think that
it would be enough.

Nor was it. There was mocking laughter at his words,
and, "Hasan must take his chance. If he recovers, he may
join us or not, as he sees best. The Dancers serve the God,
and so do we; if Morakh won us this opportunity, he is
among the blessed in Paradise."

"Will you serve the 'ifrit, as he did? They tried to destroy you at Rhabat; now they will use you to destroy the
Patrics. Is this wisdom?"

"It is as the God wills it. Do not stand between us and
our own lands, Shadow, unless you desire to follow
Rudel sooner than you might."

That was it, that was all he could do; he had lost, as he
had been sure that he would. He stepped off the road and
stood watching in silence as the Sharai began their slow
ride across the border into Surayon, going quietly in single file past Rudel's body, each man offering a salute or
a blessing before lifting his eyes towards the country so
long hidden, so long desired.

✠ ✠ ✠

IMBER WAS A deserter, he supposed. For sure that would
be how his uncle treated him, when—if ever—he went
back: as a milk-sop and a coward both, a weakling who
ran away from family and duty at a time when danger
threatened, who went in search of a fled woman without
even the poor excuse of dragging her back. He was rec-
onciled, never to live with Julianne; she'd slipped away
from him twice, and he wouldn't be so cruel as to force a
third time on her. He'd find out why, though, he was determined on that. She had seemed—well, not unagree-
able to the wedding. Not distressed, as some girls were
when they were forced to the altar. Sometimes—brief
times, they'd only had brief times together—he'd
thought she might return his own affection; something
surely had burned the air between them when their eyes
locked . . .

First he had to find her, though, before he could understand her. Find her and rescue her. *Great danger,* the
djinni had said, and so he had come at great speed; and
the major, the overriding surprise to him was that his
cousin Karel had come with him, and half their men beside.

"They're more or less the names I would have chosen," Karel had said the first night as they walked the
bounds of the camp together, "if I'd had my pick of the
squad. They would have come for me, if I'd ordered
them; and I'd have done that, you know, if you'd tried to
sneak off alone."

"I know," which was one reason why he'd asked for
more than Karel's blessing. Better to ride in company
than to be hunted. "But you didn't need to order anyone."

"No. They volunteered. They'd have obeyed me, because I'm a soldier," which was the other reason Imber

had wanted him along, "but they follow you because of who you are."

"Because of what I am, you mean." The Baron-heir, the Count's son, too valuable to be let wander unprotected in the Kingdom or outside it.

"That's not what I mean at all. You're too young yet to see it, but the men know. They fear your uncle, and so they obey him; they respect me, and so they obey me; you they simply love, as they have loved your father. You give them cause for it, without realising what you do. Can you imagine your uncle riding patrol as you have these last weeks, living with the men and sharing their work, their food, their discomforts . . .?"

Imber smiled briefly. "No, perhaps not—but it was only because of Julianne. I couldn't find her, and I couldn't sit in the palace and do nothing. Besides, there was need, we have to watch our borders . . ."

"Exactly, that's my point. The men understand all of that. They'd have known, if you were doing it to win their favour; they're hardy souls, and hard to fool. But you came because your girl had driven you to shame and anguish, and they've all been burned by women in their time. And you came because it was your duty, and that's something else they're glad to share with you. And then a will-o'-the-wisp from the desert sends you on a mad ride south, the wrong side of the mountains in a time of war; of course they follow you, how could they not? They're glad to have me here, but they'd have come without me if I'd stayed. If I'd ordered them to stay, I'd have faced a mutiny. And that's the difference between us, Imber, and by the time you hold the County you'll have learned how to use it as your father does, and then it'll be all the difference in the world."

Imber wasn't accustomed to having his character so dissected—except perhaps by his uncle the elder Baron Imber, who held a far less flattering view of it—nor to hearing such plain speech from his merry cousin. Startled and embarrassed, he could say only, "They didn't all come."

"Of course not. Some had to stay, to watch the border and to send word back on the fanciful and foolish doings of the young Baron-heir." That was better, the teasing was back in words and voice together. "Though I think whoever carries the message to the palace may be surprised by his reception. You're loved there too, and not only by your father. Your uncle will condemn your wilfulness, and his friends will support him, but even he will say that our duty lay in protecting the County's heir-apparent. I tell you, Imber, there's only one man who'll come out of this adventure with his reputation entirely gilded, and that's my own virtuous self. Which is, of course, entirely why I came with you."

"Of course it is . . ."

THAT HAD BEEN days ago: days of hard riding in a hard and dry country, with the mountains an impassable wall to bar them from the safety of the Kingdom—riding wrong-handed, Karel called that, and grumbled about the impetuosity of boys who wouldn't take an extra day to put that same wall between themselves and trouble—and the open desert on their left ever a threat. They passed settlements with caution; the few people they met were Catari, vassal clans to the Sharai. Those were reluctant—reluctant with reason, Imber thought—even to speak to an armed troop from Elessi, but at least there was no sign of their masters.

THE GROUND WAS seldom difficult for horses here in this half-world, between the wide sand and the high rock. Often it was easy, hard-packed shale with a smoothing of

sand, and there they rode long hours and at speed, resting
only once in the heat of the day and again through the
deep chill of the night; their big destriers had the stamina
to take that pace, and Imber refused to slack it until they
must. The only real trouble came to Karel, whose mount
found the only pit in miles for its hoof to trip in. Their fall
was spectacular. Karel was bruised and shaken, no worse
than that; the horse's leg had snapped, which was the
worst possible news. Imber slit its throat himself, and
then insisted on putting Karel up on his own beloved stal-
lion while he rode a spare horse from the string. The
commander needs to draw the eye of the men, and this
was still Karel's command. His Mutassar was a pure
shimmering white, unmistakable, the obvious and only
choice; only later did he recognise that this was another
gesture that the men would love in him.

SHORT OR LONG, serene or panicked, every journey
has its looked-for end, though that may not be the end of
the journey.

　　Some few of Karel's men had been this way before, on
a mission for the Count; there came a night when they
promised him Selussin in the morning, and the castle before noon.

　　Sunlight woke something in Imber that he thought had
been awake and afire already, but had only been smoul-
dering after all. *Today I shall see her, somehow, though
all the men and spirits of the desert defy me.* The thought
was like sundazzle on bright water, fierce enough to draw
tears from his eyes. The slender height of her and the
long dark fall of hair, skin soft as rose-petals and
coloured like the roses of his mother's treasured garden,
all the pure image of a tender girl who had made him love
her from the moment of their meeting; and then the gaze
that pierced, the tongue that was as sharp as the mind be-

hind it, the joy in him to have found a girl with whom a lifetime of days and nights would never be enough to explore every complicated corner of her . . .

More than anything he wanted only to meet Julianne again, to sit and speak with her and learn his future from her lips: whether they could be married in body as they were in law, whether they could ever be married in love. This time there could be no demands, no question of forcing her to anything. He would ask, as plain and simple as his nature, and trust to her subtlety to see that he could make her happy.

Soon, now. Soon . . .

NOT SOON ENOUGH, but eventually they did see the tawny outline of mud walls and towers rising to the east of their path, and the cold grey shadow of a castle on a height to the west. *Great danger,* the djinni had said. They were half a company, and that castle could withstand an army's siege for months if it were garrisoned.

Even so, he turned his horse towards the rise, and the road he could see climbing up from town to castle. After a minute, Karel drew up level and gestured for him to rein in. He did so reluctantly, and his cousin said, "We should go into Selussin and speak with the people there, Imber, learn what we can before we approach Revanchard."

That was right, of course, but he shook his head despite a lifetime's training. "No. Send a man, send all the troop, go yourself if you want to. I'm going up."

"Imber, your safety is my responsibility."

"As Julianne's is mine. Karel, I will be careful; I don't intend to ride straight to the castle gates and beat on them with my sword-hilt. But we've been a full week on the march; we may be too late already, and I won't waste another half a day in seeking out some braggart who claims

to know more than eyes and wits can show me. Julianne
is my wife and needs my help; it may be wisdom or stupidity, but I will go."

Karel gazed at him levelly, thoughtfully for a moment.
"What would be wisdom," he said, "for an ambitious
captain and a cousin to the Count, would be to knock you
from the saddle and have my men bind you until I was
certain how the land lay, before us and behind. However," grinning suddenly, "I too have been in love, and
mad with it. Besides, life has been too dull lately, and
overcaution has lost as many battles as foolhardiness.
Very well, my lord Baron-heir, I am with you—but cautiously. I'll send two Catari-speakers into the town, to
learn whatever they can; the rest of us go up together.
And you ride in the centre of the troop, and if we find an
ambush waiting, then the men around you take you down
again, whether you will or no. I do not want to be the one
who confesses to the Count—or to your lady mother the
Countess, which would be worse—that I have lost their
infant son and the hope of all the County."

Karel made his dispositions swiftly; two men peeled
away while the rest reformed and began a more steady
advance, scouts ahead and a rearguard behind and Imber
safely nested at the heart of all. He resented both the pace
and the protection, he yearned to be racing on like a hero
from a ballad, leaving all his companions in his wake—
but heroes from ballads often expired in their ladies'
arms, mortally wounded in the course of their bold res-
cues. He would be little use to Julianne with an arrow in
his throat, dying without ever knowing whether or not
she could have loved him.

THEY SKIRTED FIELDS and reed-beds, and made better
speed once they reached the road; Karel trusted his own
judgement, in a way that Imber thought he himself never

would. *The God preserve that man for when I must be Count*—which was the first time he had thought that or anything like it, and he couldn't decide if this was a strange or a likely time to be having such a thought.

But it was there in his head and it seemed to make sense, to fit a pattern. There was Imber, Count Imber; and there was Karel, holding whatever title he might choose so long as he held his place at Imber's right hand, as—thinking back—he always had done; and there on Imber's left, holding his left hand literally was Julianne, Countess Julianne, and it was all so clear and right that it felt like a sending.

The God grant that it was no false vision. Imber felt that he was looking at Karel with new eyes suddenly, measuring him against men a generation older, and finding him in no sense wanting. He almost opened his mouth to speak, to say something of what he saw; but just at that moment the road turned around a jut of rock and ran out onto a plateau, and there was the castle in all its grim menace, directly ahead of them.

There were the castle gates, and they stood wide open; and all around were the ashes of many fires, and there was movement both within the gates and on the plateau, and none of it was at all what Imber had expected or imagined.

THEY WERE PEASANTS, who were so busy here: Catari and his own people mixed, so they couldn't all have come from the town below. They were men largely, with a few young women among them; and they were all in grief, silent and distressed.

There must have been a battle here, or a slaughter rather. The people were carrying bodies out from the castle, a terrible number of bodies that they laid out in line on the ground. From his saddle's height Imber could see old men and women among the dead, and children too. Most seemed to have no mark of death upon them; perhaps it had not been a slaughter after all, perhaps it was poison or sickness that had carried them off. After a moment, it didn't seem to matter. He scanned the line feverishly, and didn't see her face; he turned his eyes to the gates and spurred forward, crying, "Julianne . . ."

"Imber, wait! Come back—"

There was, there could be no going back. He rode into the castle forecourt and found more corpses, in a jumbled pile. The people there fell back and gazed up at him mutely, accusingly, *you came too late.*

That he knew already. One hasty glance assured him that Julianne did not lie among the bodies here, but there was small comfort in that. The djinni had said that she was here, and he had all the castle yet to search. *In great danger,* the djinni had said, and he had been too slow, too careful on the road . . .

He was neither slow nor careful now. He flung himself from his horse, heedless of the sound of hooves behind him and Karel's voice yelling; he raced madly in through the nearest open doorway yelling himself now, crying Julianne's name and hearing nothing but echoes returned to him.

He ran through darkness and through sudden beams of light, as though his own despair and occasional flickers of hope—*not here, not yet, I have not found her yet, so perhaps she is not here*—had been turned physical in the air around him. He plunged up stairs and down, turning corners where they came and taking passages at random, never stopping for thought or balance, so that he was swiftly lost within the castle's defensive maze. He stumbled over risen flags and fallen corbels, once he fell sprawling over an unexpected step; but he touched nothing but stone and old wood, he discovered no one living and no one dead, his hoarsening voice raised no answer but the dust.

The second time he fell, it was in the deepest dungeon and the deepest dark that he had found thus far. This time he had tripped over a simple bucket; he heard its hollow rolling and sobbed suddenly for more than breath, sobbed for the loss of all that was most precious, light and faith and dreams and Julianne.

He was still lying there, still sobbing when there was a light brought into the darkness by the sound of boots, and then a voice; and that was Karel, of course, come to find him, and he said, "Oh, get up. How dirty do you want to be, for the men to see you?"

"She, she isn't here, Karel . . ."

"No, she isn't. At least, if she is, we haven't found her yet, though we're more likely to do it than you were, running and screaming like a child playing lost. Torches are good, in dark places; so is the patience to search in corners. So is it good that we haven't found her, Imber. There are no bodies in the castle; all the dead are out in the yard."

"You don't know that. Perhaps those are only the ones that they've found so far and carried out. The djinni said that she was here . . ."

"I think they died out there—but perhaps you're right, or perhaps the djinni was wrong, or deceptive. Let's go and find out, shall we? Those people seem used to men of Outremer, unless they're just too distressed to be frightened. We'll ask them. You may want to clean yourself up first."

THERE WAS A scullery above, with a well that drew clean water. Imber washed hastily, rubbed a little at the stains on his surcoat, then shrugged and walked out into the stabbing brightness. No matter what the men saw:

they knew already, and he would not, he would *not* be ashamed of his feelings, his lady or himself.

Among the peasants, one man—bearded, middle-aged, lean and sinewy—seemed to have taken charge. Karel approached him to ask, "Who are these dead, fellow, are they yours?"

"Ours, aye, every one. Our mothers, our children, my wife."

"My friend here, he is looking for his own wife . . ."

A swift assessing glance, a shake of the head. "Not here, not among these. We know all of these, between us."

Not his face, but something in the man's look was very familiar, if utterly out of place; his accent confirmed it. Imber spoke haltingly, reacting without thinking: "You're Elessan."

"I am, and my wife—was. I know you too, my lord Baron. You came to our village once, we saw you, I lifted my boy up to give him a better view of you . . ."

He nearly broke then, as Imber had broken already; he would have done for sure, his mouth was twisting out of his control when Karel interrupted.

"I am sorry for your loss, but tell me, I must know: what is a man from Elessi doing here, in this company? How is it that you left your land, your family, your little boy? And what caused all these deaths?"

"Truly, sir, we don't know. We found them so, after we had followed them for so long. They should have died before, but they were saved, we thought; and there were promises made, to those of us who followed . . ." Promises that were all dust now, that much was clear even to Imber, who had come here in pursuit of a promise also and knew the bitter taste of betrayal too well himself.

"I don't understand," Karel said.

"No more do I, sir. I will try to try to tell the tale, but

it is hard . . . There was a sickness came to the village, a cold kind of death. And then a healer, blessed by the God's favour, he claimed, and with a holy relic of great power. He gave life to the dying, and not only to those who were sick; my wife hurt herself working in the fields and should have died of the bleeding, but he touched her with his saint's hand and she was whole again, except that she would not speak to me or anyone, not even to our child. Those he had healed before had followed him thus far, and so did ours when he moved on; and so did we. I left the boy with my brother and went after my wife, though she was strange to me now. I hoped to bring her back, but the healer preached a great war against the Folded Land, and said that we were the God's army to strike against heresy. We were no soldiers—there were old men and children he had healed, and we had few weapons between us—but we had seen the power of the God in him, and so we believed. He said we should strike from here; but he led the healed ones on at a great pace, and we fell behind. When we arrived this morning, we found this as you see it, all our kindred dead and the healer too, we found his body outside the castle. He had been killed with arrows, but not these. We don't know how they died, except that my wife had bled terribly from her old injury. Perhaps when the healer died, all his healing was undone; but that cannot have been the God's work, sir, he would not treat us so . . ."

"No. There is a devil in this, man."

"Yes, sir. What can we do?" He had been strong too long; now suddenly he was lost, too far from home and from the life he understood, bewildered by finding tragedy where he had looked for hope. Imber understood him perfectly.

"Do what you have been doing, it's all there is for now: take out your people and find a place to bury them decently. My men will help with the digging, once we have thoroughly searched the castle. And I can say the funeral service over those you have lost, if you would like it, in the absence of a priest. I have done that before."

"Yes, sir. Please, if you would . . ."

IMBER WENT ALL through Revanchard again in the hours that followed, this time with a torch and a companion. He found nothing, not even the scant evidence of occupation that others turned up, indications of a small party staying recently.

The men Karel had sent to Selussin came back with news of more moment. Julianne's father, the King's Shadow had been in the town this last week, along with three companions whose descriptions tallied with the jongleur, the renegade Ransomer boy and the girl Elisande from the Roq, all of whom had accompanied Julianne in her flight.

"That's proof positive," Imber said, feeling his spirits lift for the first time since they had come to Revanchard. "The djinni did not lie to me; she was here, and she was taken away before this happened," with a gesture towards the great burial pit that was being dug close by. "But taken where, where is she now?"

"Wait, there's more. Yesterday an army came out of the desert, the Sharai on the march behind their warleader Hasan. The town is full of rumours. Some even claimed that he had married Julianne, which must be nonsense; but what is certain is that they brought siege to the castle last night and went on into Outremer this morning. They sent messengers back, who said that the Folded Land lies open now. I don't know if that's true, Imber, but if it is, I think we must look there for Julianne. In any case, that way lies our duty. The Sharai are in Outremer, and we must follow; every man will be needed. These, too," with a glance of his own at the people laying their dead in their last home. "They were promised a holy war, and they shall have one, if they are still willing. We can arm and equip them, from the town and our own supplies; they may not be soldiers trained, but dispersed among our own men, they'll be fit to fight. Half of them are Catari born, but even the Catari fear the Sharai. I'll take any who swear loyal to the King."

Imber nodded distractedly, impatient only to be mounted and on the move again, in pursuit of Julianne, though all the Sharai of the desert and all the wizards of Surayon lay between him and her.

The Liaden Universe®
by
Sharon Lee and Steve Miller